PAMELA HARTSHORNE

◆

THE CURSED WIFE

Complete and Unabridged

CHARNWOOD
Leicester

First published in Great Britain in 2018 by
Pan Books
an imprint of Pan Macmillan
London

First Charnwood Edition
published 2019
by arrangement with
Pan Macmillan
London

A catalogue record for this book is available
from the British Library.

ISBN 978–1–4448–4022–3

Published by
F. A. Thorpe (Publishing)
Anstey, Leicestershire

Set by Words & Graphics Ltd.
Anstey, Leicestershire
Printed and bound in Great Britain by
T. J. International Ltd., Padstow, Cornwall

This book is printed on acid-free paper

THE CURSED WIFE

Mary is happily married to a wealthy merchant, living a charmed life in Elizabethan London. But there's a part of her past she can't forget. As a small girl, she was cursed for causing the death of a vagrant child — a curse that predicts she will hang. Mary's carefully curated world begins to falter; her whole life is based on a lie. One rainy day, she ventures to London's Cheapside, where her past catches up with her. Suddenly, the lies and deception she has fought to bury begin to claw their way to the surface. As the wronged enact their vengeance, Mary must attempt to break the curse. Can she right the wrongs of her past before the curse wreaks its revenge?

In loving memory of my father,
B. K. Hartshorne, 1923–2017

Prologue

London, Little Wood Street, November 1590

Outside, a blustery wind is shoving clouds across the sun. The light comes and goes, comes and goes, sweeping stripes of sunlight and shadow across the city like bars across a prison window.

Inside, the chamber is empty except for the two of us. Once as close as sisters. One fair, one dark. One a mistress, one a maid.

One alive, one dead.

Before, the air was rent with fury, with the sourness of resentment, of jealousy, of fear. Now there is nothing, just the jerking of my heart and the shriek of her absence and a muffled rushing and roaring in my ears.

She lies unmoving on the rush matting, one arm bent awkwardly beneath her, her cap askew. Her eyes are open, fixed on the chest where the sunlight skims the belly of a silver jug and moves on, but they do not blink. Her lips are parted as if she is about to speak, a tiny thread of green silk trailing from the corner of her mouth, but she is not going to brush it irritably away.

She is dead. The light has gone from her, snuffed out, as easily as pinching a wick between your fingers. I knew it straight away, a bright shard of terror slicing through me then falling away to leave me numb.

I must move, I must think, but I can't. I can

1

just stand here, turning the embroidered cushion between my hands, around and around and around. My fingertips graze the piping, slide across the damask, skip over the piping once more, on and on until I am sure that I can feel every thread in the weft, every curve of the pattern. My gaze flickers frantically around the chamber, looking at anything but the crumpled lack of her on the floor.

There is a clog in my throat, hard and unyielding. I can't swallow it down, can't choke it up. A vicious pressure is building behind my eyes, and in my chest fear is rising, swelling unstoppably.

Dear God, what have I done?

The wind bangs accusingly on the glass panes, rattling at the casement, as if it knows exactly what happened. If it gets in, it will swirl up the truth that has been hidden for so long and shout it along the streets, and all will be lost. I cannot let that happen, but what can I do?

What can I do?

I pushed her, yes, but she pushed me too. I was just trying to make her understand, but she would not listen. I did not mean this to happen. I had no idea. If I could go back to quarrelling, I would. I wish that I could. I wish that I could unravel time, pull the thread back and back and back through the years to when we were little maids and we loved each other and we still had the chance to do things differently.

PART I

1

Mary

London, Little Wood Street, March 1590

Sometimes I forget that I am cursed.

It seems at first as if this will be an ordinary day. The rain is thundering onto the roof tiles when I stir, and I am tempted to pretend that I haven't woken and to burrow closer into my husband's warm back for a few more minutes. But above the sound of the rain I can hear the household stirring: rustling, a cough, the clang of a pot. Footsteps down the narrow stairs from the eaves. The telltale creak of the door into the yard.

From somewhere below comes a bump and a crash and a muttered oath. That will be Sarah, the new maid, coney-brained and clumsy, with a longing for her village and the life she knew.

My husband mumbles as I ease reluctantly away from him and grope through the curtains for the clean shifts I left close by on a stool. Sucking in my breath at the coolness of the linen, I pull them under the covers to warm them.

'It's dark still,' my husband grumbles. To the world Gabriel is a shrewd merchant, stern and severe, but here in our bedstead he is just a man who does not like mornings. He turns over and throws a heavy arm over me, pressing his face into my shoulder and pinning the shifts between us. His warm breath huffs against my skin and I lift a hand to stroke his beard. Small touches, that is all that I allow myself. It is my penance.

'It's raining. If it were not, the sun would be well up, and you would be springing out of bed, eager to get on with your business.'

With a grunt he hauls himself up onto the pillows and scrubs his hands over his face. 'There will be little enough business today if it keeps raining like this,' he says. 'I might as well stay snug at home with my wife.' He tickles my waist suggestively and I laugh as I push his hand away and wriggle into my shift, telling myself I have not noticed the quick shiver down my spine, that I do not remember another time when I pushed someone away.

Every time you change your smock.

'Your wife has better things to do than lie abed all day. The household will not run itself.'

I am still smiling as I kneel to pray by the bedstead. I clasp my hands together, resting my forehead on my steepled knuckles, and I thank God from the bottom of my heart for blessing me with a home and a family, for making me safe.

For turning the curse aside.

Afterwards, I call Amy to help me dress, but she is heavy-eyed with toothache and her jaw is so swollen that I send her down to the kitchen to make a warm clout to press against it.

'What about your laces, mistress?'

'Cecily can help me. Go on now, Amy, and

send Cecily to me. I will look at your tooth later.'

In truth, I can dress myself for the most part, but it is good for my daughter to learn how to serve. She chatters happily as she lays out a petticoat and disentangles the laces on my bodice. She is in a gay mood this morning, and why should she not be? At thirteen, Cecily is still the pampered baby of the household and indulged more than is good for her, I fear. I try to harden my heart, but it only takes one dimpled smile or tears shimmering in the beautiful eyes, and my resolve melts. Gabriel is no better. He lets her coax him into a ribbon for her hair or some other pretty geegaw that has caught her eye as if he really were her father.

'She brings sunshine into the household on the dreariest of days,' he says, and it is true. Cecily has the ability to brighten the room with her smile. She is so passionate in her desires, in her laughter, as well as in her tears. There is no middle way for Cecily. Her tantrums can be terrible, I know, but her sweetness is a joy for us all.

She helps lace me into my kirtle and pins my lace into place. I straighten Peg, the one-armed wooden baby that sits on the chest, as Cecily shakes the covers on the bed and pulls the curtains back.

'Why do you do that?' she asks, and I turn in surprise.

'Do what?'

'Touch the wooden baby.'

'Do I?' I ask startled.

'Every morning,' she says. 'Before you go

downstairs. I have often noticed it.'

I laugh, half embarrassed. 'Really? I don't know why.'

But I do know, I think. Peg is my only link to the truth of me, to the family that was my own. After all these years, the memory of my parents and my sisters has rubbed away and left little more than flickers of light in a blurry shade: a gentle hand resting on my head; my sisters' squeals of laughter; the boisterous boom of my father's voice when he came back from St Bartholomew's Fair. I remember being swung into the air, breathless with the terror and delight of it, the feel of his big hands at my waist. 'See what I have bought you, lambkin!'

I bought Cecily a wooden baby at the fair when we first came to London, and I sewed it a tiny gown, just as my mother sewed a gown for Peg. But Cecily never cared for her baby the way I cared for Peg. She dropped it in the street one day and we never saw it again.

Every few years I repaint Peg's face and give her a new smile, serene and friendly. I make her a new miniature cap and gown at the same time, but I have never replaced the missing arm. Sometimes I long to forget what happened to it, but I know that I need to remember.

Now I give Peg's skirts a tweak and pat her wooden head, and I could almost swear that she smiles back at me. 'It's just a habit,' I tell Cecily who crosses her eyes at me.

'I hope nobody else ever sees you do that, Mamma. They would think you quite mad!'

'You are saucy, miss.' I try to frown in reproof,

but I end up smiling, as Cecily knew that I would. I can never resist her laughter.

She is so like Cat in that way.

I am glad she does not look like Cat. Her curls are dark and lustrous, while Cat's were the gold of ripening corn, and her eyes are bright and brown as a puppy's, not cornflower blue. There are times when her hands dart and dance in the air, when she sits at the virginals and her lovely voice fills the chamber, when the dazzle of her smile makes my chest hurt, those times I cannot help but think of Cat, and the thought of her is a finger pressing on the puckered scar on my hand, poignant with remembered pain more than pain itself.

It must have rained like this when Noah was building his ark, I think, as Cecily follows me down our fine new staircase. I cajoled Gabriel into having it built, and a little thrill of possession shivers through me every time I walk up and down it. I like to imagine how it will be when the wood has darkened and the smell of seasoned oak has mellowed and generations have smoothed their hands over the banister just as I do.

But my good mood evaporates as the morning wears on. It is so dark that we have to light candles at nine of the clock, and the constant drumming and splattering and dripping outside are a wearisome backdrop to a day full of small disasters: butter that will not churn, a broken jug, Cecily tearful about a rent in her petticoat. The gloom puts everyone on edge, and I snap at Sarah when she hums as she sweeps the kitchen floor while I'm trying to look in Amy's mouth.

'Sarah, please *stop* that.'

Her mouth drops open and she freezes mid-sweep. 'Stop sweeping?'

'Stop singing that — ' I bite down on a curse. ' — that . . . *song.*'

Sarah looks vacant. 'Oh, John, Come Kiss Me Now' is sung everywhere. The tune floats out of alehouse windows and from street corners. Wherever the waits are playing or an apprentice is whistling, whenever a maid picks up a lute or a rogue his fiddle, that is the song they choose. She probably doesn't even know what she has been humming.

I cannot tell them that every time I hear the tune, fear and guilt twist and tangle in my belly. That my throat thickens and I struggle for breath. I try to close my ears to it, but this morning the rain and the darkness are pinching at my nerves and I cannot find my usual even temper.

'Hum something else,' I tell Sarah shortly and turn back to Amy. 'Cecily, do you hold the candle still. I cannot see anything if you wave it around like that. Come closer.'

Cecily and Amy exchange wary looks as my daughter steps obediently closer and holds the candle over my shoulder. Sarah resumes sweeping, mutinously silent now, and the rasp of the broom across the tiles scratches in my ears almost as irritatingly as the song. I hiss in a breath and twitch my shoulders to loosen the tension there before I bend over Amy once more.

I prise open her mouth as gently as I can and

10

peer inside. 'The tooth must be drawn,' I say as I straighten.

Amy's eyes roll in her head and she claps a hand to her cheek where it is puffy and red. 'Oh, mistress, no! No, I beg you! The pain is not so bad. It will go away soon.'

'Amy, the tooth will not unpoison itself,' I say, exasperated. 'You will not feel better until it is gone. I will go with you to the barber if you are afraid.'

She looks wildly around for an excuse. 'It is too wet to go out.'

'What is a little rain compared to the pain in your tooth?'

But Amy digs in her heels like a hound being dragged away from a scent. 'If you please, mistress, a plaster like the one you gave Tom when he had the toothache will be all I need.'

I sigh and shake my head, but I can hardly force her to the barber surgeon if she will not go. Amy is a strong, sonsy lass, broad of face and broad of beam, dogged in her devotion to the household but immovable as an ox when it comes to doing what she does not wish to do. There is no point in telling her that Tom's gum was not swollen and oozing.

'I have no time to argue with you, Amy,' I say instead with a severe look. 'If you choose to suffer, so be it.'

★   ★   ★

Dinner is late, just one more vexation in a vexatious day. I am chivvying Sarah and Cecily

11

to set up the table in the hall when there is a knock at the door. I am closest, so I open it myself and my irritable frown is wiped away by a smile of pleasure. 'Richard!' I stand back and hold the door wider open. 'Welcome back!'

Richard Martindale is captain of the *Catherine*, one of Gabriel's ships and named for me, or so my husband thinks. The *Catherine* is a sturdy cog that sails to the Baltic laden with fothers of lead and bales of cloth, and brings back oils and spices, salt and copper, glass and books, anything that catches Gabriel's factor's eye. Richard himself is a bluff seaman with deep creases at the edges of his eyes and a weathered air. Behind him bobs his servant, Jacopo, a tiny wiry man, his face seamed and brown as a nut. Even sheltered under the jetty, they are both dripping.

'Come in out of the rain.' I beckon them in and call for Sarah to take their wet cloaks. 'What brings you out in such weather?'

'The wet is nothing to us, is it, Jacopo?' Richard claps him on his sodden doublet, splattering raindrops onto the floor. 'There is more water than this at sea, I can assure you, my lady! And as we are newly docked, I thought your husband would want to know of our voyage.'

'He will be glad to see you.' I point Richard towards Gabriel's closet, which he knows well. 'You see that we will be eating soon. Will you dine with us?'

He bows. 'With pleasure. Jacopo, make yourself useful.'

12

'Always, captain.'

Jacopo waits until Richard has knocked on Gabriel's door before shooting me an expectant look. He reminds me of a monkey I saw in the market once, sitting on a sailor's shoulder, a quick, bright-eyed creature, but a little frightening too.

'What have you brought me this time?' I relent with a smile and he flicks his wrist and a seashell appears in his palm as if by magic. He bows as he offers it to me.

Jacopo always brings me a gift from his travels. His leg was broken by a load that fell from a crane onto the quayside some seven years ago now. Gabriel was standing right beside him. The barber surgeon wanted to cut off the leg, but Richard shouted at him and would not have it, and Gabriel sent a boy running for me instead. I cleaned the wounds and gave Jacopo some powdered poppy to help him sleep as we strapped his leg straight. In truth, I did not think he would survive, and the lack of fever was due more to his robust constitution than to my skill, but Jacopo believes that I saved his leg and yearns to repay the debt. His gifts, he says, are paltry things: I am to ask a service of him, anything, and he will do it. And he looks at me with an intensity that makes me uneasy. It is as if I owe *him* now. I owe him an outrageous demand, a sacrifice.

How old Jacopo is and where he comes from are a mystery. Richard says Jacopo had sailed to the edges of the world and back before he became his servant. He had been to Batavia where the ships filled their holds with spices, and to Africa where they filled them with slaves. He was familiar with ports from Acre to Amsterdam, from the West Indies to the Cape of Good Hope. He fell in with Richard at last in Genoa. 'Or was it Sicily?' Richard says sometimes. It seems that Richard rescued Jacopo from two attackers, and in gratitude Jacopo attached himself to Richard as a manservant, much to the sea captain's bemusement.

'Queer little fellow,' Richard confided to me once. 'I told him he didn't need to serve me, but he refused to listen. If he thinks himself in debt to you, he'll do anything — anything! — for you. Why, once I fell into an argument about a bill, and the next day the innkeeper was found with his throat cut. Might have been coincidence, of course, but I've learnt never to ill-wish anyone when he's listening.'

I have never told the children about that, but Tom in particular is fascinated by him, and likes to make up stories to explain his past. Jacopo was a mercenary, he thinks. Or perhaps he was a pirate, or an assassin. I would like to dismiss such ideas, but I know why Tom imagines him that way. There is an intensity to Jacopo, an alert, coiled quality, like a wild animal that might spring at any moment. I have seen him spin round at an unexpected movement, his eyes wild and his lips drawn back in a snarl, a dagger flashing in his hand, only for the dagger to vanish in an instant when he realised there was no danger after all. The menace was wiped from his face and he was smiling, and it all happened so

14

quickly that I have sometimes wondered whether I imagined it.

The children mock his devotion to me. 'You cannot ask him to take a letter to John in Hamburg,' Tom said. 'That is not enough for Jacopo. Much too tame a service. He would rather do something bold for you. Why don't you ask him to *kill* for you? That would be much more in Jacopo's line.'

'I wish you would ask him to rid you of Mistress Parker,' Cecily said, too pertly. 'She is hateful!'

'Or my French master.'

'Or that tedious Goodwife Blake, always fretting about her child and sending for you at the most inconvenient times.'

'Hush,' I broke in firmly. 'You speak of a sin.'

These children, they think murder is a laughing matter. They know nothing.

Now I take the shell from Jacopo and try not to notice how strong and quick his hands are. Hands that might twist a garrotte or spin a knife.

I turn the shell carefully. It is a fragile thing, much lighter than I expected, curved like a snail's shell but twenty times the size, with curious red stripes as it curls into itself. 'It is beautiful,' I say.

'Hold it to your ear, my lady,' Jacopo says. 'You will hear the sea.'

I tilt my head and cover my ear with the shell. A gentle rushing, roaring sound fills my head and I close my eyes and imagine the sea that I have never seen. But then through the rushing comes the sly echo of the tune Sarah was

15

humming earlier — *Oh, John, come kiss me* — and my eyes snap open as my heart jolts in horror. I want to throw the shell away from me, but instead I force a smile.

'Thank you, Jacopo.'

It is a poor meal that we sit down to when Gabriel and Richard emerge at last with the satisfied air of business well done. It must have been a profitable trip. I view the table with dissatisfaction. Poor little Sarah is still nervous and clumsy in the kitchen and Amy too preoccupied with her toothache to be any help at all. Between mending the petticoat and making sure that Sarah swept up all the shards of the broken jug, I boiled pigeons with cinnamon and ginger. There was some veal pie left over from the day before, but Sarah let the cream for a custard curdle and the tart I made with some wrinkled apples burned at the edges while she was attempting to comfort Amy.

The men do not seem to notice. They eat heartily as they compare memories of dipping their hands into barrels of peppercorns and cloves, of clinging to masts as their ships bucked and reeled through monstrous storms, of bargains struck and risks taken and profits made. I listen, rubbing the scar on my hand absently as they swap stories spun on distant quaysides: cities paved with gold, savages gorgeously attired, monstrous snakes and strange fruits. Tom listens wide-eyed.

Gabriel had three sons when I married him. John, the eldest, is lately returned from his apprenticeship in Hamburg. I sent him away a boy, and he has returned a man, his shoulders broader, his neck thicker. I am biased, I know, but he is a fine-looking fellow, with Gabriel's steady eyes, an open face and a good-humoured mouth. Cecily adores him. When he first returned she was shy of him, after four years apart, but now everything is 'John says' or 'John thinks'. Gabriel pretends to be sad. 'It used to be 'Pappa says',' he teases her. 'But you do not care what your pappa thinks now, do you, sweetheart?'

Twelve years ago, John was nine and Tom only three. And between them, quiet Nicholas, so like his father and closest to my heart. When he died of an infected wound at fourteen, I grieved for him as if he had been my own son. Now Tom is older than Nick was then, and wild to start his own apprenticeship in Hamburg. It seems no time at all since he was a small boy, sturdy and tousle-haired, trailing home from school with his shirt billowing out of his muddied hose, his laces trailing and his cap askew. I tell Gabriel that Tom is too young still to go away, but he is fifteen and a child no longer. He is ready to leap.

I will miss him. There will only be Cecily left a child, and at thirteen already, it will not be long until she, too, will leave. I can hardly bear to think of her married. I look at her beauty and her innocence, and I shudder to remember her father. We must choose a husband for her with care.

But not yet.

I pick fretfully at a piece of pie. Oh, I am all raw edges today, scratching against the slightest

17

thing: the scrape of stools over the tiles, the clunk as Sarah sets the pie too heavily on the table. I put the seashell on the chest to keep it safe, and it catches irritatingly at the corner of my eye. Every time it does, I seem to hear that whispery echo of the tune pressing like a cold knife at the back of my neck and the scar on my hand twitches and throbs.

When the men have out-marvelled each other at last, Gabriel notices Amy, who is slumped wanly on a stool at the end of the table, pressing a linen clout to her cheek.

'What is wrong with Amy?' he asks, picking out a choice piece of pigeon and offering it to Richard.

'She has the toothache, Pappa,' Cecily tells him. 'Mamma says she must go to the barber surgeon, but Amy will not go.'

'She is afraid,' I say, but Gabriel only nods.

'I had a tooth drawn once,' he tells Amy. 'I was afraid too.'

'I would rather sail into waves twenty yards high than let the barber surgeon at my mouth,' Richard adds, ignoring my warning frown. 'Jacopo once had to tie me down and take out a tooth for me himself, did you not, Jacopo?'

'Aye, and you cursed me for it up and down the seven seas, cap'n.'

'I'll pull Amy's tooth out for her,' offers Tom, his mouth full of bread. 'We can tie a thread around her tooth and tie it to an open door, and then slam it closed very quickly and the tooth will be out before she can say barber surgeon,' he suggests. 'Why pay for his services?'

18

'You will do no such thing,' I say firmly as Cecily and Sarah squeak, round-eyed with horror, and Amy whimpers.

'Fear not, Amy.' John leans forward with a kind smile. 'I will be your knight errant and keep Tom away from you.'

Amy only manages a wan smile. Ordinarily she would have been blushing with pleasure at John's attention. Her tooth *must* be hurting.

'I will give her something for the pain,' I say, 'and if the tooth be not better tomorrow, I will ask the barber to come whether she wills it or no.'

But when Richard and Jacopo have taken their leave and I go to my still room, I find only a few dusty seeds of poppy head in the drawer of the little cabinet where I keep my roots, seeds and herbs. In spite of it being daylight still, I have sent Amy to bed but she will not sleep without a syrup of poppy, and there is not enough here to make it. I sigh, pushing the drawer closed with too much force. I wish I could go back to bed and start this day anew.

Foolishly, I find myself blaming Sarah. If she had not been humming that cursed tune, the drawer would be full of poppy, I decide. Or Amy would have agreed to go to the barber straight away, and the dinner would not have been such a hotchpotch. It might even have stopped raining by now.

I am absurd, I know.

'Where are you going?' Gabriel asks when he sees me coming down the stairs with my heavy cloak over my arm.

19

'To Sopers Lane. There is a woman there who sells seeds and roots, and I need more poppy.'

He cocks his head towards the door. Outside, the rain can be heard crashing still onto the roof and splashing from the eaves. 'In this?'

'Amy will not sleep otherwise.'

'Send Sarah.'

'You know what Sarah is like. Poor girl, she is so lost still. She will bring home the wrong thing, or trip over the gutter and spill it.' I shake out the cloak and throw it around my shoulders.

'At least take her with you.'

'There is no point in two of us getting wet, and I am respectable enough to walk out alone, am I not?'

Gabriel sighs and helps settle the cloak into position. 'You are a stubborn woman, my lady.'

'Amy is in pain,' I say. 'And it is my fault that I did not check my cabinet.'

A faint smile plays around my husband's mouth as he sets his hands on my shoulders. 'You may be stubborn, but you are a good woman, wife.'

Familiar guilt rolls queasily in my stomach. He does not know what I am, and I dare not tell him. He is a decent man. He may not be a gentleman but he believes in compassion and kindness, in fairness and in truth.

And truth is the rub.

My eyes slide painfully away from his. His hands are warm and solid through the cloak. I stare at his collar instead, to where the pulse beats steadily in his throat. The temptation to lean against him, to rest my cheek against his chest is overpowering, but if I succumb, I might tell him everything. Sometimes the truth festers like pus in a boil, and I think it would be a relief to burst it and let the poison out, but I cannot take that risk, not for Cecily, not for me.

So I keep myself laced tight, I wear my guards high. Only at night, lying in the dark with my husband, do I let my passion for him loose. The rest of the time I keep my secret safe and I make myself the wife he wanted, a gentlewoman who has brought him status, a woman of good repute, respected in the neighbourhood. I am modest, I am demure. I do not laugh too loudly or berate my servants. My neighbours ask me for advice, for recipes and remedies, they ask me to attend them in childbed. I am blessed.

But they do not know the truth.

They do not know what I did.

I pull the cloak over my head to hide my face and Gabriel opens the door for me, grimacing at the scene outside with the rain coursing from the eaves and splashing into great puddles on the paving. The mid-part of the street is running like a ditch, the gutters full of it, brown and churning.

'We should clear the grate,' I say, and he is standing so close that I feel his body shake with laughter.

'My practical wife,' he says, and he lets his hand rest for a moment on my back. 'Are you sure you want to go right now?'

His question makes me hesitate, and I falter, my stomach swooping with the sudden sense that I am poised on the brink of something

21

terrible, with the conviction that if I step outside the shelter of the house, there will be no paving beneath the puddles and that I will find myself twisting and tumbling into a terrible void.

I don't want to go, no. But how can I say that now? I shake the strange sense of foreboding aside. 'I will be back soon,' I say as I tug the cloak closer around my face, put down my head and step out into the rain alone.

And I forget that I am cursed.

2

Cat

London, Cheapside, March 1590

I am sulking, huddled under the eaves of a goldsmith's shop while I wait for the rain to stop, but it still falls as if a solid sheet hanging from the jetties above, crashing and splashing into the street. It is raining so hard that I can barely see the great conduit opposite, or the cross with the poor Blessed Virgin, her arms broken and her son wrest from her knees, held in place with some old ropes. I feel like that too, as if a few lazy ropes are all that is holding me together.

When I think back to Steeple Tew and how the countryfolk would bob and doff their caps when Pappa took me out riding, I can hardly believe that I am here, like this. I would sit perched in front of his saddle and wave back at the countryfolk like our Lady Queen herself, and Pappa would roar with laughter. 'Is she not the fairest lady you ever saw, and the most gracious?' he would demand. 'I will marry her to a nobleman at least, you mark my words. Do you hear that, Kitten? Would you like to marry a great man and live in a fine house with all the gowns and jewels your heart desires?'

'Oh yes, Pappa,' I used to lisp. 'I should like that above all things.'

What a ninny.

Look at me now, my shoulders hunched against the cold. My gown is of wrought velvet, my kirtle embroidered with flowers, but both are threadbare now. I have no guards for my skirts and they drag at me with their sodden weight. My shoes are ruined and my feet so cold I can barely feel them. I wish I could not remember what it is to be warm, but I do, and the memory is piercing: how once I would hand over my cloak without registering who would take it, how easily I would move towards the fire and hold out one slippered foot after another to it, letting the delicious heat warm me from my toes.

Once all that had been mine. Now there is no fire, no servant. Just Anthony, with his empty promises. We live on the turn of a card, the throw of a dice. When he wins, he spends it on wine; when he loses, we drink ale, but we always drink. If we can scrounge a pie or a piece of bread and cheese, we count ourselves lucky. When I think of the feasts my mother would throw, the banqueting house she built to impress the neighbours, my throat burns and sometimes, yes, I weep hot tears.

Oh, I am weeping now . . . but it might just be the rain. I dare say it is. I knuckle the wetness from my cheeks and remember how pleased I was to return to England. I truly thought it would all be better once we were back.

Yes, I am a ninny still.

It seemed so easy when we boarded the ship at Calais. Twelve years we lived in France, moving from city to city as the whim took us. I eked out my jewels, and for much of the time Anthony earned plenty playing cards. We lived in style when we could, moved on when we could not, but still, we were gentlefolk. We had servants.

But then the last pearl was sold, and the last maid ran away when she saw that she would not be paid. How disloyal servants are nowadays! They would not have treated Pappa so. And Anthony's luck with the cards turned too, the way it does. He killed another gentleman in a drunken brawl over dice, and so we ran.

We were sure we would have better luck in London. All Anthony needed was a run of good cards and we would be in funds again. We could make our way to court, he said, his eyes alight with dreams.

Hah! I am not the only ninny.

We have been in London near three months now, and there is no sign of luck, just a succession of ever more squalid lodgings and the dull ache of hunger in our bellies.

It was Anthony's idea to come to Cheapside for a change. This is where the wealthy come, he said. In a tavern in one of the streets to the side, there would be gentlemen aplenty who would gamble away their gold for the pleasure of shaking the dice in their hands, or the sons of fat citizens he could fleece at cards, he was not proud. Since we arrived from France, we had been frequenting inns in the wrong part of the city. Now our luck would change.

I did not want to come here today, but Anthony insisted. He said there was nothing else to do in the god-forsaken rain, and it is not as if there is any pleasure to be had in staying in the wretched room that we have rented with our few remaining coins. The rain comes in through a hole in the roof and drops onto the bare boards right next to the mean mattress. When I complained to the widow who owns the house — if you can call such a hovel a house — she curled her lip at me and said that I should be grateful that the likes of me had a room at all. She said she would be glad to avoid the pair of us if we did not care for it.

How is it that a common goodwife is able to look down her nose at *me*?

Anthony was impatient with me. 'I will make us a fortune today,' he said. 'Then you can be a lady again and turn up your nose at any goodwife you choose, but until then, Cat, you must hold your tongue. I am weary of being moved on.'

He is weary of it? I am wearier, I swear. Weary of wretched lodgings and stinking taverns where I must smile and lure wealthy gentlemen to sit beside me. Anthony is all charm and good cheer and the men are more interested in cards than in me in the end. They fondle my knee absently and call for more wine and, if we are lucky, for food, but what they really want to do is to play. So I sit and I smile while the fiddlers scrape away in a corner and the slurred voices rise in song, and if I have to listen to 'Rogero' or 'Tom Tyler' or 'Oh, John, Come Kiss Me Now' one more time, I will scream.

I stare miserably out at the rain. I told Anthony there would be little luck to be had in such weather, but he would not listen. Only the hardiest or the most desperate of folk are out today.

Folk like me.

And a woman who does not look desperate at all. My gaze sharpens, my interest caught. She keeps her eyes lowered as a modest woman should and she does not draw attention to herself, but she walks as if she has a right to be here. No busybody will summon the constable to move her on, no men will leer and thrust their hips suggestively at her. She will not be jeered at or spat upon. Her cloak is drawn up over her head against the rain so that I cannot see her face, but something about the straightness of her back, something about the way she moves kicks at my senses and sends a jolt of recognition through me, sharp and sure. My heart stumbles and then soars so hard and so fast that my breath stops in my throat.

Mary . . . Mary, is that you?

I *am* befuddled with ale. My head wobbles on my neck as I nod at the truth of my observation. My ears are still ringing with the raucous din of the Dog's Head, my nose stinging with the rank smell of sweat and wet cloth and spilled ale and the hot pies being passed over heads, and now, yes, the world is blurry and disconnected. I am glad of the wall behind me to prop me upright. So perhaps I have imagined you. It is very possible that I have.

But what if it *is* you?

You lift your skirts to hop over the gutter. I can't see properly through the rain but I am sure

27

it is you. I even step forward to call to you, but the hollowness inside me swoops and spins in my head and I lurch, stumble and just manage to grab onto a carved beam before I fall. By the time I right myself and the dizziness settles to nausea, you are already walking on, across the far gutter, along the footway, towards Sopers Lane.

Without knowing why, I am following you, dodging unsteadily out of the shelter of the eaves and crossing the street after you, careless now of the rain. I am so wet now, I cannot get any wetter, and I could not stand there shivering and sick any longer with the relentless rain pounding around me. I nearly trip over the gutter and stagger from side to side to stop myself falling into it. Anyone watching would think that I am a lightskirt, sodden with drink, but it's not that, Mary. I am ill. I think my courses may be coming, and you know how bad they always make me feel. You used to have a remedy to make me feel better.

Please, make me feel better. If it *is* you.

You have stopped at Sopers Lane end, in front of a little cottage, dwarfed by the five-storey houses around it. It looks absurd, as if it has been transported out of some woodland clearing. I stop too, dragging my arm under my nose, drenched and breathless with the effort of staying upright.

It might not be you at all. But there are bunches of herbs hanging by the door. Seeds and herbs are the kind of thing you would be buying. You were ever good with remedies.

And poisons, of course.

A brisk knock and you are ducking your head to go inside. I am left blinking owlishly at the space where you were.

What am I doing here, stumbling through the rain after a stranger, while the world tilts and heaves around me? I feel as if I am floating outside myself, looking down at the drunk and dishevelled woman in disbelief. That woman cannot be me, Catherine Latimer, Lady Delahay. This has to be some terrible dream. Any moment now, I will wake up. I will be home, at Steeple Tew, with the sun pouring through the window, and the wood doves burbling contentedly on the roof. Down in the courtyard, there will be bustling and joshing and horses whickering. I miss the lovely clop of their hooves on the cobbles and the jingle of harness and Pappa's voice. How I miss his voice. How I long for the lush countryside, the gentle hills dipping to glinting, gurgling streams and dappled woods, and up again to the ridgeways where the sheep nibble the grass, their bleats carrying across the still summer air and mingling with the sound of bees busy in the lavender. You should be there too, Mary, when I wake. But you should be there to comb my hair and help me dress, not striding around Cheapside like the lady you are not.

Heartsick, I squeeze my eyes shut. Please, please, let this be a dream. Let me go home, I pray, but when has God ever answered my prayers? When I open them again, I am still standing in Cheapside, drenched to the bone, gulping back snotty sobs and my throat raw with longing.

I blot the rain from my face with my sleeve. I should go back to the Dog's Head. Anthony's mood may have improved. There were few pickings today. Even foolish gamblers had stayed at home, and I made the mistake of telling him that I had said that it would be so. Anthony can be vicious when disappointment sours his temper, which happens all too often nowadays. We both had too much to drink, and passed the hours snipping and sniping at each other until we were screaming about I cannot remember what. I know it felt as if it mattered at the time. Even in the Dog's Head, where arguments are two a penny, heads turned our way, and when the back of Anthony's hand caught me across the mouth to quiet me and I fell squalling across the table just as the fiddlers fell silent, the innkeeper had enough. He pushed his way through and told us to be quiet or he would call the constable. I hauled myself up, dabbing at my cut lip, and vowed never to see Anthony again, but he knows I will be back. Where else can I go? I can slink back into the inn and have some more ale. Maybe that would make me feel better.

Still, I linger. I just want to know if it is you or not. It seems to me that the rain is easing a little and I wipe my face again pointlessly as I lurk on the other side of Sopers Lane. I wait for the door to open, and when it does and you come out and I see your face for the first time, and it *is* you, the sight of you is like a slap, waking me out of the stupor I have been in for twelve years now.

Mary. After all these years, there you are.

And here I am, frozen into shyness, not knowing whether I long to embrace you, or dread the expression on your face when you see what I have become.

You haven't noticed me. Why would you? To you I am just a beggarwoman, scuttling along the skirts of the street, picking at the filth in the gutters, scrabbling for a crust of bread. You tuck your little packet of seeds into the purse that hangs from the girdle under your cloak, and pull your cloak closer over your head before heading back across Cheapside and up the street that leads north away from the famous conduit. I do not know this part of the city, but I follow you anyway, past one lane, and then another, and across a wider street. How far have you come, Mary? I almost give up, but now we are in a prosperous street with fine houses and orchards behind brick walls. Is this where you live now?

I could let you go. I don't want to see the disgust in your eyes, or worse, the pity. But you look prosperous. There are coins in that purse, and there will be more at home, I warrant.

You are a *maid*, Mary. The world is turned upside down, and the two of us with it. I was born to be a mistress, not to beg from you, but I am tired and cold and hungry and wet and the injustice of my situation rises up inside me, swelling unstoppably. It is not right. The unfairness of it is likely to *choke* me if I do not call out, and so I do. Your name lurches off my tongue, out before I can stop it.

31

3

Mary

Oxfordshire, August 1562

I was six when I was cursed.

Until I was cursed, I was blessed. I had survived the sickness, after all. Before then, I only have clots of memory: my mother's deft fingers sewing a tiny gown for my wooden baby; my father all bombast and good cheer, but a twitch under his eye when he thought no one was watching; my sisters, Nan, the eldest and self-important, and Frances, the peacemaker. I remember the stifled giggles under the covers in the bed we shared, how we would burrow together like puppies. The way Nan tossed her head, the anxious line between Frances's brows. I was the youngest, desperate to catch up and be included in their games, forever relegated to the lowliest role or to fetching and carrying.

Who fell sick first? One day we were playing Hoodman's blind, and then my memory jumps to tossing and turning in a bed, the fever hammering in my bones, the heat of it shrivelling me, thirst burning in my throat. I called for my mamma, but she did not come. There was only Emmot, her maid, her face drawn, laying a rough hand on my forehead. 'The fever is broken,' she said. 'Good.' But she did not smile and she

32

sounded like an old woman.

After that there is only greyness, when I was not quite asleep, not quite awake, and all I could do was to lie listlessly, wondering at the eerie silence of the house. 'Where is Nan?' I asked when Emmot came in with broth. 'Where is Frances? I want Mamma.'

All dead, Emmot told me at last. My father, too. My bold, boisterous pappa with his big hands and his big laugh. My foolish pappa who had gambled away all his money, and my mother's with it. There was nothing left to pay the rent.

Grim-faced, Emmot put me on a cart laden with hessian sacks and sent me to Steeple Tew, where Sir Hugh Latimer was kin to my mother and would take me in. My father was the second son of a second son, and improvident with it, but he was a gentleman and had charm enough to win a gentlewoman for his wife. She was a cousin of sorts to Sir Hugh, Emmot told me. The connection was remote, but it was all that I had.

'Be grateful,' she told me. 'Nowadays there's plenty of folk like you end up sleeping in barns and hedgerows and roaming the country. You remember little Susan Pollard you used to play with? Someone said they saw her and her brother begging on the road to Banbury the other day, poor lass.' She shook her head. 'Used to be it was just countryfolk turned to vagrants. The sheep got their fields and they was turned off the land, and that was bad enough, but now, now it can happen to anyone. A neighbour one day, a vagabond the next. Nowhere to live, nowhere to go, moved on from town to town because decent folk don't want to look them in the eye and realise how easily they could be living like savages too. So don't forget your good fortune, lambkin. It is God's will. You ent got much, but now you'll have a roof over your head and food to eat. You be thankful for that.'

She pushed the wooden baby my father had bought me from St Bartholomew's Fair into my hands as I sat uncertainly next to the carter. 'You take your Peg and you be good, Mary.'

The carter slapped the horse's rump with the reins and the cart lurched into movement. My throat was so tight that when I called a farewell it came out as barely more than a squeak, and I don't know if Emmot heard it over the creak and rumble of the wheels on the cobbles. When I swivelled on the seat to look back and wave instead, she was standing with her lips pressed into a very straight line, not moving. The expression on her face made my stomach ache with the longing to jump off the cart and run back to her and bury my face into her apron.

'It is as it is,' Emmot had said. 'Be grateful.'

The carter's name was Jack. He had a weathered face with a hairy wart on the side of his nose and a most pungent smell, although whether that came from him or the battered leather apron he wore I couldn't decide. He was a taciturn companion, but as I was shy and had never been on a wagon before, I was content to sit silently beside him, holding Peg on my lap and looking about me.

Our progress was slow through the clamorous

streets of Oxford, but once out into the open countryside we made better speed. I was used to looking up at the world, but now I was up high, I could look down and everything looked different, smaller and more distant: the kine in the meadows, the sheep on the hillsides, the countryfolk miniature versions of themselves as they cut the last of the crop, their scythes glinting in a swinging rhythm while the women and the children pitchforked the hay into stacks and the air blurred with dust that stung my eyes as we trundled past.

After a long, dry summer, the colour had leached out of the countryside. The trees looked ragged and the yellowing grass along the hedgerows collapsed onto itself, bedraggled and untidy. Only the elderflowers seemed to be thriving, bowing under the burden of their berries.

There were deep ruts in the track in places, and Jack would curse as the cart lurched in and out of them. I held on tight to Peg with one hand, and to the edge of the cart with the other, mesmerised by the steady bob of the horse's head, by its flicking ears and the rounded rear with its twitching tail. Its plodding hooves kicked up a fine layer of dust that coated my skin and settled into the creases in my apron.

Beside me, Jack whistled tunelessly through his teeth, breaking off only to throw a desultory curse at his patient horse. I knew the song. Nan and Frances used to sing it often: *Oh, John, come kiss me now, now, now*, they would sing it as they danced around with me. *Oh, John, my*

35

love, come kiss me now. I remember the sticky warmth of their hands clasped around mine, how they dissolved into squeals of laughter at the idea of kissing a boy.

They would never kiss a boy now.

My world had shrunk to this small space on the hard wooden seat, with Peg tucked under my arm and my legs dangling. There was nothing but the creak of the cart wheels, and the squeak and groan of the wagon as it lurched up and down and from side to side, a ship on an earthen sea where the mud had dried into crumbling brown waves. I could smell the horse and something piquant and spicy in the barrels behind me, and after a while Jack's whistling faded to a comforting background noise, blurred with the sound of the wagon and the chittering birds and the plaintive bleat of the sheep along the ridgeways.

I was half asleep. Perhaps that is why I don't remember exactly what happened. One moment we were travelling along an empty section of the highway, the next, it seemed, the wagon tipped into a deep rut and Jack was shouting and cursing and I jerked properly awake to find that we were surrounded by beggars who had swarmed out of the ditches. The drowsy summer afternoon was suddenly cracking with danger, as violence sprang out of nowhere, raw and red, snapping and snarling like an unmuzzled mastiff. I caught my breath as I shrank back against Jack in terror.

These were the vagrants and vagabonds Emmot had told me about, folk so poor they had nothing left to lose and who roamed the country like wild beasts, folk I might have been destined to join were it not for the fact that I was blessed and had kin who would take me in. But they did not seem folk like me as they grabbed at the edges of the cart and reached up to me, as if they would pull me down and eat me alive. Horror scrambled over me, snapping shut my throat so that I couldn't breathe, and darkening my mind. I think I may have whimpered, but my chest was so tight I could do no more than watch, frozen, as Jack swung his whip furiously from side to side.

'Get out of the way!' he bellowed. 'Go on, git out of it, you whoreson rogues!'

The vagrants were shouting and jeering back at him, their faces feral and twisted. To me they seemed barely people at all. Many were grotesquely disfigured with suppurating wounds, or so encrusted with dirt and grime it was hard to tell if they were men or women. Terrified, I let Peg slip onto my lap so that I could put my hands over my ears. The horse was straining at the harness to pull the wagon out of the rut. I was willing it on, desperate for it to keep moving.

I didn't see how the girl appeared. Perhaps she scrambled up, perhaps someone lifted her. All I know is that quite suddenly she was standing on the cart step in front of me while the air splintered viciously with desperation and hate.

'Git off!' Jack tried to swipe at her wildly, but he needed both hands on the reins as he urged the horse forward and the urchin ducked easily.

For one still moment, I stared at the girl, and

she stared back. She was so dirty that I could barely make out her features, and the stench of her so close made me gag. In a strangely detached way, I found myself remembering what Emmot had told me about Susan Pollard, begging on the road to Banbury. This could not be her, surely? Susan had always been so dainty and neat. Her cap was always straight, her apron always pristine. There was no spark of recognition in those blank eyes, but I thought it might be her. I don't know why.

What if it *was* Susan? What could I say? What could I do? I had nothing to give her.

'Susan?' I said tentatively.

She didn't answer. Instead she bent and snatched Peg by her leather arm from my lap.

I knew that I was fortunate compared to the vagrants. My skirts might be let down as far as they would go, and my apron might be worn, but at least I was not dressed in rags. I had a clean linen smock and a seat on a cart. To the girl I must have seemed rich indeed, and perhaps she just wanted a wooden baby of her own to play with.

But Peg was all I had. Already my mother's face was fading from my memory, but I had an impression still of gentleness and warmth, and seeing those dirty fingers close around my wooden baby's arm brought a surge of feeling that I could not name: horror, fury, grief. It roared in my head so loud that when my hands rose to grab Peg back they didn't seem to belong to me at all. They might have been another child's hands observed from a distance, one closing around Peg, the other palm raised, drawing back, pushing forward . . .

The cart lurched violently from one side to the other as it was pulled out of the rut at last and the girl was gone, a jagged shriek rending the air. Did she cry out or did I? My palm was tingling as if I had slapped it against a wall. Behind us, a chilling wail of anguish rose, and as the horse laboured out of the next rut I twisted in spite of myself to see where it was coming from. I was trembling violently, Peg pressed so hard into my chest that it hurt. She had lost an arm. It must have come off when the girl fell (*was pushed*).

Behind us, the vagrants were clustered like flies around a shapeless bundle of rags on the track. The girl. A woman was on her knees, keening. As if sensing my gaze, she looked up and even from a distance I could see the malevolence snarl her features. Struggling to her feet, she started after us, catching up with the cart easily in spite of her limp, her hand near my foot. I could see the dirt seaming her face, the hate in her eyes, and I wanted to look away but I couldn't.

'You've killed her!' she spat at me, her voice low and more frightening than if she had screamed. 'How does that feel, eh? No more than a bairn and a murderer already! What harm did my daughter ever do to you? She were just a lass like you, and now she is dead.' Her voice was clotted with grief, her words tumbling from her lips, drowning out Jack's snarling attempts to whip her away from the cart. 'My Ellen might have ridden on a cart too until last year. She had a wooden baby, just like yours, but that is long gone, sold for a crust of bread. It might have been *you* in filthy rags,' she told me, 'you scrabbling through the mud for a coin, did you think of that, you whey-faced trull?'

My first reaction was relief: it had not been Susan. Then I felt ashamed. I wanted to tell her that I had not meant it, that I did not know what had happened, but my tongue cleaved to the top of my mouth and I could not utter a syllable. All I could do was cover my ears with my hands but it did no good. I could not shut out her words as they went on and on.

'A curse be on you!' she cried, breathless, as Jack lashed at the horse which broke into a trot. Unable to keep up, she fell back at last. 'A curse on you, I say!' she screamed after me. 'You *and* that wooden baby of yours!' She flung Peg's leather arm after the cart. It bounced off the wooden wheel and tumbled into the dust.

'May you never have a child of your own, you little devil. Think of my Ellen every time you stir a pot, every time you change your smock. By God's blood, may you never be safe, *never*. The truth of what you have done this day will stay with you always,' she cried. 'It will haunt you until you die kicking and choking on the gibbet. *A curse on you!*'

Her wail curled up into the air behind the cart, a terrible keening sound that chilled me to the core. I was shuddering, my breath coming in jerky little gasps. I looked down at Peg for comfort, twisting her until I could see her face,

40

but her blank eyes seemed to look back at mine in horror.

A curse on you.

'Don't you pay her no mind.' Jack spat into the dust. 'One less beggar brat stealing honest folks' money.' And he went back to his whistling.

Oh, John, come kiss me now, now, now.

Oh, John, my love, come kiss me now.

The blood was still booming in my ears, and my heart thudded frantically in terror.

I would never have a child of my own.

I would never be safe.

I would die choking on a gibbet.

My hands went up to circle my neck. I could almost feel the noose tightening.

It could not be. I shook my head to clear it of the woman's shrill accusation. The girl had jumped, or she had slipped. I had not pushed her. I did not mean to.

Did I?

But the image of that spread palm, of my arm drawing back at just the right angle to give a good shove played over and over again in my mind.

My palm, the scream, the jolting cart, the anguished, all too human lament.

The curse.

★   ★   ★

Steeple Tew was an old manor tucked into the fold of a hillside not far from Banbury. By the time the wagon lumbered into the courtyard, I was too tired and wretched to take in much

41

beyond forbidding stone walls when Jack lifted me down and deposited me ungently on the cobbles. The ground seemed to shift and tip beneath my feet after so long sitting high on the lurching cart.

My clogs were caked with dust and my apron was brown and grubby from the journey. Emmot would have scolded me for getting so dirty, but Emmot was not there. I was alone, and I was cursed. That was all I knew.

The housekeeper, an angular woman called Bridget, came to take charge of me. She took me to the kitchen where I had my face and hands roughly scrubbed, and she made me take off my apron and kirtle so that one of the maids could beat the worst of the dust from it. Naked in my shift, I clutched Peg and sat miserably on a stool. I did not want to be there. I wanted to go back to Emmot, back to a time before I had killed, before I had been cursed.

But going back would mean taking the highway once more, and the vagrants would be there still with their sharp faces and their hands like claws and their vile stench. They would remember that I had been on the cart, that I had been there when the girl fell, that my hand had been thrust into the air where she had been. They would tear me to pieces until I screamed the way she had screamed under the cart's wheel. I imagined them crowding together under the hedgerows, shifting restlessly like cattle, waiting for me, and dread gripped me. I did not want to stay, but I could not go back either. I could just sit there and hold Peg for dear life, while the tune Jack had been whistling all day went round and round in my head until I dug my fingers into my scalp, wanting to claw it out and throw it into the fire.

That was when Cat found me. She danced into the kitchen, an exquisite fairy creature with huge blue eyes and guinea-gold hair, so enchantingly fair and so different from the vagrants that I could only stare and wonder if I had tumbled into another world.

'Are you Mary? I'm Catherine,' she said before I could answer. 'But you can call me Cat, like my pappa does. Sometimes he calls me Kitten to tease me.'

'Cat,' I repeated wonderingly. I had never met anyone called after an animal before. 'Do you live here?'

She looked blank as if it had never occurred to her that anyone could live anywhere else. 'Of course, and now you will too. Pappa says you are to be my companion.' She spoke the word very clearly as if she had just learnt it. 'Do you know what that is? It means a friend,' she said, again before I could tell her that I did. 'You will be my friend.'

Susan Pollard had been my friend.

'Will you be *my* friend?' I asked her, intrigued in spite of myself that you could order a friendship, and she smiled at me, such an open, sunny smile that for the first time since I was cursed, I felt something hard and tight loosen in my chest.

'Of course I will,' she said.

4

Mary

London, March 1590

The rain has eased a little when I come out of the small house, tucking the packet of poppy seeds into the purse that dangles from my girdle, but the cobbles are still slippery under my clogs as I cross Cheapside and turn into Wood Street.

The quietness of the city makes me uneasy. Sensible people are hunched over braziers, their shutters sparred against the weather. The goodwives have been to market, and the gentlefolk who come here in search of silver and gold, of velvets and silks and sumptuous satins have stayed at home in their warm houses. The smoke straggles out of the chimneys, beaten back by the rain.

If this were Steeple Tew, I would not even notice, but in London, the lack of noise has a wrongness to it that sets up a twitch between my shoulder blades. The streets are usually thronging with carts and wagons making their way through the press of people and animals, with traders and goodwives and servants and hawkers and everyone who can find an excuse to be out and about. There should be a clamour of conversation, of curses and quarrels and laughter mingled with bleating sheep or bellowing cattle

44

and the squabble of poultry and the raucous cries of the hawkers, but instead I see only a miserable lad with a rope of onions round his neck and a maid with a basket of roasted apples under her arm. 'Hot codlings, hot!' she cries half-heartedly every now and then, but nobody is in a mood to stop and buy.

A gaggle of unruly apprentices jostle each other into the gutters, pushing and shoving until all their feet are wet, and I glimpse a dishevelled whore leaning drunkenly against the wall opposite, careless of the rain. Poor woman, I know I should frown at her, but I cannot help wondering where she came from, and what brought her to Cheapside in only a thin, tatty gown. I remember the woman who cursed me, how her face had twisted with bitterness. *It might have been you in filthy rags.* And she was right. If it had not been for Cat and her father, that might have been me shivering in the rain with nowhere to go.

I draw the cloak closer around me and remind myself of my family, of the warm house in Little Wood Street at the sign of the three swans. I am not cursed, not now. Still, the memory of it loops around my throat and just for a moment I feel myself choking.

There is no reason to feel this press of unease, lowering over my head like the dark grey sky. The damp air is dense with disquiet. It is all Sarah's fault, I think again, exasperated with myself. If she hadn't insisted on humming that wretched tune this morning, I wouldn't keep thinking that I can still hear it. Snatches of the melody tickle

45

me, whisking out of earshot the moment I stop and turn, haunting my brain as soon as I go on my way again. I try to hum a different tune as I walk briskly up Wood Street, but it is no good. Even the cart wheels splashing through a puddle in the middle of the street seem to echo with the rhythm of the song: *now, now, now.*

I want to be home. I put my head down and pick up my pace. I have crossed into Little Wood Street and am thinking about the syrup I will make, when I hear someone call my name.

My real name.

'Mary!'

I so nearly betray myself. I stop myself from faltering just in time. Why would I turn? I am not Mary any longer. I am Mistress Thorne, wife to an upstanding merchant. Mary does not exist any longer.

'Mary! Mary, wait . . . '

I increase my pace as if I have not heard, but there is something in the woman's voice that sets foreboding pooling like ice in my belly. I know she means me. I want to run the last few yards to the house, but I can't. Respectable Mistress Thorne, running through the streets? Impossible.

But *she* is running. She is coming after me. I can hear her panting over the sound of the rain, the slap and squelch of her feet through the puddles on the footway, and I gasp in shock as her hand closes over my arm and pulls me round.

'Mary!' It is the whore, her hair straggling loose from her cap and plastered to her head, her face streaming. She dashes the rain from her cheeks with the back of her hand while I am still catching my breath. 'Mary, do you not know me?'

'You are mistaken,' I say shakily. 'My name is not Mary.'

'Is it not? Mary, look at me! It is I, Cat!'

I stare at her, uncomprehending. Cat? No, this bedraggled creature reeking of ale cannot be Catherine, my mistress, my friend. I try to pull my arm away. 'I do not know what you mean,' I start, but her fingers close around my sleeve like talons.

'You know,' she says. 'Look at me.' She wipes her face again. 'Mary, *look at me*!'

Perhaps it is the imperious note in her voice, perhaps it is my eyes catching up with my ears, but I do look at her, and my mouth falls open as a great swell of emotion rises in me: astonishment, joy, disbelief, shock. And slithering between them, to my shame, horror.

'Cat! My God, *Cat*!' Without thinking, I reach out and grasp her arms, and a tremulous smile breaks over my face. 'Cat, I thought I would never see you again! Is it really you?'

'It is.' She laughs a little wildly. 'Have I changed that much?'

'Yes, you . . . *Yes*.' I shake my head. I cannot think straight through the thoughts that are jumbling and tumbling around in my head. How can I possibly start? I don't know what I think, what I feel.

My eyes search her face. It is her, but not her. There are lines around her eyes that I do not remember. Her lip is puffy around an angry-looking cut, and a bruise is blooming on her cheek. My smile fades. 'Dear God, Cat . . . what has happened to you?'

Her eyes fill with tears and she looks away. 'I should not have discovered myself to you,' she says. 'I am ashamed.'

'Do not be. I am so glad to see you, Cat,' I hasten to reassure her. 'It is just . . . well, come inside. We cannot stand out here in the rain. Come in and get warm at least.'

Come out of sight is what I really mean. Now the first jolt of surprise has faded, I am all too aware that the Parkers' house is just across the way. Edward Parker is a pompous little man who serves as coroner, and his wife, Isabella, is no friend to me, for all her sugary words to my face.

'She is jealous of you,' Anne says. Anne Hawkins is my gossip, as dear to me as a sister now. As dear as Cat once was. Like me, Anne married a widower and has a daughter, Bess, who is the same age as Cecily. She has no kin nearby either, so we have been family to each other. We have sat in each other's parlours, and stirred each other's pots, laughing. I helped her son into the world; she sat vigil with me after Nick died. But even Anne's brows would rise to see me with a harlot, and it is all too easy to imagine how Isabella Parker would whisper news of it around the ward.

Taking Cat's arm, I urge her along the street, glad of the rain that keeps my neighbours from their doors. I keep my head down as we pass Anne's house as quickly as possible, and until we reach the sign of the three swans. Cat is drenched and shivering. I can feel the fine tremors through my hand and I have to make an effort not to wrinkle my nose at the smell of stale ale and sweat that hangs around her. Pity for her grips my heart.

It is only when I reach for the door that a warning rings, high and shrill at the back of my mind, and I falter. Too late, I realise what her reappearance will mean. A chasm yawns at my feet, but what can I do? I cannot turn her away, not now that I have brought her to my door. This is *Cat*, swaying beside me, shivering, lost and afraid. I remember the little girl who found me in the kitchen at Steeple Tew when I was terrified and lonely and she made it better. I asked if she would be my friend, and she did not hesitate. *Of course I will*, she said.

So I turn the handle and push open the heavy front door, to be greeted by the sweet, clean smell of home, of polished wood and warm wool and the lavender woven into the fresh rushes. 'Come in,' I say to Cat, ridiculously nervous. 'Come inside.'

The water puddles onto the tiles from her skirts as she stands looking around her in a daze. I clap my hands and call for Sarah. Please let not Cecily come instead, I think, and I smile with relief when Sarah appears, bumping into the doorway as she hurries into the hall, clumsy as ever. Her eyes widen at the sight of Catherine with me.

'Bring hot wine and cakes to the parlour,' I say firmly, as if it is normal for me to return with a bedraggled whore. Taking off my cloak, I hand it to her to hang up. 'This is my old servant, Cat, come to visit me,' I improvise when Cat just stands dully. 'No, wait!' I put a hand to my head, changing my mind as Sarah turns to go. Gabriel might come out of his closet at any point, and Cecily might choose to play the lute in the parlour. I must talk to Cat alone before anyone else comes. 'Bring the wine to my chamber instead. Come, Cat, I will see if I can find you a dry shawl at least,' I add when Sarah has blundered off.

Cat still hasn't said anything, but her eyes come back to me and there is a spark of something unfamiliar in her face. She follows me obediently up the new staircase, and out of the corner of my eye I see her trail her fingers wonderingly up the carved banister.

'Sit down,' I tell her, and urge her to the chair while I bustle around the chamber, poking up the fire, pulling a shawl out of a chest, shaking it out and tucking it round her shoulders. Playing the maidservant I once was. When Sarah brings the wine, I pour out a glass and set it in Cat's hands, closing her fingers around the warmth as if she is a child, and she squeezes her eyes shut with an expression that is something like pain.

At a loss as to what to do next, I pull up a stool and sit on the other side of the hearth. It crosses my mind that we have reverted to old positions without thinking, Cat in the mistress's place, I at her feet, and I am conscious of a pinch of resentment. I am mistress here now.

The wet wool of her gown is steaming gently

in the heat of the fire. Cat sips the wine and opens her eyes at last. 'Thank you,' she says in a wavering voice. 'You do not know how I have dreamt of being warm like this.'

'Cat, what has brought you to this?' I do not know any other way to ask, and bitterness races across her face, although whether it is at my question or some other memory, I cannot tell.

She does not answer directly. 'What is this place?' She sips at her wine as she looks around the chamber, at the tapestries and the velvet that hangs around the bed that I share with Gabriel, at the gold thread and the embroidered cushions.

'It is my home now,' I say.

'Yours?'

'My husband's,' I amend.

'You have a husband!' she comments. 'And good wine.' It has given her a sly, slurring edge. I should have ordered ale. 'Pray, where did you find one so wealthy?' There is a slackness to her face as she holds her feet in their tattered shoes towards the fire, one after the other.

I hesitate. 'I married Mr Thorne.'

'Mr Thorne?' Cat's brow wrinkles and then clears. 'The merchant?'

'Yes. You had gone, I had Cecily to think of . . . What else could I do?' I hate the defensive note in my voice.

'But he was to marry me!'

I set my teeth. 'You told me to take your place. You said I might marry him with your goodwill.'

Cat stares at me. 'I did not think you would take me at my word!'

'You did not want him.'

'You let him believe you were me?' There is gathering outrage in the blue eyes, and I swallow.

'He still believes that.'

'You have *lied* all this time, Mary? Taken *my* name?'

'I had to! Or I would have become as you are now,' I say deliberately, letting my gaze rest on her stained skirts, her bedraggled hair.

Her jaw tightens. 'What of my brother? Avery must have known who you really were.'

'He died, Jocosa too. I did not know if I could take Cecily to Steeple Tew, or if the new Lord Delahay would support her. You had gone. I had nowhere else to go. Gabriel — my husband — said that you could write if you changed your mind, so I did, in your stead.'

Cat's gaze returns to the flames and for a while there is only the spit and crackle of the logs as they settle, and the relentless patter of the rain outside.

'All this time,' she says slowly at last, the corner of her mouth curling in a way I do not quite like, 'you have been living as *me*. I do not know what to say, Mary. You were quick, it seems, to take advantage of the situation. That was clever of you. But then, you always were clever, weren't you? And you have done well for yourself.' She looks around the chamber again. 'Very well.' Her eyes come back to my face. 'Wealth suits you, Mary. You have been luckier than I.'

She drains her glass and holds it out, and I cannot help myself. I get to my feet and pour her more wine. I even offer her a cake.

'Cat,' I say clearly. 'You must not call me Mary.'

'What shall I call you then? Mistress? I heard you tell that serving wench that I was your maid.'

'I had to say something! Call me mistress or Catherine, but not Mary, I beg of you.'

'Very well, m-*mistress*.' Cat laughs at my expression. She drinks her wine, eyeing me over the rim of the glass. 'We have changed positions, it seems.'

And there was I thinking the opposite.

She puts down the glass and gets to her feet so that she can shake out her damp skirts. I swivel on my stool to watch her walk around the chamber. Her head is blurry, I guess, and she is moving with exaggerated care, but she touches things lightly: feeling the weight of the velvet hangings, pressing the bed to test its softness. She smooths the tassel on a cushion, runs her palm over the turkey-work carpet on the chest.

A gasp of laughter. 'Is that really your old wooden baby? And still with only one arm, I see!' Cat carries Peg over to the fire and for one terrible moment I think she is about to throw her in, the way Avery once did. 'Do you remember how you held onto it when you first arrived at Steeple Tew? You would not let me touch it — not that I cared. I had one much finer of my own.' She waggles Peg's arm at me. 'Why do you keep such a poor thing?'

The firelight flickers over Peg as Cat turns her dismissively, and I am certain I see such an expression of horror on the wooden face that my

53

heart lurches into my throat and hammers there.

A trick of the light, no more.

Still, I take Peg from Cat and lay her in my lap and smooth down her gown before setting her on the floor beside me. 'I like her,' I say.

Cat flits off again, jittery now. This is how she was at Haverley Court, lurching from a blurry slackness to feverish intensity. She stops in front of the looking glass and examines her reflection. Does she see the split lip, the bruise, the bedraggled hair beneath her cap, or does she see herself as she was, glowing with beauty, a-sparkle with wit and promise?

And yet, even in this state, she *is* beautiful and bright, the sun to my moon. Everything about Cat is vivid: her eyes are the bluest blue, her hair the goldest gold, while I am dim in comparison to her. My hair is an unremarkable brown, my eyes an unremarkable grey. I have straight brows and a mouth that is too big for my face. She is a summer day, I am a misty winter morn.

'Cat?' I say tentatively at last. 'What of Anthony?'

She does not answer at first, but her shoulders stiffen. When she turns, the confidence has dropped from her like a discarded cloak, and her eyes are full of tears. 'I cannot talk of it,' she says, a crack in her voice. 'I beg of you, do not ask me about him.' Her voice drops to a choking whisper. 'I have been so scared . . . '

I touch my lip, where hers is split. 'Your lip . . . ?' I ask, and she nods.

I remember Anthony when I first saw him at Steeple Tew, how he bowed low. The boyish

54

looks, the lock of hair that he would push back with a glinting smile. And Cat, whirling frantically, her eyes wild. 'I love him! I *need* him. Oh, you could not understand, Mary!'

I could not then, but I do now.

'I am truly sorry,' I say, 'but you are safe from him now. I will give you some money and some clean clothes before you go.'

'Go?' Cat's mouth trembles. 'You would turn me away?'

I stare at her, stupefied. 'But, Cat, you cannot stay here,' I stammer.

'Why not?'

Why not? I want to scream at her. 'You cannot be yourself here,' I say carefully instead. 'Gabriel married me thinking that I was you. I am you now,' I say, and in my head I hear that sickening refrain again: *now, now, now.* 'We cannot go back, and my husband must not know the truth.'

I am trying to sound calm, but my voice cracks with desperation. If Gabriel finds out that I have been lying to him all these years . . . Panic scrabbles at the edges of my mind. It cannot happen. It *must* not happen.

I will not let it happen.

'I will not tell him,' says Cat. 'Why would I?'

The answer leaps into my head: *to punish me.*

I rub my temples. This is not what I was thinking when I invited her in. But then, I was not thinking at all, was I?

'Please, Mary,' she says in a small voice, and I look up sharply. Her blue eyes are blurred with tears, and guilt jabs at me. What is wrong with me to think such a thing of her? This is Cat, and she is suffering.

Cat crosses the room to drop to her knees beside me and bury her head in my lap. 'Please, please let me stay. Just for a while. I have been so cold, and I am so *tired*.' Her voice cracks and tears. 'I cannot go back to Anthony now that I have left him. He will kill me, Mary.'

She sobs into my skirts and I stroke her head. Her cap feels gritty with dirt and I am ashamed of myself for wishing that I could wash my hands. 'Hush now,' I say helplessly.

'He *will*!' She lifts her face to me, beseeching. 'I am not how I was. I ask for so little now: shelter, some warmth, something to eat. Can you deny me those?'

Of course I cannot. I am a Christian woman. I cannot turn her away, but the scar on my hand has begun to itch.

'Just for a short time?' Cat pleads. 'Until I am stronger? And then I will go away and not trouble you any more, I promise.'

'Cat, of course you can stay,' I say, and her face lights up in a dazzling smile. Ah yes, that is the Cat I remember.

'Thank you! Oh, I thank you!'

'But, Cat,' I go on warningly, 'there is much to be thought of. How are we to go on?'

'Well, you have already said that I am an old servant of yours.' Cat sits back on her heels, buoyant once more. 'We will change places!' She laughs excitedly, a frenetic ripple of notes up the scale. 'You will be the mistress, and I the maid.'

'You would not like being my servant,' I say.

'It would just be for a short time. Come, will it not be amusing?'

I think of the years I spent as her maid. Of a sore back and sore fingers. Of aching feet and bone-tiredness. Of emptying her chamber pot and preparing rags for her courses. I did it willingly, but it was not amusing, no.

'What of Cecily?'

'Cecily?' Cat looks blank, then her face clears. 'Oh, my daughter.'

'*My* daughter now,' I correct her, biting out the words. I do not know whether to be relieved or furious that Cecily can mean so little to her. 'You gave her to me. You begged me to care for her, and I have. She is mine now.'

Now, now, now.

I shake my head to clear it of the tune.

Cat takes both my hands in hers. 'Mary, do not fret. I will do nothing to betray you. All I ask is some shelter for a few weeks, in memory of the shelter we gave you at Steeple Tew.'

And my name, which you stole.

She doesn't say that, but I know she must be thinking of it. And she is right. I have everything that was once hers: her name, her status, and the rest. She threw them away, and I picked them up, but that did not make them mine.

A shameful part of me is wishing that I had taken Gabriel's advice, that I had let Amy suffer and stayed home where it was warm and dry, where Cat would not have seen me. But it is too late for regrets. She is here now, and I cannot throw her out into the rain and send her back to a man who beats her.

And she might tell Gabriel the truth if you do, a voice whispers at the back of my mind. We both know what happened twelve years ago, and now I have more to lose than she does.

Much more.

And Cat knows it.

5

Cat

Little Wood Street, March 1590

I have a chamber of my own. You wanted me to sleep squeezed in with Sarah and another maid, who share with Cecily, and I listened, astounded, as you proposed who would share which beds, as if I really was just another servant, or a child come into the household. You cannot seriously have supposed that I would want to do that, after all that I have been through?

I hung my head, but not so quickly that you would not see the tears of self-pity that stung my eyes. 'Of course,' I murmured, biting my lip, making sure you could see my efforts to disguise my disappointment. 'If that is what you think best.'

You hesitated. 'Unless you would rather sleep on your own?'

Oh, Mary, Mary, you are as easy to manage as ever.

I confess, I was still a little drunk when you brought me here. The warmth of the house left me befuddled, and I hardly knew what I was doing at first. I have a vague memory of you hurrying me up a staircase, and then putting a glass — a glass! — of hot wine in my hands. It burned comfortingly down my throat, and the fragrance of cinnamon and cloves cleared my head, and I began to feel myself again.

I looked around your chamber and I could not help but compare it with the squalid lodgings I left this morning, with its stink of tallow and piss, and the scuttle of rats. While I have been tossing on a mean mattress, you have been sleeping soundly on three feather beds. My hand sank down when I tested them. It must be like sleeping in the clouds that billow across a summer sky.

You have had all of this, *all of it*, because of me, Mary. You have stolen my name! You have been masquerading as me all this time. I could hardly believe it when you told me what you had done, and so coolly too, as if it were nothing to take my name and my life and make them your own, you a mere maidservant too! Who would have thought you would have dared to impersonate a lady?

Nothing but the best for you now. Your chamber smelt of sunshine even on a day like today. What is that fragrance? A special mixture of your own, no doubt. Some lavender, I am sure, and roses, perhaps? The scent reminded me of the garden at Steeple Tew anyway. It made me think about the way the slanting sun would turn the stone walls to gold, and throw long shadows across the fields. The memory is a jagged ache in my throat and I have to swallow hard.

This is no manor drowsing in the summer sun. It is just a tiny chamber in the roof, barely more than a wedge of space between the rafters, with a roughly hewn bedstead and an old chest that I have nothing to put in. It smells of wood rather than summer, but at least there are no rat droppings on the floor and no leaks in the roof. I am better off than I was this morning, with Anthony labouring over me.

I wonder if he is still in the Dog's Head? Has he gone to look for me? He will be angry, I fear, when he realises that I have gone. He is very possessive. He likes to hold onto what he has. He is like you that way, Mary. I could have taken your money and gone back to him, I could have shared the purse of silver I know you would have pressed on me, but he would have gambled it away, do you see? I am better off here.

Thinking of Anthony, I chew my thumbnail. He is all charm until he is crossed. I have learnt this well over the past twelve years. You told me it was madness, but how could I have known it would turn out like this? You have not said 'I told you so', but I could tell that you were thinking it.

Well, it has not all been bad. As long as my jewels lasted, as long as there was wine, and a servant or two to care for our needs, there was laughter and lust and even love. But I wonder, sometimes, if Anthony and I did not secretly conjure George up in our heads while we were making the beast with two backs. As if we somehow needed him to make us *feel* like that.

I sigh a little, remembering how once I craved Anthony's touch, how I thrilled at how possessive he was. Now . . .

I have nibbled a shred of nail and I tear it free impatiently. I wish I was sure that I have not made a terrible mistake. What if he tries to find me? But how will he know where I have gone? Our lodgings are in Southwark, far from here. In all the weeks we have been here, I have never seen you until now, Mary. We have moved in different worlds, it seems, so there is no reason that Anthony's path should cross yours as mine did. And even if it did, would he even remember you, my modest maidservant? I dare say he never even looked at you.

No, I think I will be safe. Besides, for all I played the terror-stricken wife to you, I can manage Anthony. He is clever at cards, but for all his gloss, he has no ambition beyond a full glass of wine and a woman to satisfy his needs. He might be angry, but he desires me still. That gives me power over him. I can use that if needed.

When I saw you first, I had no thought of abandoning him, but then you brought me inside and your chamber was so comfortable that the thought of going back to that hovel was unendurable. And so I had to persuade you to let me stay. I did not think it would be so hard, Mary. Anyone would think you did not want me here.

Who would have thought that you would have done so well for yourself? I imagined you as a maid to some other lady, not pretending to be a lady yourself! I am angry with you for using me that way, but I admire you, too, I must confess. You took your chance, and it has paid off. No wonder you do not want me here, putting all you have gained at risk, but you gave in, as I knew you would. I did not need to threaten to tell your husband the truth. I did not even need to hint at it. You know what I can do.

So Roger, your husband's serving man, was sent to sleep above the stable, and a new flock mattress was dragged up here for me and slung onto the ropes. It will serve, but when I prod it, it is lumpy and hard, and I think of your bed with its velvet curtains and cushiony softness and the injustice of my situation burns in my belly.

You stood in your bedchamber and put a rough coverlet into my arms.

'Where is the sheet?' I asked.

'Servants do not have sheets, Cat.'

'Please,' I said in a small voice.

I should not have had to beg for a *sheet*, Mary. Why did you make me do that? Have you forgotten the times I was a kind mistress to you?

You bit your lip as you turned away to lift the lid of your linen press, and the scent of lavender wafted out. 'Do not let the others see,' you warned as you tucked a sheet beneath the coverlet in my arms. 'We do not want them to wonder about you.'

You do not want them to wonder about me. Be honest, Mary. You do not want them to ask how someone like me could be a servant. You do not want them to wonder if there might be some secret between us, do you? Or what that secret might be.

I thought at first that you had not changed at all, but you have. You have grown into those severe brows and that lush mouth that always sat so oddly with your oh so modest demeanour.

The mouth of a whore, Avery always used to say. You are no beauty, but you are striking, and there is a sheen to you now, and a confidence in the way you clapped for your servant.

Now you may clap for me if you wish, and I will have to go. I sit abruptly down on the bed. Have I made a mistake, insisting that I stay and be your servant? *You will not like being my servant*, you warned me, and I fear you may be right. But it will not be for long. I will find some way.

And in the meantime, I have this chamber. I have a clean linen shift to wear, a petticoat and a gown, a pair of stockings and some velvet pantofles that are too big for me. My feet have always been daintier than yours.

You gave me a comb and a cloth to rub myself with too, and the little maid, Sarah, was sent labouring up the steps with a bowl of scented water, most of which she slopped onto the floor. I gather from the careful way you haven't said anything that I must stink, and I set my teeth as I scrub myself furiously and comb the lice from my hair. Somehow this is more humiliating than anything George ever did to me. I know I should feel grateful to you, but instead I hate you for pitying me, for seeing me in my shame.

It feels good, though, to feel cool, clean linen against my skin once more, and I sit on the edge of the bed in the shift to pull on the stockings and tie the garters at my knees. Once you would have knelt to tie them for me. Once you would have pinned my sleeves, and pulled my laces. Now I have to do it all by myself.

Two floors below I can hear a girl protesting loudly to you. 'Who is this new servant? Why should she have her own chamber? Let her share with Amy who snores, and leave Sarah with me. That would be more fair!'

I am surprised that you let her speak to you like that, but then, it seems you are an overindulgent mistress altogether, tolerating clumsy maids and sending others to bed with little more than a toothache. They take advantage of you, that is clear. You murmur placatingly in response, but the girl continues to complain. 'And why did you give her your second-best gown?'

Second-best, is it, Mary? I think, jerking the laces of the bodice tight. The gown you gave me is fine-quality russet, better by far than the one I had. The thought that you wear a better one rankles, though.

But a chamber of my own, a roof over my head, a warm gown: these things are a start. The certainty of a place in this comfortable house as long as I have a tongue in my head that can tell your husband and your neighbours that you are living a lie. The chance to plan and take my chances.

By the time I make my way down the narrow stairs from the attic it has grown dark, and in the great chamber the clumsy maid has lit a mass of candles. Beeswax candles, of course. It is so long since I have sat in the light of anything but stinking tallow that the brilliance almost blinds me.

You are sitting in a chair in the great chamber,

some stitching in your hands. Always busy, always *good*.

Except when you are lying, of course, and come to think of it, that is all the time.

You seem composed, but I can see the tremulous pulse in your throat. Your husband is standing before the fire, holding out a booted foot to the warmth. He is bigger than I remember. More solid.

You both look up at my entrance, and I see relief cross your face to see me modestly dressed and with my hair decently covered. What did you think, Mary? That I would come down with my breasts bare and hair hanging loose?

'Husband, here is the servant I was telling you about earlier,' you say calmly. 'Cat has fallen on hard times and I have offered her a place here for the time being. You have no objection, I trust?'

'None if you have work to occupy her.'

For a wealthy merchant, your husband is dressed as soberly as a monk, in a plain dark doublet and hose, and a gown lined with nothing but budge. He is a dull-looking man, quiet of face, quiet of feature, but he holds himself easily and his eyes are shrewd. I did not notice that before. The lack of interest in them as they rest on me is a needle prick of pique. He is a man, after all, and I am fair, even in your second-best gown. Even with a torn lip and a bruise on my cheek. He ought to *notice* me.

Strange thought that this man might have been my husband. Not that I would ever have lowered myself to marry him. For all his faults, Anthony is at least a gentleman. And this house

66

is comfortable, but it is nothing compared to Haverley Court, or even to Steeple Tew.

Still, there is money here, and security, and now that I know you have been lying to your husband all these years, I see no reason why I should not have both.

You lay your sewing aside and get to your feet. 'You look better, Cat,' you say. 'Are you warmer now?'

'I am, thank you . . . mistress,' I add after a moment. The word feels grudging on my tongue.

'Do you come with me to the kitchen then,' you say briskly. 'You can help prepare supper.' You turn to the merchant. 'Husband, shall I send in more wine?'

'Thank you, no. I will go to my closet.'

'Come then, Cat.'

I follow you out although something in me bridles at being given orders by you. It comes to you so naturally now. I do not care for it when you are brisk like this. I think after all that I prefer you when I am the mistress and you are the maid.

The kitchen is warm and smells of bread and a mutton broth that is simmering over the fire. Sarah is on her knees, mopping a puddle of cream from the floor, watched by a girl with an enchantingly pretty face and a rosebud mouth.

'Oh, Mamma, look what Sarah has done now!' She spreads her hands, casting her eyes up to the bacon pieces hanging from the ceiling.

Mamma? I glance at you. Your face may be calm, but there is a rigidity to your shoulders and I look back at the girl with more interest.

67

This then must be Cecily. My daughter.

My daughter, you said, your voice hard.

Well, well.

I remember little of her birth. A red haze of pain, of pushing and wrenching and tearing and stretching. The muscles in my throat taut with screaming. Sweat rolling down my face and my body leaden, and all you could say was 'Just one more push'. Easy for *you* to say. You should not even have been there, as an unmarried woman, but none of the respectable neighbours would have anything to do with us by then, would they?

You kept telling me it would be worth it when my babe was born, but you were wrong. After all that, I had only a daughter to show for my trouble. A daughter was no good to me. You never understood that, Mary. Your voice lifted when you told me, as if it was something to be joyful about.

If only I had had a son instead! Everything would have been so different. You told me it would be a boy, you and that old witch you brought in to help. My right breast was plumper; that was a sure sign, you said. The babe stirred at the beginning of the third month; another sign. When I stood up from sitting, I used my right foot first. I rested most readily on my right hand. Clearly I was carrying a boy.

Oh, I am out of all patience with you just remembering how you raised my hopes, only to dash them with your smiling news: *you have a beautiful daughter*. Faugh! I had it all planned out, and then to be told that the babe was a girl . . . What use was a daughter?

I barely saw her after that. You tried to interest me in her, but what was there to see? A screaming infant, red-faced and tightly swaddled. You were besotted enough for both of us, in any case. I think you even named her. George was no more interested than I. He had only married me for a son, after all.

Now the girl must be thirteen or so, and is bidding fair to be a beauty. I feel a twinge of pride in spite of myself. She has her father's dark eyes and dark hair, but still, she has the look of me, doesn't she? You must think that every time you look at her and the thought pleases me. You cannot have forgotten me, Mary, not with Cecily there to remind you of what you did.

And how you have been lying ever since.

Sarah is stammering out an apology for her clumsiness with the cream, and instead of rebuking her, you comfort her. 'It cannot be helped,' you tell her. 'Do you make sure it is all cleared up, and then you can help me prepare the meal.'

I meet Cecily's eyes across Sarah's bent head. I half expect her to share my incredulity at your softness, but she only looks coolly back at me. It must have been her I heard complaining to you earlier. She is not pleased that I am here, that is clear.

'This is Cat,' you tell her when you have finally finished fussing over Sarah. 'We were children together, were we not, Cat?' you add nervously. 'Cat was with me when you were but a babe, Cecily.'

Cecily raises her brows and looks at me,

unimpressed. 'Cat?'

'A pet name,' I explain. 'I am Catherine.'

'Like Mamma?' There is a sharpness in the brown eyes that sits oddly with the sweet face.

I glance at you and smile. 'Exactly like Mamma,' I agree.

6

Cat

Instead of sitting up by the fire with your husband as a gentlewoman should, you tie an apron around you and bustle around the kitchen, quartering a roasted chicken, throwing onions in a pan for a sop, mincing carrots for a salad. You direct your husband's serving man, Roger, to put up the table in the hall and fill the tubs with fresh water for rinsing the glasses. Having cleared up the creamy mess on the floor, Sarah is to pull jugs of small beer — and yes, of *course* you have brewed it yourself to a special recipe. She is kept busy trotting backwards and forwards to the larder to bring out the remains of a tart and some preserved quinces.

Cecily is set to fetching a tablecloth and damask napkins. I am to help her set the table, and I smile brightly as I am handed the pepper box and the salt, as if I am used to doing such lowly tasks. She is clearly not pleased at my arrival. You are probably counting on that fact. Something tells me you won't like it if she grows too close to me, so it will be amusing to win her over. A little challenge for me, if you will.

I set out to charm her as we move around the table, setting out pewter plates in every place. No trenchers for you, I see, Mary. I am surprised you do not set out knives, forks and spoons for everyone too. Little touches of luxury are evident everywhere: plates, glasses to drink from, silver gleaming on the chest. I admire the girdle Cecily wears and she cannot resist boasting that it comes from Venice.

'John bought it for me while he was away. It was a gift.'

'John?'

'My eldest brother. Well, I call him my brother,' she amends, polishing a spoon on her sleeve, 'but he is not. My father is not my father either, but I always think of him as such. I was only an infant when Mamma married him.' The brown eyes rest on my face, their expression hard to read. 'But you know that, of course.'

She is sharper than she looks. I nod. 'I remember when you were born,' I offer.

'So you must have known my real father?'

'I did, yes.' I smooth out the tablecloth, knowing that she means George, but thinking of Anthony. Not as he was in the Dog's Head, but as he was then, dark and comely. The smile that warmed me, that fluttered along my veins. The mouth that could make me shake with pleasure in the days when he cared to pleasure me. 'You have the look of him,' I tell Cecily honestly.

'I have supposed so,' she says, and flicks at a speck of something on her skirts. 'I am not much like my mother.'

I smile. 'Oh, do you not think so?'

'You see a similarity?' She looks surprised, as well she might. You are both dark, but otherwise you have nothing in common.

'In character rather than in looks,' I say. 'There

is much about your mother that you do not know.'

Well, perhaps it was mischievous of me, Mary, but she is intrigued now. I imagine you squirming under her questioning and laugh to myself.

You set a good table, I must say. The entire household sits down to supper in the hall, even the kitchen boy, an urchin apparently rescued from the streets and now dressed in a canvas shirt and patched hose. I have to sit on a bench separated from him only by Sarah. At least I do not have to serve him: that would be too much.

The servants admire and respect you, that much is clear. I am already tired of hearing what a good mistress you are, how kind, how devout, how *worthy*. If they only knew what I know about you, Mary, they would not be so impressed, would they?

Your children, too, are all one could wish. Gabriel's son John is a fine-looking young man, even I must admit. I keep my eyes demurely lowered for the most part, but I can feel his gaze on me and I cannot help preening myself a little. Your dull husband may not have the wit to admire me, but his son clearly does. John is well set-up with a handsome pair of legs and a courteous manner, even to servants such as I am supposed to be. He is young still, of course, no more than one and twenty, I judge, and so fair that his beard is no more than down on his cheek. When I smile at him, he reddens.

There is a boisterous lad a little older than Cecily too, and, of course, Cecily herself, a beautiful, lively daughter who clearly dotes on John.

How charming you all are together. The perfect family.

Under my lashes, I watch you as you sit quietly next to your husband. You are toying with your glass, but drinking little and eating less. We servants have pewter goblets, and ale instead of wine. I find myself staring at the wine in your glass, imagining the taste of it hitting the roof of my mouth, sliding down my throat, and the need for it throbs down to my fingertips. I gulp at the ale instead, but it is not the same.

Cecily is telling some story that is making the others laugh, but my gaze is fixed on the wine, and that is how I see the merchant lean towards you and murmur something as he presses a crumb from the corner of your mouth with his thumb. You touch the tip of your tongue briefly to the place where his thumb was, and you look back at him.

Well.

So you are afire with passion for him, this dull man, and he for you. You did not tell me *that*, Mary. Neither of you smile, but even from the end of the table I can see how the air heats between you. All it would take would be a graze of a finger, a breath warm on skin, and it would burst into a blaze.

My cheeks burn as if I am watching you naked together. Warmth pools in my belly, and there is a disturbing tug in my privy parts that makes me shift uneasily on the bench. No man has ever looked at me the way your husband looks at you.

74

He is not a gentleman, true, but when he looks at you like *that*, I feel envy, yes, I do. It seems that all you have to do to earn his desire is to sit there like a pudding, quiet, covered up, eyes modestly lowered.

So you have wealth and respectability and children *and* a husband who desires you — and all because of me. Rage and misery bubble in my throat. I stab my knife into a piece of chicken. It will not do. You have everything and I have nothing. It is not fair, Mary. You must feel it too.

Hand clenched around my knife, I look up, and I catch you watching me, almost as if you can hear my thoughts. There is a crease between your brows, and you smile anxiously at me, but I am not fooled. You do not want me here. You are wishing that you had never invited me in. You are thinking that you should have given me money and hustled me back out into the street. Perhaps you are even wondering how soon you can persuade me to go.

But that is not going to happen now, Mary. I let my fingers relax and smile sweetly back at you. I like your warm, comfortable house. I am here now, and here I will stay.

★   ★   ★

I sleep well on my flock bed, in spite of the lumps. It is a great improvement on what I have been used to of late, but still, I think of you lying with your husband high on your feather beds, the curtains closed around your bedstead, warm and close under your sumptuous coverlets, and it

75

seems unjust that I should be up here under the eaves with just a plain bolster and coverlet.

For all that you are the mistress and I the maid, you are up ahead of me. The household is abustle with activity before I have pulled on the clean shift. I have to lace myself into the bodice. I know, I have become used to dressing myself, but to have to do it here, while you are below, it feels all wrong, Mary. Why are you not here to help me rise?

I am hungry again, but no, we cannot break our fasts until the whole household has prayed together, and then the barber surgeon has been sent for and the missing maid, Amy, has had her tooth pulled to much screaming and wailing. I have to wait while you fuss around her afterwards, making up a calming posset and preparing another clout to comfort her and insisting that she stays in bed, as if she has not already been lolling around for too long. You are such a weak mistress, Mary. They cannot respect you.

Later, you tell me that I can accompany you to the market. How gracious of you! You are going to show me how to shop, you say. I have to walk behind you and carry your basket. Do you have any idea of what that feels like, Mary? Well, of course you do. You were a servant for long enough. But you do not know how it feels to have been a mistress and be now reduced to a maid. You have no knowledge of how humiliating it is to trail after you like a little dog.

I am a little anxious at first in case Anthony should see me, but it is early. I do not think he will be out and about yet, and anyway, he would never think to look at a maidservant demurely following her mistress.

Yesterday's rain has cleared and in the weak sun, the sky is reflected in icy puddles that gleam in the street. A brisk wind cuts through to my bones and I stand and shiver while you dig your hands deep into sacks of grain to check the quality, and lean over the butcher's stall, pointing out precisely the cut you want. He is all deference: Yes, Mistress Thorne. No, Mistress Thorne. That is the best cut, Mistress Thorne. For roasting, is it? Stewing? Lifting his cleaver and bringing it down through the bone with a dull thwack.

'This is as good meat as you will get anywhere in London,' he tells you proudly.

And you, you ask him about his apprentice who was sick, and you seem to know his wife. How can you be interested in these dull little people? I huddle deeper into my cloak and will you to hurry.

It all takes so *long*. Weighed down by the basket, I follow you along to the market, where the countrywomen squat by their baskets, huddled under their hats, their faces swathed in neckerchiefs. You don't seem bored at all.

'Pay attention now, Cat,' you say as you inspect cabbages — cabbages! — closely, turning them over in your hands and sniffing them with as much care as if you were buying a precious jewel. 'This one is rotting already, do you see?'

I don't, but I nod and pretend to listen. What do I care for cabbages?

Now I have to stand while you bargain with a toothless woman squatting next to a wicker cage of clucking, burbling hens. She plucks out two, snaps their necks efficiently, trusses their scaly feet together and hands them to me with a sly smile. She knows that I do not belong in this crowded market with its pushing and jostling and bleating and shouting and quacking, and its smell of rotting vegetables and mud and banked aggression.

I am expected to carry these dead birds? I glance at you in disbelief, but you are wishing the woman a calm good day as you hand over a coin. You keep careful track of the money in your purse, I notice. You were born to be a merchant's wife, it seems. The knowledge that you have taken my name and made Lady Catherine into a prudent housewife burns and scrapes like a bone in my throat.

Everything takes twice as long as it should. Women keep stopping to greet you respectfully, and you inquire after their children and their coughs and their caudles as if you really want to know. I see how they defer to you and ask your advice, even the matrons whose gowns are as well-trimmed as yours. One or two gazes flicker over me, sharpening at the unfamiliar face, narrowing further at the bruise blooming on my cheek, the scab on my lip.

'My servant, Cat,' you say smoothly. 'She is but newly arrived in London.'

My cheeks mottle with the humiliation of being looked over by women like these, women I would not even acknowledge in my own life. My

78

real life. When would I have ever had occasion to carry my own basket in a market? Even when money was short in France, I had a servant to shop for me. I begin to think you have done this deliberately, Mary. You must have known how I would dislike this, but if you think this will be enough to get rid of me, you must think again.

I shift the basket from hand to hand, swapping with the chickens, and wait while the women pay court to you. They dip their heads and smile admiringly while their eyes grasp at every detail of your gown. There is nothing for them to sniff at. You are modest, which they approve of. You do not flaunt yourself, but the cloth is of the best quality, and your trimmings discreetly expensive. Dark it may be, but the gown still shouts prosperity. You wear it well, I will give you that, and black becomes you. I would have chosen a brighter colour myself.

Oh, you are quite the lady here, are you not? The queen of the parish, of the whole ward, it seems. While I have been suffering, you have been laughing with your gossips. Where once you would have told me all your secrets, now you confide in a mere Mistress Hawkins, a plump housewife with a merry laugh whose eyes rest on me curiously. She may think you will tell her all about me when you are alone, but you won't, will you, Mary?

At least there is one who dislikes you. A Mistress Parker, who is too grand to acknowledge a mere servant, as she thinks. She is all smiles and honeyed words, but her face is clotted with envy as she looks after you. You do not like her either, do you? No one else would be able to tell, but I see the slightest tightening of your shoulders, the way you are able to withdraw into yourself, so subtly that you would have to know you really well to notice. I doubt Mistress Hawkins knows you well, Mary, no matter how close a gossip she may be.

Nobody knows you the way I do.

All this clamouring and clattering and chattering are making my head ache. My back aches too, and my feet, rubbing in unfamiliar shoes. I wish we could go home instead of listening to the interminable news of sickness and adultery by people I do not know. There are mutterings about the misgoverned women the minister keeps in his house, the state of the gutters, how one woman called another woman a whore in the open street. Your neighbour, a fat goodwife who waddles up to accost you breathlessly, has a daughter who is in labour and, by the sounds of it, is hollering like a beast.

'I would take it kindly if you would step in to see her,' she says wheezily, laying an overly familiar hand on your arm. Her chins wobble as she speaks and her fingers are dimpled and swollen around her rings. 'You are so skilled, mistress. You would be able to quiet her.'

'I will go to her now,' you say instead of reprimanding her for her insolence. You turn to me. 'Do you take all this home, Cat, and tell Sarah to start preparing dinner. You can help her. I will come in a while.'

And that is it. It takes me a moment to realise that you have dismissed me. *Dismissed* me! As if

I am nothing. You turn away as if there is nothing more to say, and you go off with the grovelling goodwife and you do not even turn back to see if I have everything I need. You leave me standing here ridiculously in the street, holding two dead hens and a basket of cabbages and turnips. An apprentice pushes past me with a casual insult, a woman at her door leans into her gossip and they both look over at me and snicker behind their hands.

I glare back at them. What do I care for their snide looks? They do not know who I am. I will not be treated like this. You should know better.

I watch you walk off, straight-backed as ever, and I feel something turn over and settle inside me, cold and hard.

7

Mary

Little Wood Street, May 1590

Outside, the sky is turning a dark blue over the rooftops and the casement is open to let in the soft evening air. All day the sun has been shining. The trees are bursting with greenness and blossom powders the streets while the herbs in my garden are budding up nicely. My husband's business prospers, my family and friends are in good health. We have eaten well tonight and now we are gathered cheerfully in the great chamber. Cecily is at the virginals, and Cat and John are singing together. Cat has a beautiful voice, sweet and pure, the kind of voice that makes people stop in the street below the window to listen.

I should be content.

Instead, I am afraid.

At Steeple Tew, I loved to hear Cat sing. It meant that she was happy, and when Cat was happy, the whole manor was happy too. It was a gift that she had, to make us share in her feelings. But now the sweeter the melody she sings, the more jagged I feel, as if the music is scraping against me, jarring in time with the uneven beat of my heart.

Go from my window, my love, my dove, Cat

sings, smiling at John. *Go from my window, my dear.*

At the virginals, Cecily strikes a chord that jangles harshly through the chamber and makes Cat break off in mid-note. 'Your pardon,' Cecily calls after a moment. 'My fingers slipped.'

'No matter,' says Cat gaily. 'We will start again.' And she smiles at John, who turns the dull red of bricks drying in the sun.

I rub at my hand where my scar itches. 'Just for a while,' Cat said, but two months have passed and still she is here, at the heart of the household. She is a poor servant, as I knew she would be. She wrinkles her nose when set to plucking chickens or to filling a scuttle for the midden or sweeping out cobwebs. Her seams are sewn crookedly. She is careless in the kitchen, forgetful in the market.

She mocks me behind my back. I was on my way into the kitchen the other day when I heard the servants laughing, and I paused, smiling, pleased that they were enjoying themselves, even though it sounded as if Cat was hectoring them.

'Do you sweep the floor, Amy,' she was saying briskly. 'No, wait, I will do it because I sweep best. You cook the meal instead. No, I cook best. Bring water from the conduit . . . no, no, I do that best too. Roger, put up the tables, no, wait, I will do that too. *I* put up the tables best.'

It took me a moment to realise that she was imitating me, and hurt swiped the smile from my face. Amy, loyal, steadfast Amy, was honking with laughter. I imagined her wiping her eyes with the corner of her apron, and I knew that I could not bear to step into the kitchen and pretend that I had not heard. I turned away instead and went up to my bedchamber, my throat tight with tears that I refused to shed. I am not a *child*. I am not going to cry because they are laughing about me behind my back.

But my vision was wavering when I closed the door to the chamber and leant back against it. I could see Peg, sitting in her usual place on the chest, and I could have sworn that her smile had slipped, that instead of curving upwards, it was turned unhappily down, just like mine, and my heart tripped with the impossibility of it. Blinking the tears furiously away, I looked again. No, I had imagined it. Of course I had. How could a painted smile change?

Picking Peg up, I stared down at her familiar face: two round eyes, wide and staring, two little dots to mark the nose, a curving red line for a mouth. It is a little unsteady in the centre where my paintbrush wobbled, but that quirk has always been there.

Hasn't it?

The more I stared, the stranger the wooden face seemed. Had her expression always looked that dismayed, her smile that anxious? Suddenly repelled, I put her abruptly back down on the chest and stepped away, my hands shaking.

Since then I have found myself looking askance at Peg whenever I pass, turning my head without warning as if I will catch her expression changing even though I know it won't. It can't.

I was sharp with Cat when I found her in the parlour this morning. I have tried to teach her some skills in the still room and she pays attention there at least, but she does not spin, she does not sew. She would much rather be sitting at her ease, or singing. Only this morning I found her in the parlour, lounging on the window cushions and plucking idly at the lute. Sometimes I think she deliberately plays that tune that disquiets me so, and a clogged feeling rises in my throat, almost like panic, and I was shorter with her than I usually am.

'What are you doing in here? I thought you were helping Amy with the brewing.'

'Amy said she doesn't mind doing it by herself.' Cat didn't even stop playing. It wasn't the tune, but it was almost it. Straining, I was convinced that I could pick out the *now, now, now*. 'Brewing is dull work. I could not bear it.'

It was all I could do not to snatch the lute from her hands. 'I told you that you would not care for being a servant,' I said.

'Well, and you were right as you always are, Mary,' she said tartly, and to my relief she laid the lute aside, although I was sure that I could still hear that miserable tune jumping and jarring in the air. 'I do not care for it at all.'

I sank down onto a stool. 'Cat,' I tried again. 'If you do not wish to be a servant, I will give you some money. You can go away and start afresh.'

'Go away?' She stared at me, the blue eyes filling. 'Is that what you want? To send me off with a few coins and be rid of me! What am I, your sweepings to be brushed out into the gutter?' Her voice rose and I shushed her.

'Of course not. I thought merely that if you were unhappy . . . '

'I am sorry indeed that I am not a better servant, but I am not born to it,' she said. 'You do not know how hard it is.'

I thought of the years I spent as a servant at Steeple Tew. 'My father was a gentleman. I was not born to it either,' I reminded her, but Cat waved that away.

'Oh, you were but a child. It is not at all the same.'

I let that go. Cat sees the world not through a window as others do, but in a looking glass that reflects back only what she wishes to see. 'I know it is hard for you,' I tried. 'That is why I wish to give you some money so that you may live as you are used to. Gabriel owns some houses in Finsbury. You could live there with a servant and be comfortable, perhaps.'

'Comfortable? So I, Catherine Latimer, *Lady Delahay*, am to be reduced to a tenement in the country and a single servant, is that what you propose?' she asked tearfully. 'Do you think that is fair, Mary, when you have taken my name and my connections and the life that should have been mine?'

You did not want it, I wanted to cry. My fists were clenched in my skirts and I made myself relax my fingers and smooth the fabric instead. Cat is contrary at the best of times. I could not risk making her angry. It would take very little for her to go to Gabriel and curtsey low. 'There is something you should know about your wife,' she would say, and that would be that. She has said nothing, made no threat, but we both know that she could.

'Besides,' Cat went on, 'I would not be safe on my own. What if Anthony were to find me?'

I had forgotten about Anthony. 'He has not found you so far.'

'He will be looking for a woman on her own. It would never occur to Anthony that I disguise myself as a servant, why would it? But if I live alone, I fear it would only be a matter of time before he found me. You do not know him,' she told me. 'He will not give up. I am afraid every time I go out.'

I have not noticed her fear, I confess. It seems to me that she has been quite at ease, but I know better than to say so.

'But what then are we to do?' I said. 'You will not want to stay here forever.'

Cat examined her nails. 'Perhaps I may marry.'

'Marry?' I gaped at her. 'But you are married to Anthony!'

'Not so,' she said airily. 'There were no witnesses.'

'But . . . ' I shut my mouth. I did not know what to say.

'You need not look at me like that, Mary. Your own marriage has little to recommend it either.'

'Our vows were witnessed. We had a nuptial mass,' I said, my face stiff. 'The minister blessed our marriage. I am married before God.'

'But under a false name,' Cat pointed out with a sweet smile. She brushed at her sleeve. 'Can you not let it be known that I am a widow — which I am, as you know?'

'Yes, I know,' I said dully.

'You must know some wealthy men in search of a wife.'

'Cat, these are practical men. They are looking for a woman to run the household, care for their children, help with their business. A woman who will work and add to their reputation.'

'I'll warrant some look for skills in the bedchamber too — and do not try and tell me that your husband does not care for that,' she said with an arch look. 'I have seen the way you look at each other. You are not as prim and proper when the bed curtains are drawn, are you, Mary?'

I set my teeth. 'I would be glad to find you a husband, but I do not know any gentlemen.'

'I will settle for a merchant now I have seen how comfortable you are,' she said, to my dismay. 'One like your husband, perhaps?' she added airily. 'Although I would manage him very differently, I can assure you. Your husband is rich, but you put on an apron and bustle around like a goodwife. If I were married to a man of his wealth, I would have whisked him off to an estate long since. I would have had him build me a fine new house, or buy a fine old manor like Steeple Tew. If I were you, I would have a housekeeper to stock my larder, someone else to poke over turnips or sniff at pickled eels. But you have no such refinement,' she said almost sulkily. 'I do not understand why Gabriel would bother to marry a gentlewoman if he just wanted to stay in London. Avery would have pushed for every penny he could. I cannot see that having Lady

Catherine Delahay to wife would be worth anything unless he wanted to move up in the world.' She sounded baffled. 'I never expected to find you here. I had imagined you on an estate in the country, but no, here you are as if he had done no more than marry a baker's daughter! What have you done for his standing?'

'I am respected. I have added to his reputation.' I was offended, but in truth I have often wondered myself why Gabriel wed me, even after he had discovered that the sickness had taken Avery and his wife and the marriage portion agreed with them. I had been too grateful to question him closely, too afraid to reveal that I was not the woman he thought I was. I told myself that he was a man who had set his heart on a gentlewoman and was determined to get what he wanted.

Now that I know him, I think the explanation is much simpler. My husband is a kind man. And he wanted me.

I think of how he turns to me in the night, and heat floods through me. He does not know my name, but he knows what turns my bones to honey. He knows how I arch beneath him, what makes me catch my breath, and smile and sigh. He knows *me*.

He wants me still.

In the end, Cat had her way, as I knew she would. We have agreed that she will be a companion more than a servant. That I will treat her as my kin. 'As we are,' Cat reminded me.

There will be no rough work for her now. She thinks she may help me in the still room as she has done before now, and she may go to market, but there will be no plucking of chickens, no chopping of onions. No beating of carpets or churning of butter.

I stretched my mouth into a smile. 'But you must sing and play for us in the evenings,' I said. 'That will be your task.'

She clapped her hands together, her smile brilliant. 'Of course! Thank you, Mary.' Impulsively she embraced me. 'I am grateful to you for taking me in,' she whispered in my ear, her arm around my neck, and when she drew back, the cornflower blue eyes were warm as summer skies as they looked into mine. '*Thank* you,' she said.

I thought about arriving at Steeple Tew, the curse ringing in my ears. How I had clutched Peg as the only familiar thing in a world turned dark and bitter. How Cat had danced in and taken my hand and made everything right.

'How could I not?' I said, drawing her back into a tight embrace. I pressed my cheek to hers. 'How could I not?'

I am glad that I have been able to offer her shelter and repay the welcome that she gave me. I am glad that she is not alone and friendless and cold on the streets of London. I *am*. But everything has changed now that she is here, and I am not glad about that.

Now I watch as Cat sings, her face upturned to John, her hand to her throat. Her lashes flutter extravagantly as she acts the part of the lover to make everyone laugh.

Everyone except me — and Cecily, I notice, but then, she is concentrating on the keys of the virginals. She is still learning how to play.

I let my gaze wander around the chamber. At the back, Amy and Sarah are listening to the song, rocking gently from side to side, their shoulders bumping every now and then as Sarah misses the beat, but they are smiling, content. Richard Martindale has come to supper. Gabriel is taking Tom to Hamburg to learn the business from his factor there, just as John did, and the three of them have their heads together, discussing the journey. Jacopo is squatting outside the door. He prefers to be outside, he says, with his back to a wall. The smoke from his pipe drifts up past the open casement and the smell of it catches at the back of my throat. He seems peaceful, but I think of the knife that he keeps at his waist, how quickly it appears at the first whiff of danger.

Some friends of John's came to supper too, young men who are sprawled on cushions or have made themselves comfortable in the window seat as they listen to Cat and John sing. They are all laughing, enjoying themselves.

John is dazzled by Cat, of course. Gabriel tells me not to fret. 'He is a young man and she is a beautiful woman. She knows how to keep him at arm's length and he will grow out of it. When I come back from Hamburg we will think on a marriage for him, but for now, let him make calf's eyes at her if he will.'

I hope he is right. I hate to see John's ready smile falter as Cat turns carelessly away from him, the reddening of his cheeks when she bestows a smile.

The song ends at last, and the chamber erupts with clapping and laughter. Cat bows, smiling, and gestures towards Cecily at the virginals to include her in the applause. Everything is as it should be.

Am I the only one who feels the air constantly atremble with disquiet?

I am in the chair, the best seat, but I cannot shake the feeling that the chamber is shunning me. I stare at the silver jugs on the chest, convinced that they have swivelled to face Cat instead, and that there has been a subtle shift in the tapestry figures whose eyes turn away from me to her. They look to her now, not me.

At urging from the others, Cat has started another song. She is doing nothing wrong, I remind myself as my thumb frets at the scar. She is just singing. But there is something precarious in the air now, a whiff of danger, like a drift of smoke that makes you lift your nose but dissolves into the air before you can point to it and say 'There!'

How complacent I have become! I thought I had turned the curse aside, but it is still there, written bone-deep. Cat's arrival has shown that my world is unstable, slippery. A careless word, less than a fingernail flick from her, could bring it skidding out from beneath me to shatter like pottery dropped on cobbles. I can hardly breathe with the terror of it.

But what can I do? Sometimes I let myself think how different things would have been if only Amy had not had the toothache that day. If only I had checked my store of poppy seeds. If only I had taken Gabriel's advice and sent Sarah.

If only, if only, if only . . . Oh, what is the point of if onlys? I think bitterly. It is done now. I cannot unspool time, unweave the tiny moments that make up the warp and weft of life. It is knitted up now, and Cat is right in the centre of it.

I will never be rid of her now.

'Another!' my guests call when the song finishes. 'One more!'

Cat demurs prettily, but allows herself to be persuaded at last. 'Very well,' she says, and picks up the lute. Even before she opens her mouth, I know what the song will be.

Oh, John, come kiss me now, now, now, she starts, and then they all join in, even Tom who cannot usually be bothered with singing.

Oh, John, my love, come kiss me now.

I cannot sit here any longer, as if my stomach is not curdling with a dread I cannot explain. 'I have the headache,' I murmur to Gabriel as I get to my feet as unobtrusively as possible. 'I will go to bed.'

But alone in the bedchamber I share with my husband, I can still hear them singing, and I could swear that behind the lute, behind the voices, are the creak of the cart's wheels and the scream of a child and a curse called over the years.

Gabriel's deep voice, Cecily's laughter, the bright spill of conversation through the open windows. My family are all next door with Cat, and I am here alone with only Peg for company. I lift her up from the chest for comfort, but her

93

painted smile seems fixed and her expression so desolate that I shudder, and for one horrifying moment I can feel a noose tightening around my neck.

PART II

8

Mary

Steeple Tew, 1562–1576

With Cat as my friend, I was safe at Steeple Tew, and I was grateful, just as Emmot had told me to be. Sir Hugh, Cat's beloved Pappa, was distantly kind to me. Her mother, Lady Ursula, never cared for me, but she was correct. I was clothed and fed, I slept with Cat in a comfortable bed, and I was allowed to share lessons with her and her brother, Avery. Avery's tutor, Master Gregory, taught us in the schoolroom at the top of the manor, a small, dank chamber but good enough for children. Cat had no interest in learning, and sat making idle scratches on her tablet, but I loved to copy letters from my hornbook and she would imitate the way the tip of my tongue stuck out when I was concentrating.

I learnt to read quickly, but Avery struggled and hated me for making him look foolish by comparison. He was a sturdy boy, golden-haired like Cat, but meaner of spirit, with a tight, cruel mouth and meaty hands that were ever quick to cuff. Sometimes I would pretend that I could not read a word just to stop his face mottling with rage. At others I squirmed on my stool with frustration at how dull his wits were and I would have to bite my lip not to prompt him, but I might as well have spoken out, for Avery would find a way to punish me either way. After our lessons, he would pinch and push and play tricks on me. Once he took Peg and threw her on the fire. I burned myself badly getting her out. A puckered scar has blotted the side of my hand ever since; I cannot bend my little finger properly, even now, and Peg's wooden stump is singed still underneath her skirts.

The building of the banqueting house at Steeple Tew brought an end to my childhood. Lady Ursula was commonly considered to have married beneath herself and she pinched constantly at Sir Hugh for his lack of ambition. To quiet her he built a banqueting house in the garden. Made of the same honey-coloured stone as the manor house, it had three storeys — one for dining, one for drinking and conversation and one for dancing — and was bigger than many of the houses in Little Wood Street now. When it was finished, all the neighbours around were invited to be impressed by the latest fashion. As was the purpose. There was to be a feast in the hall, and then the guests would repair to the banqueting house for sugared comfits and sweetmeats. Cat and I thrilled at the idea and practised dancing in the long gallery, touching our finger-tips together and sweeping down into curtseys while we hummed the music as best we could.

'A banqueting house is no place for children,' Lady Ursula said sharply when Cat begged to go, but as always Sir Hugh took Cat's side, promising her a dance after the banquet and letting her wheedle a new gown out of him too. Lady Ursula was very tight-lipped about that.

Cat wanted me to go too, but there Lady Ursula drew the line. 'Mary can help the servants,' she said curtly. 'It is time she learnt her place.' I was ten.

After that, we slept together still, but Cat lay in a curtained bed, while I was on a truckle bed at her feet. I combed her hair, but she did not comb mine. I stood with a mouthful of pins while I fixed her collar and sleeves into place, but I had to lace up my own kirtle. I brushed her gowns and made sure she had a fresh linen shift to wear every day. I brought her perfumed water to rinse her face and hands in the morning, and I helped rub her body to cleanse it. I kept her company and read to her and fetched her cakes and wine. So it was not so different to what I had done before.

But it was not the same.

I did not have to wash the laundry, which was bitter work that left your hands cracked and raw, or turn the spit or scrub the pots. Much of what I did should have fallen to Cat. Lady Ursula tried once or twice to suggest that she should learn how to run a household, but Cat was not interested in tedious tasks like cooking or casting accounts. She saw no need to learn how to brew or run a dairy or administer medicines. When would she have to make cheese or polish silver? Sir Hugh had told her he would make a good marriage for her, and she was as certain that it would happen as she was that the sun would rise every morning. She would preside over a great house and there would be others to worry about what everyone would eat and drink and how often the rushes were changed. As she grew older and ever more beautiful, and all the young gentlemen in the area paid determined suit, she did not hesitate to refuse each and every one of them.

'Country squires,' she would tell me, dismissing their pretensions with an elegant flick of her fingers as I dressed her hair.

She could have been mistress of a solid manor nearby, with an indulgent husband. If it had been me, I would have taken the first who asked, to have known that I would be safe and my future assured, but when I said as much, Cat only laughed at me.

'Oh, Mary, you are such a timid creature! You might be content to spend your life churning butter and inspecting crops, but I wish for more,' she told me. 'Pappa does not want me to hasten into marriage. He is content for me to make my own choice — and so I will.'

She studied her reflection in the looking glass as I set a combing cloth around her shoulders, lifting her chin and turning this way and that to better admire her pure profile. Cat's dreams glittered with richness and excitement. She imagined herself at court, sinking into a curtsey before the Queen, married to a great nobleman, with a coach of her own and a long gallery for when it rained, but for many years the most excitement Steeple Tew had to offer was the occasional visitor or travelling pedlar.

If Cat coaxed and wheedled hard enough, her father would take us to Banbury for the Michaelmas Fair where there were stalls selling trinkets and ribbons and hot pies to be had, and the countryfolk jostled elbows with townspeople as they celebrated their hiring. I remember squeezing through the press of people, clutching onto Cat's gown, while the babble of voices beat at me, and the smell of wool and straw and dung and cooking apples, of hope and pleasure and disappointment and sweat, tangled together in the crisp autumn air.

I would have gladly stayed at home. I did not like riding pillion along the country lanes with the curse ringing in my ears, but Cat always insisted that I go too. 'I would not enjoy myself without you,' she said. 'It would be as if just half of me were there.' I knew what she meant. We loved each other, then, though we fought each other too, as sisters do. But we were not sisters, of course. The tenuous link of blood between us stretched thinner and thinner as the years passed, and my future dwindled to service while hers was bright with possibility.

My own dreams were more practical. I wanted only security. I was always dutiful, always good, always careful. I did nothing to risk my place at Steeple Tew. I knew that I had to apply myself and work hard. So I did everything I was asked, and I found pleasure in learning household skills. I liked the kitchen with its warmth and busyness. I watched the cook and learnt how to make a custard, to stew an ox tongue and roast a deer. I plucked ducks and chickens and pigeons until my fingertips split and stung. I chopped onions and gathered herbs for salads. My favourite task was to go to the spice cabinet in the still room and bring back pepper or cloves or a finger of dried ginger for the cook.

Sometimes the housekeeper, Bridget, would set me to reading recipes, knowing that I had learnt my letters and was quick, and I would help her mix up salves or measure out the spices to distil the special water she swore was a sovereign cure for every ailment. Even today, the smell of fennel and caraway seeds, of ginger and galingale, of pennyroyal and wild thyme, takes me back to the familiar fug of the still room at Steeple Tew, and to Bridget, angular and brusquely kind.

So I was not discontented with my lot — until Avery came back to Steeple Tew.

I was almost seventeen when he returned. For three years he had been in service with Lord Fairhurst, who had a large estate near Stow-on-the-Wold. We heard a good deal about how fine Lord Fairhurst's house was and how fashionable their manners. The way Avery told it, our Lady Queen herself would be overawed by the state they kept. Certainly Avery felt himself too grand for Steeple Tew now. He spent a lot of time telling us how slow and old-fashioned we were, while Lady Ursula nodded along. Had she not been saying the same thing for years?

The years away had not improved Avery. He was bigger, broader, meaner. There was a new sneer to his mouth, a calculating gleam in his eyes, and when I first saw him after his return, sprawled insolently on his mother's cushions, my stomach tightened with foreboding. I kept my gaze downcast and tried to make myself unobtrusive, but it seemed that Avery had not forgiven me for having a sharper wit in the schoolroom, no matter that six years had passed and Master Gregory had long since gone. He sought me out, standing four-square in the passage so that I had to squeeze past him, or deliberately spilling ale onto his hose so that I had to fetch a cloth and dab at him close to his privy parts. Once he shoved me into a doorway and grabbed my hand to press it against his trunk hose where his yard reared hard and horrifying. Nauseated, I tried to pull away but his fingers clamped around my wrist, holding my hand in place as he rubbed it up and down over the wool, his eyes glazed. I had to kick him hard on the shin before his grip slackened enough for me to snatch my hand out of his grasp and back away.

'Do you touch me again like that and I will go to Lady Ursula,' I said, low and angry, rubbing my sore wrist.

'Pah, what does my mother care for you?' sneered Avery. 'I will tell her you tried to seduce me, and she will turn you off for your insolence.'

She would, too. Lady Ursula hung over her son just as dotingly as Sir Hugh favoured Cat. I could have told Cat, I suppose, but what could she have done? Sir Hugh might indulge her, but I was but a poor connection, a servant, easily disposed of, easily replaced. What would become of me if I had to leave Steeple Tew? I would end up huddled under the hedgerows like a beast, scratching in the earth for a root, begging for a crust of bread.

Panic darted around my belly, but I managed to lift my chin. 'Leave me alone, Avery,' I said.

But he would not. It seemed that I was an itch that he could not stop scratching. I tried to make myself invisible, but what could I do? I had to go where I was sent, do as I was told, accept what I was given. And be grateful for it. Bridget did what she could to help. She sent other servants when Avery shouted for wine, and she kept me out of the way as much as possible, but I was still Cat's maid. Avery would throw himself down onto a seat if I was keeping Cat company in the parlour, and he would stare at me while we sang or read as if reliving that sordid scuffle in the passageway. I kept my expression wooden, but I could feel his eyes scouring me, stripping the clothes off me one by one. When I heard that marriage negotiations for him were taking place, I was limp with relief.

'They are talking of marrying him to Jocosa Lismore,' Cat told me. 'She is very folderol they say, and no beauty, but all previous arrangements have fallen through and if they do not marry her off soon it will be too late. She thinks herself too good for Steeple Tew, but Avery may be the best she can do.'

Poor Jocosa, I remember thinking. Imagine being married off to Avery. 'Mamma says that it would be a good marriage,' Cat chattered on. 'I dare say she will have her way. I hope Avery does marry her. It would be a grand wedding and the

Lismores have *connections*. Perhaps I will meet someone with more to offer than a little manor. It would be a fine thing, don't you think?'

I did. I wished fervently for the negotiations to succeed, hoping that Avery would turn his attention to his betrothed instead, and when a date was announced for the wedding, I let myself feel safe.

May you never be safe, never. I forgot what the vagrant woman had said.

I forgot that I was cursed.

9

Mary

Steeple Tew, January 1574

It was a bitter morning early in January when I carried Cat's chamber pot outside to empty it in the jakes before she awoke and complained of the smell. A few stars still sprinkled the sky to the west, but to the east beyond the water meadows, the horizon was flushed pink. The air was iron-hard and unrelenting, every blade of grass, every twig, every reed in the stable thatch aglitter with frost. My clogs skidded on the icy cobbles in the yard and I had to pick my way carefully past the stables to the privy. I wished I had thought to put on some mittens. Pressing my lips hard together, I tried to breathe through my nose. If I forgot and sucked in a breath, the cold jabbed at my teeth and made me wince.

There was blood in the pot that morning. That meant that Cat's flowers had come down, and I would need to go in and prepare her rags. I knew her body as well as my own by then, and I could read the stretched look around her eyes when her head ached, could track her monthly cycle by changes in the scent of her skin. That was the one time her sparkle dimmed and she lay still and sluggish. For three days a month she would lose her beauty. Her skin dulled and greyed, and her hair grew lank, and she lay on her bed tormented by vicious cramps, clutching the warm plaster I made for her belly. When she was like that, the whole manor seemed to fall silent. But then she would be bright and gay again, and her sweet voice would fill the house as she sang, and her laughter as she rode out on the spirited grey mare that Sir Hugh gave her made us look at each other and smile indulgently. When Cat suffered, the whole world suffered with her, and when she was joyful, we were all cheered in spite of ourselves. It was a gift that she had.

On the way back from the privy I paused, empty pot in hand, to listen to the silence. In the distance, I could hear the faint sound of Hob, the kitchen boy, being berated for not stoking up the fire quickly enough, while the cook bad-temperedly banged pots around. But out beyond the stables, all was still. There were no birds hopping and twittering, no bleating sheep or cattle grumbling to each other in the barn. Every living thing seemed to be holding its breath against the cold.

I was thinking about making a purge that Bridget taught me. I had already infused the powdered rhubarb overnight, knowing from the signs that it would be needed that morning. I had noticed that my own terms happened at almost the same time as Catherine's, and the purge helped me, although I was not allowed to curl up in the bed and hold my stomach. I had to continue with my own tasks, however leaden the pull in my belly, although in truth I did not suffer as badly as Cat did.

107

I rarely had a moment to myself, and I stopped to savour it, that was all. Just for a minute. I was alone, but the manor was just there. I didn't feel unsafe.

More fool me.

I had spent so long being afraid of the vagrants outside that I forgot that danger sometimes comes from the inside.

I remembered little of my arrival at Steeple Tew by then, just a muddled impression of the carter and the mob pressing around me, of the feral creature who had appeared in front of me and then was gone. But if anyone ever shoved at me, or pushed past me, however accidentally, it sliced through me afresh, a butcher's knife flashing high, spilling out memory, gleaming and steaming like a pile of entrails: my hand thrust forward, the tingle of my palm where it had touched the stinking rags, that scream. My gut would twist sickeningly then, and I would choke as an invisible noose tightened around my neck and I would push the thought of it away like a physical thing, sparring the door to my mind so that I could breathe again.

The sound of hooves and the jingle of harness brought me back to myself with a start. I turned to hurry back into the warmth, but it was already too late. Avery was upon me, bearing down on a great horse, laughing as I was forced to flatten myself against the wall while he clattered past me into the yard and shouted for a stable boy.

He must have been carousing all night. He was still drunk and dishevelled, and even from a distance he stank of stale wine. Vexed at having put myself in his way, I tried to slip past unnoticed, but he had pulled up his horse between me and the door into the back of the house.

'Well, look who it is,' Avery slurred as he slid clumsily from the saddle. 'Mistress Know-it-all carrying my sister's slops!'

I said nothing, merely ducking my head and making to go round him, but he barred my way, swaying slightly, and ignoring the boy who ran out to take his horse and led it quickly away.

'What, no set down? No clever reply?' he demanded. 'That's not like you, Mary.'

I set my teeth. 'No, sir.'

'What, do you still look down your nose at me?'

'No, sir.'

'*No, sir. No, sir*,' he mimicked me. 'Is that all you can say now? You were quick enough to show me up in the schoolroom. There was no *No, sir* then, was there? It was all *look at me, look how clever am I, oh, Avery, how can you be so slow?*'

I thought about saying 'No, sir' again, but that would have only enraged him further. I stayed silent instead and wished that the stable boy would come back. But why would he? He had the horse and was probably glad there was someone else to take the brunt of Avery's ill humour while he hunkered down in the warm hay.

'What good does all your lettering do you now, eh?' sneered Avery. 'You look at me as if you are a queen and I a peasant, but that lewd mouth of yours gives you away. You're nought but a harlot.'

I could not help myself. My eyes flashed up in protest, but it was a mistake to show a reaction. Slow and drunk as he was, Avery did not miss my fury. 'Oho, not so demure now, are you?' he leered, staggering towards me, and hurt my pride as it did, I took a step back and then another until I came up against the wood store. 'Swiving and slopping out pots is all you're good for now, Mistress Mary.' He laughed wildly. 'No answer for that, eh? I wouldn't mind swiving you myself. That would teach you a thing or two!'

'No,' I said before I could help myself. Another mistake. His small eyes lit with excitement.

'No, sir,' he prompted me, leering closer, and his breath enveloped me in a stinking cloud that hung white in the frozen air.

I turned my head away. 'No, sir,' I said woodenly. The smell of his breath mingled with the smell of the logs stacked in the store behind my back and I felt my gorge rise.

'You're a servant now, Mary. You don't get to say no.' Gleefully he brought up a hand to squeeze my breast, and I didn't stop to think.

'Don't touch me,' I said and I pushed (*pushed*) at him hard with my hand. In his unsteady state he teetered back, his boots skidding on the cobbles and sending him crashing to the ground.

There was a catastrophic silence and then he roared with humiliation and lumbered to his feet. 'You will pay for that, Mary,' he said.

I could not move at first, but I felt the air shift

and splinter with menace, and something fixed in his face made me cast the pot aside and turn to run while the crack of shattered pottery still bounced around the yard and my clogs slipped over the cobbles and panic pounded in my ears.

I must have known there was no hope of escape, but I ran anyway. Avery caught me up with ease. His hand clamped on my shoulder and he span me round.

'By God, you have asked for it now!' he said, grabbing my waist.

'Leave me be!' I cried out as I struggled against his painful grip, but he only backed me against the stable until I could feel the timber frame digging into my spine.

'Still giving orders, Mary? Perhaps it is time you used that mouth of yours to do something instead of answering back.' Then his lips were on my face, devouring my mouth in great, slobbery kisses that had me twisting and writhing in panicked revulsion.

'Help!' I called when I could, spitting the feel and the taste of him from my mouth. 'Save me!'

Avery only laughed excitedly. 'No one is going to help you, Mary. No one cares about you. You think you're so grand because you can read and write, but all you're good for is spreading your legs like any other whore.'

I barely heard him, I was panting to get free, turning my head frantically this way and that to avoid his loathsome mouth while his hands plunged into my bodice, ripping the laces and pinching my breasts. He was breathing hard as he grabbed and squeezed my flesh. 'I've wanted to do this for so long,' he said, and he laughed, his face suffused with excitement, his eyes alight with the wrongness of it.

'If you want to keep your place here, Mary, you'll learn to please me.'

'No,' I said, wriggling desperately. 'No. Never.'

The air jangled with my harsh breaths and the coarse words and insults Avery was muttering as he pawed at me. 'Oh yes, you will,' he said. 'You are a servant wench, less than nothing. You will do as you are bid.'

My palms were jammed against his doublet which was damp and sticky, the embroidery ruined. I could smell wine and vomit. I was trying to kick him but I was hampered by my skirts.

'I am more than you, Avery,' I spat back at him. 'You are too doltish to learn your ABC!'

It was foolish of me, I can see that now. I invited the stinging blow he dealt to my jaw that whipped my head to one side and left my ears ringing.

'Bitch,' he muttered, and clapped a sweaty hand over my mouth as he thrust me round and shoved me against the stable wall. 'Let's see who is clever now.'

He took his hand away so that I could at least breathe easier, but my face was jammed up against the timber strut and I could not even shout out. I could only concentrate on breathing while Avery panted vile words, scrabbling at my skirts, pushing them up, up, until cold air bit against my bare buttocks. 'God's bones, stay still!' he swore at me.

I tried to cry out again, but my face was squashed, and when I flailed my arms frantically, he pinned them with one hand, wedging me into place with his body. I could feel him fumbling with the ties of his hose, and then, God, then he was ramming into me, again and again, heedless of my pain. I was dimly conscious of the horses moving restively inside the stable, sensing the violence, the hate. I knew the stable boys must be able to hear my whimpers and Avery's grunts. They knew what I was suffering but they would do nothing, because Avery would be master one day and could do what he liked with the rest of us.

I remember thinking: this is what the vagrant woman intended. This is my punishment for pushing that child, and now I have pushed again and the curse has come true. But then my mind went dark, blotted out by the horror and disgust and shame that I had somehow brought this on myself. It seemed to go on for a long time, but at last Avery gasped and juddered against me and a moment later pulled out of me. No longer pinned into place, I slumped against the stable and crumpled into a heap. Wetness oozed down the inside of my thighs, and I could taste blood in my mouth. Pain beat at me everywhere as I lay on the frozen ground, drawing small, shuddering breaths.

'Look at me!' Avery's boot caught me in the ribs but I had no air left in my lungs to howl. All I could do was roll myself into a ball and clasp my arms around myself. When I forced my eyes open I saw Avery towering above me, adjusting the points of his hose with a smirk of satisfaction. 'Next time, Mary, do as you are told,' he said. He made to turn away, only to stop at a thought and turn back. 'Oh, and I will tell my mother to stop the cost of that pot from your wages.'

★　★　★

Bridget found me huddled against the stable where Avery had left me, discarded like a crumpled cloth, my face turned into the rough plaster, my body numb with cold. She helped me up and took me inside to the still room. She brought me water to rinse the blood from my thighs and from the cuts on my face where Avery had struck me, and she put salve on my grazes, and all the time I never said a word. She brought me a cloth so that I could strip down and rub, rub, rub away the feel of him and then she helped me into a clean shift and laced me back into my kirtle and tied a fresh apron around my waist.

I smoothed it down with hands that were not yet steady and spoke at last. 'What can I do?' I asked Bridget, who was gathering up the bowls and rags and bloodied water.

'Nothing,' she said. 'Endure it.'

So I finished making the rhubarb purge and carried it up to Catherine's chamber, moving as stiffly and slowly as an old beldam.

She was curled up in the bed, her eyes dull. 'It hurts,' she moaned, clutching at her belly.

I could barely stand. Inside I was raw and

ripped where Avery had thrust into me, and revulsion still pulsed over my skin when I remembered what he had done, but I murmured soothingly and coaxed Cat into sitting up so that she could sip at the purge.

'I hate this,' she complained feebly. 'Why do you make me drink it?'

'Because it makes you feel better. Come, drink some more.'

When she had finished, she lay back against the pillows with a grimace. Only then did the blue eyes focus on me. 'What happened to you?'

Your brother forced me and then left me broken and bleeding on the ground. I could not say that.

I touched the cut that throbbed painfully on my cheekbone and then the corner of my mouth. I dabbed away blood that still oozed there. I had not looked in a glass but it was just as well. My eye was beginning to swell.

'I fell,' I said carefully. 'It is icy out. I fell and broke the chamber pot. I fear your lady mother will send me away.'

Cat closed her eyes wearily. 'I will not let her send you away over a pot. Do not be foolish, Mary.'

I squirrelled her words away, taking them out to turn them over in my memory whenever I felt anxious.

Lady Ursula said nothing about the pot but I could feel her cold stare on me sometimes, and I wondered if she knew how her son tormented me. Avery would not let me alone. He appeared when I was going about my business, and pushed

115

me into doorways or under the stairs, against the pigsties or under a tree, shoving up my skirts and forcing himself into me, careless of anyone who might see. I quickly learnt not to fight him. I let him do what he would, and after a while it did not hurt so much, but I hated it, and I hated him. I kept my eyes fixed on a far point while he pumped into me, and told myself that one day I would feel safe again. I did as Bridget advised and I endured, but I was not grateful any more.

Steeple Tew, June 1574

Lady Ursula took to her bed one fine summer day, complaining of pains in her stomach. Bridget sent me into the garden to find endive and mint which she steeped in white wine for a day before straining and adding cinnamon and pepper. Another day I had to grind up cumin seeds into a fine powder so that she could mix it with red wine, but none of it did any good. You could feel death in the room, leaning over the bed, smell it in the sour darkness of the chamber. She had lost all colour and was shrinking into herself as the life leached out of her. She was a wasted candle, barely flickering.

Bridget persisted with her remedies even though it was clear to all that Lady Ursula was dying. My steps dragged with the exhaustion that seemed to dog me then as I took the sorrel and spinach she had asked me to pick into the kitchen, where she was ferociously stirring a pot on the fire.

'You took your time,' she grumbled. 'What's been keeping you?' A knuckle of veal and some mutton were boiling for a broth, and she took the sorrel and the spinach and threw them in the pot along with some sage and hyssop. 'Mace, saffron . . . ' she muttered to herself. 'Get me an egg, will you?' she added to me. 'Oh, and some sugar while you're at it. Look sharp, now, Mary,' she went on when I didn't move, and she looked up from stirring the pot in time to see me clap my hand to my mouth. The sweat stood on my forehead and my stomach heaved at the smell of the broth.

Bridget dropped the spoon she was using to stir the broth and hooked a stool forward with her foot. 'Sit,' she ordered, pushing my head down. 'Don't you be casting up your dinner in my nice clean kitchen.'

I kept my head down as instructed while she sent one of the little maids to fetch wine and made sure the other servants were busy once more. 'Drink this,' she said. 'It will make you feel better.'

'Thank you.' I sat up, but my hands trembled as I took a small sip.

Bridget glanced over her shoulder to check that no one was listening and lowered her voice. 'How long have you known?'

My eyes slid miserably away from hers. There was no use in pretending any longer. 'A month, maybe longer.' I had tried leaping from a wall, but all I got was a twisted ankle. I had jumped up and down and run as fast as I could, but nothing happened. I just got tireder and tireder.

117

Even Cat had commented on my grey face.

'Can you . . . can you give me something?' I knew that what I was contemplating was a sin, but what else could I do? Sick as she was, if Lady Ursula found out that I was with child, she would send me packing, whatever Cat said. Never mind that it was all Avery's doing. The unfairness of it burned me while dread churned sickeningly in my stomach to add to the constant sense of queasiness.

'What am I going to do?' My voice rose in spite of myself and I saw the kitchen boy glance over curiously from where he was scouring the pots.

'Hush now,' Bridget said firmly. 'If you want to be rid of the babe, there is still time I think. I will make you something. Try not to fret. You're not the first maid to be in this position, and you won't be the last. But you're a good girl, Mary, and you deserve better than this.'

Lady Ursula died the next morning. They rang the bells for her in the parish church, and as word spread, the neighbours came to pay their respects. Sir Hugh, Avery and Cat were gathered in the chamber with the minister, and the household servants shuffled past the corpse. With all the coming and going, we were kept busy providing wine and cakes, and I was on my way back to the kitchen when Bridget pulled me aside and gave me a cup which contained a bitter-smelling drink. It had herbs floating on the top and I sniffed it cautiously.

'What is it?'

'Best not to know,' said Bridget. 'Take it

tonight while they are all sitting with the body. It should loosen the babe, but be prepared, Mary, it is a violent potion. You will suffer.'

The light was fading from the summer sky when I carried the cup carefully outside to the privy. Careless of the stench, I sat down on the wooden seat and bent my nose over the cup again. It looked innocuous enough but the smell made my belly churn.

I thought about the babe growing inside me and I ached for it, but what could I offer it? Nothing but poverty and despair. I tipped the cup to my lips and swallowed the potion in one go. It left me coughing and choking and curiously resigned. For a while it seemed as if nothing would happen. I even left the privy and wandered along to the pigsties to lean over and scratch the old sow's back. There was no one else around as the household gathered around death.

In spite of myself, my heart lightened at the thought that Bridget's potion had not worked. I imagined the baby, how it would feel to hold it. Would it be a boy or a girl? A boy would have a better chance, I decided, but I would love a girl just as much. I would call her Catherine after my mistress and my friend.

No sooner had I chosen the name than my body was seized with a terrible cramp, so painful that I could not even spare the energy to call out. I only just made it back to the privy in time. I hugged myself as I rocked backwards and forwards, my teeth chattering with the effort of not screaming.

It did not take long in the end, but the

after-effects were as bad as Bridget had warned. I bled and bled, and my body was shaken with violent fits. I was desperately thirsty but dared not cry out for water.

At length I managed to drag myself back to the chamber. I packed rags between my legs to staunch the last bleeding and crawled into my truckle bed, unsure whether I feared death or would welcome it. I could not even rise to help Cat when she came in after sitting with her mother's body. I told her that I had eaten something that disagreed with me and she called one of the other servants to help her undress. It was another day before I could stand on shaky legs and by then Lady Ursula had been buried.

I have never conceived again. Whatever Bridget gave me to drink that day rid me of the child, but it rid me too of any hope that I might be a mother and hold a baby to my breast. I knew it even then. My only baby would be a wooden one. Heartsore, I lay in the little bed and clutched Peg to me, and the vagrant woman's curse shrieked at me through the years: *May you never have a child of your own. May you never be safe, never.*

10

Cat

Steeple Tew, May 1576

I wanted a noble husband, and I got one. George was titled, he was elegant, he was cultured. He read Greek and Latin, and he wrote poetry that I could not understand. He had inherited a great estate in Wiltshire where he was building a house in the latest fashion. He was a prize far out of my reach. Or so my brother's bride, Jocosa, told me.

'Lord Delahay is not for the likes of you,' she said.

I did not care for Jocosa, nor she for me. She was older than Avery, pinch-mouthed and whey-faced with pale, lashless eyes, and she was not happy to find that the groom's sister would far outshine the bride. But how could I help it? Pappa and I travelled all the way to Lismore House on the border of Wiltshire for their wedding, but she showed me no courtesy. At the wedding feast, she put me a long way down the table, stuck between a minister and a decrepit old tutor, and opposite a stammering cousin who sprayed me with spittle whenever he spoke and a tedious plain widow who bored us all, even the minister, with her devotion.

The feast dragged, with course after course of tepid dishes and dreary conversation. The only interest for me was the gentleman who sat near the top table on the opposite side of the hall. I could just see him between the widow and the cousin. Whenever I glanced up, he would be glancing up too and my eyes would snare on his. I waited for him to smile at me, but he never did. His hair was so fair it was almost white, and his features bland in a girlishly pink and white face, but there was something eerily intense about his gaze. I was reluctantly fascinated, but when it became clear that he would not smile, I ignored him, peeping only the occasional glance.

When the feast was over and the tables cleared for dancing, I waited for him to come over, but no. I tossed my head and let a succession of callow boys lead me out into the dance. I made sure I smiled brilliantly at them all as I danced and not once did I look at him, although I was aware of his gaze on me all the time.

Jocosa noticed, of course. 'You are wasting your time,' she told me. 'Lord Delahay needs a son, it is true, but he will not be interested in a country wench like you. He is a man of great distinction, and it is an honour to my father that he came to the wedding at all. He *never* dances, Catherine, so you may spare yourself those inviting smiles.'

By which I understood that she herself had not been asked to dance.

After that, of course, I was determined to make him notice me. And I succeeded. It took all evening, but for the last dance he came over and led me out, and I made sure to smile sweetly at my new sister. But his hands were as cold as his eyes, and although my triumph was great, I did not enjoy dancing with him as much as I thought I would. That should have been a warning.

I told you all about it that night when you unpinned my sleeves and unlaced me. Do you remember? You had been watching from the sidelines with the other servants, and you had seen it all. 'Jocosa is jealous of you,' you told me, as if I did not know that.

'What do the other servants say of Lord Delahay?' I asked, holding out my arms obediently as you eased the pearls from my waist.

'His servants are afraid of him,' you said, between the pins clenched in your teeth.

'Afraid? Why?'

'They will not say. They say nothing at all. That is how we know they are afraid. Most servants will talk freely enough about their masters, but these ... they are too close-mouthed. Do not toy with him, Cat. He is too secretive for you.'

I pouted. 'What do you say about me?' I asked, and you smiled. You look different when you smile, did you know that? It is almost startling, the change from guarded to warmth, from darkness to light. I always said you should smile more often.

'I say you are a young lady of beauty and charm,' you said. 'I say you are as bright and gay as a daisy turning its face up to the sun.'

I liked that. I thought you meant it, Mary. I thought you loved me.

George sought me out the next day and

invited me to walk in the gardens of Lismore House. I struggled to keep up a flow of chatter in the face of his stern silence. He made me nervous, I can admit that now, although at the time I strove to think myself sophisticated. But when his eyes rested on me intently, my mouth would dry and I would falter, pinioned by his stare, and there rose in me a strange trembling that was part fear, part excitement. When his fingers pressed mine, I jolted at his touch. I was his prey, dreading the moment he would swoop down on me but afraid, too, that he would veer away to some other dangled bait and leave me alone after all. And there were plenty of other maids there. He could have chosen any of them, but he chose me, and I was glad of the chance to prove Jocosa wrong.

I was proud of it. Can you imagine?

When you heard that he was coming to Steeple Tew to woo me, you tucked in the corners of your mouth. 'Are you sure you want this?' you asked me.

No, I wasn't sure, but by then I did not know how to say no. I thrilled at the idea of George, of his wealth and his standing, but when he was standing right in front of me and took my hand with those cool fingers, I shrank a little from him. He bought me expensive gifts: exquisitely embroidered gloves, a girdle with gold thread, a book, and you sewed a pair of gloves for me to give him in return. But he did not try to kiss me. He just watched me.

He made my skin prickle, and I had almost made up my mind to refuse him when Pappa

124

died. My beloved Pappa, who went out riding one day and was brought home on a bier. You had to tell me. You came in to my chamber where I was playing the lute and your face was quite white.

'I have terrible news,' you said with difficulty. 'I do not know how to tell you. Your pappa . . . Cat, he is dead.'

I laughed as I laid down the lute. 'Of course he is not dead! I saw him ride out not an hour ago.'

'His horse stumbled, and he fell.'

'No.' I shook my head very definitely. 'No. Pappa never falls.'

You swallowed and came towards me. You tried to take my hands but I snatched them away and put them behind my back. My pappa was not dead. I had no need of comfort.

'No,' I said again. 'Why are you lying to me?'

'They have laid him in the chapel and sent for your brother,' you said gently.

'Oh, this is absurd!' I jumped up and marched down the stairs and out to the little church that had been built on the corner of the courtyard by some long-distant ancestor in the time of the old religion. It was plainer by then but still a place of worship. I would tell Pappa what wicked lies you had been telling me and he would punish you for frightening me so.

A group of men were huddled together, talking in low voices, but they fell silent when I appeared and stood back to let me see how Pappa lay on the floor at their feet.

'Pappa?' Why did he not get up? 'Pappa!' I remember how my skirts rustled against the stones as I moved towards him as if in a dream. 'Pappa!' I dropped to my knees beside him and stared into the eyes that were filming over, emptied of warmth and merriment. A terrible keening cry filled the chapel, so chilling that at first I did not realise that it came from my own throat. 'No! No, no, no!'

You had to prise me away from him in the end, and you made me a drink with some poppy seeds to ease my torment so that I slept a little and then was dull and sluggish when I woke. We kept vigil together over my father's body while we waited for Avery and Jocosa to come back. I forget where they were — London, perhaps? — but that night we were alone with Pappa and the flickering candles. You knelt behind me. I wasn't even praying. I was just staring at Pappa in stunned disbelief that he could leave me.

'You must marry now, Cat,' you said in a low voice. 'You cannot stay here without Sir Hugh to care for you.' I thought you meant because of the memories, but you were thinking of yourself, weren't you, Mary? You did not want to stay with Jocosa as mistress. She liked you no more than she liked me, and she had seen no doubt how Avery followed you with hot eyes, as we all had, though I never understood why, such a severe, plain thing you were. Pappa always protected you, but with him gone, you knew she would try to send you off one way or another. Your only hope was for me to marry and take you with me as my maid, and George was my only suitor.

Jocosa would not want me to stay at Steeple Tew unmarried. She would want me gone, you said. George had a great house, you reminded me. He was a nobleman. I would be mistress of my own household and I would have servants and jewels and pin money. I would be safe from Jocosa's spiteful temper. But what you meant was that *you* would be safe.

I believed you. When George came to pay his condolences, he asked me if I was of a mind to wed, and I said that I was. And so it was done.

I blame *you*, Mary.

You made me believe that all would be well. George sent me costly gifts — a jewelled bracelet, a gold ring, a silver picktooth — and once a poem he had written himself which I thrust into your hands. 'Read it to me.'

'A love sonnet?' you said, looking as relieved as I felt at this first evidence that he cared for me. But your voice faltered as you read: it was a poem of love, yes, but the object of the writer's love had dark hair and dark eyes, not hair of gold and eyes of blue.

'He has forgot what I look like,' I said flatly when you had finished.

'Men do not pay notice to such things,' you said after a moment. 'What matters is the sentiment, is it not? His desire is clear.'

I let myself be persuaded. I reminded myself that I would be a lady, mistress of Haverley Court, where I would entertain in style. My husband-to-be was generous with his gifts. What matter that he could not remember what I looked like? He would not marry me if he did not want me, would he?

127

I was dull with misery in any case. I missed Pappa so! Steeple Tew was not the same without him. Avery cared nothing for me, Jocosa even less. I could marry, or I could stay unwanted in my own home.

You did your best to make my wedding day special. We were in mourning still for Pappa, so there would be no gay procession through the village. No flowers strewn in my path. No cup held aloft or attendants with their bridelaces. No music. But you tied rosemary to your sleeve and threaded pearls in my hair, and you walked with me to the chapel where my pappa had lain only weeks before.

George had come to Steeple Tew the night before and had no friends or supporters with him. He was waiting for me in the porch, laughing with one of the Steeple Tew stable boys, a darkly handsome lad I had often noticed myself, and my heart lightened to see him smiling, though you frowned. We exchanged rings, and when he kissed me, his lips were cold and lifeless against mine.

Afterwards, I saw him wipe his mouth and hoped you hadn't noticed. We went into the chapel for the nuptial mass, and I kept thinking of that, and of how his smile had vanished when he saw me.

Of how I belonged to him now.

I'd dreamt of my wedding feast for years. Pappa would be there, beaming with pride for his darling Kitten. Mamma would at least have seen to it that the feast was the best that could be produced, and all the neighbours would be invited to gaze on my good fortune with envy. There would be dancing and feasting and jollity, and through it all I would shine as the most beautiful bride anyone had ever seen. But Jocosa was jealous still that I should have captured a husband as wealthy as Lord Delahay and begrudged spending a groat more than she must on my wedding. 'We are in mourning,' she told Avery. 'Your neighbours are lubbering country louts in any case. We cannot ask Lord Delahay to so demean himself.'

So the banqueting house stayed shut up, and we ate a mean dinner in the hall instead. I smiled brilliantly throughout. I would not give Jocosa the satisfaction of knowing that she had humiliated me. I talked instead about my plans for entertaining when I was mistress at Haverley Court. George said nothing, but Jocosa did not like it at all, I assure you.

And then, my wedding night. I never told you about that, did I, Mary? You primped me and primed me and lifted a smock over my head, of lawn so fine that it slithered over me like a sigh. You left me propped up against the pillows, awaiting my husband. I was eager to lose my virginity, to know what made the village wenches tip back their heads and gasp, and when the door opened and George came in, I smiled invitingly.

He did not smile back. Instead, he crossed to the chest and picked up a peacock feather. When he turned back to me, he was pulling the feather between his fingers, and his expression was glazed.

It was only a feather, but all at once I was

afraid. I wanted to run for the door, to call for you to help me, but what could I have said? My husband has a feather? I could not explain to you how my skin crawled as I watched him.

He dragged the chair over to the bed and bade me pull up my shift and touch myself with the peacock feather for his pleasure. I did not tell you that, did I? Or how I did as he asked while he fondled himself? How I kept my eyes squeezed shut the whole time until he pushed me roughly onto my front and entered me from behind: one thrust, two and a third — just — before he gasped and collapsed on me.

That was my wedding night.

The next morning, you came to me after George had risen and gone out hunting with Avery and the other men. You brought me warm water scented with healing herbs and a soft cloth, and you helped me clean myself before I dressed.

'Are you happy?' you asked me, but I could not tell you what it had been like. What could I say? I hardly knew how to describe what had happened myself. George had not hurt me. I was not beaten or bruised, just humiliated.

So I smiled my gayest smile. 'Of course,' I said.

I was glad you did not ask me what it was like, as I half expected you would. You were a virgin as I had been, and you must have been curious. I wanted to feel that I knew more than you, but I was not at all sure that I did.

★　★　★

Two days later, we set off for Haverley Court. George had sent for his coach. I told myself that it meant that he had a care for my comfort, but I think even then I knew it was so that he did not have to converse with me. I was not sad to say goodbye to Jocosa or Avery, but Steeple Tew had been my home, and my throat closed as the coach lurched and lumbered down the track. I was very glad you were with me then, quiet and familiar in the corner of the coach. You said nothing, but you knew how I felt, didn't you? After a while, you crossed to sit beside me and you took my hand. You held it in your cool, capable one, and I felt better.

By the time the coachman pulled his horses up outside Haverley Court, I was stiff and queasy from the journey. We both sat still and stunned for a moment, hardly able to believe that the coach had stopped at last. Then the door opened with a creak and a young man stood framed in the doorway. He was gracefully built and fair of feature, with dark, dancing eyes, a neatly trimmed beard and a smile that was dazzling.

'Welcome to Haverley, my lady!'

Pathetically grateful for the warmth of his welcome, I let him help me down from the coach and I leant on him as I wriggled as discreetly as possible to release the stiffness in my limbs.

'I am Sir Anthony Cavendish, your husband's secretary, Lady Delahay,' he told me when I could stand straight at last. He flourished a bow. 'Permit me to congratulate you on your marriage, my lady. Haverley Court is in need of a mistress, but I did not expect Lord Delahay to bring home quite such a fair one.'

I blushed a little, pleased, and Anthony offered me his arm. 'Let me take you inside.'

It should have been my husband escorting me into my new home, but I did not think of that then. I was just glad that Anthony was welcoming, and I took his arm once more and let him lead me up the stone steps. Beneath my fingers, I could feel the strength of his muscles through the stiff fabric of his sleeve. I had a brief impression of looming bricks and the glint of glass, and then I was stepping into a vast hall with an imposingly carved fireplace and a staircase grander than I could have imagined.

George was already there, slapping his gloves against his thigh, but his expression lightened as he saw Anthony. 'Come, let us have some wine to celebrate my marriage!' He sounded more good-humoured than I had ever heard him, and I let myself be ushered into a chamber that I took to be my husband's study. No one thought that I might wish to wash my hands or use the privy after the journey.

I saw a chest, its lid propped open, full of books, and a desk with an inkpot, some papers and more books, and I felt a flicker of pride at last that I had married a man of such abilities. Perhaps, I thought, we could start again with our marriage now that we were at Haverley. Perhaps George would be different there, I told myself hopefully, and I could put the dismaying experience of my wedding night behind me.

And look, did not George cut a fine figure in a gorgeously embroidered doublet and slashed

Venetians to show off his good legs? What if he was not talkative? He was refined. He had good teeth. He was not disfigured. I should be leaping for joy at my good fortune.

Anthony took the wine from the servant and poured it into precious glasses. George had drained his almost before I had taken my first sip and held out his glass for more.

'So, here you are at Haverley, madam wife,' he said to me. 'I hope you will soon feel quite at home.' It was almost the longest speech he had ever made me.

I smiled uncertainly. I was trying not to look at the naked figures that romped across the sumptuous tapestries. They portrayed classical themes, that much I realised, but I did not recognise the stories. Without thinking, I looked for you to enlighten me, as you had more book learning than I, or just to raise an eyebrow in that way you did, but you weren't there. Did you jump down from the coach yourself? Did one of the servants take you into the house the back way? All I know is that your absence hit me as if I had stepped into a hole without warning. It made me realise that I was all alone with a husband I barely knew and a man bound to do whatever my husband said. My gaze flickered nervously around the room until it jarred to a halt at a jug on a windowsill.

It was full of peacock feathers.

11

Mary

There were still curls of sawdust in the upper chambers when we came to Haverley Court. When I climbed down from the coach that day we arrived and saw it looming above me, I could not help a gasp that was part awe, part fear. I had never seen a house so big or so new, all raw bricks and glittering glass and thrusting chimneys, while around it were left sad stumps of trees and expanses of mud where the gardens had yet to be built.

No expense had been spared. There was a magnificent oak staircase, lavishly carved, and a long gallery with a dizzyingly ornate plasterwork ceiling. There was a chimney for every room, and tiles on the floor. Everything was new and of the best, and yet already there was a tawdriness to it all. In spite of the light pouring in through the great glass windows, the air always seemed dense, almost spongy, and dank. A torpor lurked in the turn of every step, in the dimness of every corner.

The old house had been demolished so that the new one could be built in its place, but its presence seemed to crouch still in the air, as if Haverley Court had been but poorly painted over a ruined building, cracked and fissured with sadness and despair.

To me, the house was a living creature, watching me slyly. Its shadows tiptoed behind me as I walked through it. I would feel them like a breath on the back of my neck and my skin would prickle. Sometimes I would even stop suddenly and jerk round as if to catch them, and I could swear that walls had leapt silently back into position just in time, the tapestries faintly fluttering as the shadows slipped behind them.

The kitchen was equipped to create great feasts, but Lord Delahay never entertained. He had alienated his neighbours, insulting them and turning away their attempts to court him for the great wealth he had inherited from his uncle, a wealth he squandered on the new house and the jewels he showered on Cat. There was a deep, unpleasant coldness to Lord Delahay, but he seemed generous to his wife, if not to anyone else, and though I worried about her, Cat liked to preen in a new gown or a new necklace.

The servants were slack and slovenly, and went about their business blank-faced. It was left to me to run the household. I tried to encourage Cat to take on her duties as mistress but she just waved me away.

'You do it, Mary. You know what should be done, and you are so much better at these things.'

So I did my best to keep house in her place. I kept the accounts and I oversaw the kitchen and the dairy and the garden and the still room. I chivvied the servants to clean and tidy, to bake and to boil and to brew, to scrub and polish, and although they dragged their feet at first, in the end they liked the new sense of purpose their duties gave them. They might have grumbled about the morning prayers in the hall that I instituted while Cat and Lord Delahay were still abed, but they came. Gradually their expressions grew less blank, their manner more confiding.

'Did not the previous Lady Delahay order the household?' I asked Sindony once. Sindony was one of the laundresses, her hands were cracked and red from years of washing in lye.

'Which Lady Delahay?'

My brows rose. 'There was more than one?'

'In the old house. An unhappy place, that was.' She spat on the grass where she was stretching linen to dry.

Cat, it seemed, was George's third wife. The first had seven babes, all dead, Sindony told me, and an eighth that killed her too. The second Lady Delahay could not conceive. 'She were a thin, whey-faced lass,' Sindony said. 'Jumped at shadows. One day she went down to the river and drownded herself.'

My hand crept to my mouth. 'But . . . why would she do such a thing?'

'They *said* it were an accident,' Sindony admitted. 'But it's a strange accident that ties stones around your waist, don't you reckon? 'Course, Lord Delahay would've greased the coroner's palm for him to look the other way.' She shrugged. 'It's a kindness to her, in a way. It meant she could be buried in the church.'

I shuddered. What kind of man would casually pay off his wife's terrible sin? What sort of unkindness had driven her to the river in the first place?

My great fear was that Lord Delahay would turn out to be like Avery. As subtly as I could, I asked if any of the maidservants had been forced by him, but they only looked at me out of the corner of their eyes as if I was a simpleton. No, they said, there had never been any of *that*.

'What then?'

'Screaming,' one called Jane told me. 'Groaning. Like there's a great beast in there. Nobody knows what goes on at night, 'cept that man of his, and he ain't telling.' She leant closer. 'There's some as says Lord Delahay summons Old Nick himself.'

Devil worship. I knew how overblown servants' chatter could be, but still, I crossed myself without thinking.

'Every now and then, we hear that one of the servants has been called in and next we know, they ups and offs, and we never see them again.'

'Maidservants?' I asked, dry-mouthed.

'Men too. Lord Delahay, he'll mount any horse.'

I thought of the stable boy George laughed with on his wedding day and I worried for Cat, although she brushed all my concerns aside. It was impossible to talk to her then. There was a feverish gaiety about her, and she was so brittle that I feared the slightest tap would shatter her into jagged fragments, like a fine dish cracked on a stone floor.

'Why do you stay?' I asked Jane, who shrugged.

'Nowhere else to go,' she said. 'I heard as when the old lord was alive, the servants came from the village, but since Lord Delahay came, they won't send their sons and daughters here no more. Lord Delahay, he don't care. He just sends his man out to pick vagrants out of the hedgerows and offer us a crust and some cloth for our backs in exchange for keeping our mouths shut. And we do,' said Jane. 'I got nothing and nowhere to go back to.'

I did not blame Jane. I thought of the vagrants on the road to Steeple Tew, of Ellen's mother who had cursed me, and I knew I was doing the same as Jane. I had nowhere else to go either.

'Best keep out of his way,' Jane advised. 'You just have to look the wrong way and he comes at you. I saw him beat a servant most to death once because he'd dropped a cup. He'd take fists to you as soon as look at you. That's what he likes,' she added. 'Don't give him no reason to notice you and you'll get by. It's better than sleeping under a hedgerow.'

So I worried, but what could I do?

At Steeple Tew, the whole household ate together in the hall. It was different at Haverley Court, where Cat dined alone every night with Lord Delahay and his secretary in the chamber specially built for that purpose. I could not imagine what it must be like with just the three of them. When the last course had been cleared away, the only servant allowed to enter the chamber was Lord Delahay's manservant, Daniel, a silent man with strange goat-like eyes and a smile that made me want to wash my hands. He carried wine up to the chamber and waited there until he was sent for more, which happened often. I counted out the jugs anxiously every night, and shook my head when Daniel returned them for refilling.

No longer did I put my mistress to bed. In the mornings I would find skirts on the floor, the lace ripped and trampled, and pins scattered everywhere, while Cat slept, breathing coarsely through her open mouth. When she awoke, she would complain of a headache and send me for a plaster, or an ointment of rue to dab on her temples.

Haverley Court was so spacious that I had the luxury of a small bed to myself and a chest to keep my few possessions. I slept above the kitchens, in a small chamber right at the back of the house, but sometimes at night I thought I could hear the sound of shouting and screaming and drunken laughter echoing off the new walls and bouncing up and down the chimneys, and I would rub at the scar on my hand. I kept Peg in my chest, and whenever I lifted the lid for a clean petticoat or a cap, I would catch a glimpse of her face and it seemed to me that she looked as worried as I felt.

Once, fearing that her courses might be coming, Cat had asked for her rhubarb remedy. In truth, I forgot about it until the evening, when I hurried after Daniel as he carried wine to the chamber. He looked shocked and tried to protest as I caught him up, but I was already opening the door. I had thought to help him, that was all.

The chamber was dark, lit only by the leaping

139

flames in the fireplace and a couple of candles. Cat reclined on a cushion while Anthony, her husband's secretary, was tickling her with a long feather. They were both dishevelled and shrieking with laughter. Cat's cap had come off and her hair tumbled shockingly around her shoulders. Her face was slack and shiny in the firelight.

I did not see Lord Delahay at first. 'My lady,' I began, aghast at the sight of Cat. She looked up and defiance chased shame across her face before a figure surged out of the shadows and snarled at me.

'What are you doing here, wench?'

I showed him the remedy. 'For my mistress. I thought — '

I did not get to finish. I was still speaking as he drew back his arm and caught me such a buffet across my face that I was sent sprawling to the floor at Daniel's feet, the rhubarb decoction splashing around me as the goblet shattered and pain exploded in my cheekbone.

'You're here to serve, not think,' he said viciously. 'Now get out and do not dare come in here again.'

For a long moment, I lay there, so dazzled by pain that I could not move.

'Get out,' said Lord Delahay again, softly this time, but with such menace that I flinched. Somehow I dragged myself to my knees. I tried to look at Cat to see if she wanted help, but her eyes would not meet mine.

Daniel edged some shards of the goblet towards me with his toe, and wincing, I gathered

140

them together as I struggled awkwardly to my feet. My skirts were soaked, I had bruised my shoulder when I fell and my head was still ringing from the savage blow.

I had no choice but to leave, but I felt ashamed that I had left my mistress in such a parlous state.

Cat did not want to meet my eyes the next morning. She must have seen the bruise on my cheek but she said nothing. I dressed her hair in a silence that grew heavier with every moment that passed. When I had finished, my gaze met hers in the looking glass, and I thought I saw shame and fear in the blue eyes. I remembered how I had felt when Avery forced me, time after time, and how I had longed for her to notice, to say 'This is wrong' and put a stop to it. I rested my hands on her shoulders.

'Cat,' I said, 'what is he doing to you?'

Something flickered in her expression, but then she shrugged my hands aside. 'I do not know what you mean.'

'Lord Delahay . . . your husband . . . does he hit you the way he hit me?' I touched the bruise on my cheek where my skin felt tender and my eye throbbed cruelly.

'Of course not.' The blue eyes slipped and slid away from mine. 'He just does not like to be disturbed. You should not have come in.'

'You were drunk,' I said bluntly. 'You were . . . ' I searched for a word to tell her how shocked I had been. ' . . . acting lewdly with your husband's secretary.'

'*Acting lewdly?*' Cat mocked me. 'We were

141

enjoying ourselves, something that you clearly do not know how to do, Mary. You always were po-faced,' she said with a toss of her head. 'Oh, you would not understand! I am a married woman now. I do not have to behave like a virgin. My husband wishes me to be friendly to Anthony. He wishes us to make merry together in the evenings, and that is what we do. Would you have me refuse my own husband? Now, bring me my ruff.'

Purse-mouthed, I obeyed, but everything I did was wrong that morning. Cat would not be pleased. The ruff was soiled, the lace was torn, the wires were bent. I pricked her with the pins, she said. I tied her garters too tight. She bade me take away the shoes I brought her, even though she had asked for them only a moment before.

I set my teeth and did everything she asked. I was fastening pearls around her neck, my expression still stiff with resentment, when I saw her wince in the looking glass. She put a hand to her belly, and my anger faded with understanding. 'Is it your courses, my lady? I will make you a remedy to calm the cramps,' I said.

'It is not that!' There was a petulant edge to Cat's voice as the blue eyes filled with tears.

'Then what?'

'I am not with child!'

In my head, I calculated how long we had been at Haverley Court. She had been married when the hawthorn in the hedgerows was heavy with blossom, and now the days were short and dark. It would be Christmastide before long, although I could not imagine much celebration at Haverley Court.

'You have not been married long,' I tried to console her.

'Long enough!' Cat snapped, and then in one of her abrupt changes of mood, she swung around on her stool and grabbed my hand. 'Oh, Mary, I am such a shrewish mistress today, but you do not know . . . ' She bit her lip. 'I am frightened,' she whispered after a moment.

'George wishes for a son,' she tried again. 'I am afraid that if I do not conceive soon, he will be angry with me as he was with you last night. George has had two wives, Anthony told me, and both have failed him. He said the last wife was so despairing that she drowned herself.' She looked imploringly up at me. 'George . . . his temper is dark but if I could just have a child, it would all be better, I am sure of it.'

'Does he blame you then?'

'He is afraid that he has married another barren wife. Mary, I know old Bridget taught you at Steeple Tew and you are well versed in remedies. Can you not give me something to help me conceive? And do not tell me I must pray,' she snapped as I opened my mouth. 'I have tried prayer and still my courses come!'

I looked at her helplessly. I only knew how to rid myself of a child, not to conceive one. 'We should ask the midwife in the village.'

'She will not come. I sent for her and she had the impertinence to refuse because we are an ungodly household!'

'Perhaps if you drank less . . . ' I began, but

143

Cat turned her face away.

'I cannot. Do not ask me to explain. But please, Mary, you must help me.'

'I will ask Sindony,' I said.

Sindony sent me to a wise woman who lived in a tumbledown cottage on the outskirts of the village. The villagers muttered that she was a witch, which I dismissed, but I could not help thinking of it as I knocked on the lintel and ducked my head to step into the hovel. She was old and dirty, and the foetid smell inside made my eyes water. She looked me up and down assessingly, and I found myself shifting from foot to foot in spite of myself as I tried to explain what Cat needed.

She told me to give Cat ten juniper berries to eat every morning. When that did not work, I bruised mandrake seeds and steeped them in a cup of white wine for Cat to drink, which she did, doggedly. When her courses kept on coming, she sent me back to the wise woman, and I learnt how to make cooling drinks with barley water and blanched almonds and cucumbers and white poppy seeds.

And then came the morning when Cat vomited over the side of her bed into the chamber pot. She lay back against her pillows, groaning, and would not get up. 'I am ill,' she said tearfully.

I stroked her hair back from her forehead. 'Perhaps you are not ill,' I said. 'Perhaps you are with child.'

Cat drew in a long breath. I could tell that it had not even occurred to her. 'Could it really be so?'

'Well, we will see,' I said. 'But you must eat only wholesome foods and drink little and be moderate in all things if you wish your son to be born healthy.'

To my surprise, Cat did everything I told her. She was determined to have a son. I do not know what she told Lord Delahay, but there were no more disorderly evenings. Instead, Lord Delahay left with his secretary and his manservant, I knew not and cared not where.

The Court was a much pleasanter place without Lord Delahay. The servants lost that rigid tension that comes from being braced for a blow, and the very atmosphere seemed lighter. Cat lay on cushions and let me spoil her with dainty morsels and cakes. I watched as her stomach swelled, and I remembered how mine had never had the chance to do the same. It was almost as if the babe growing within her had taken the place of my child that had been evacuated into a privy before it could even exist, and I fussed over Cat and fretted about her health as if the babe was part of me as much as of her. For a while, it was almost like the old days at Steeple Tew. I read to her and I sewed for the baby and we looked forward to the baby's arrival together. As the months passed, we grew close again and I was happier than I had been since before Avery returned from service.

I hoped that Lord Delahay would stay away long enough to persuade the village midwife to attend the birth, but the woman was obdurate, and in the end I had to rely on Sindony and the wise woman for their help. As an unmarried woman, I should not have been in the birthing chamber, but Cat clung to my hand and grew so distressed at the idea of my leaving that Sindony told me to stay.

So I was there when Cecily was born. I watched her come into the world head first. The wise woman pulled her out of Cat's body, tipped her up by her heels and smacked her bottom until she uttered a thin wail of protest, and then she put her straight into my hands, bloody and beautiful, and my heart swelled with emotion so intense that I could barely breathe. There were tears running down my face as I gently wiped the blood from her and swaddled her, and I could hardly bear to carry her over to Cat who lay slumped against her pillows, grey with exhaustion. She lifted herself onto her elbows, though, at my approach.

'Is he healthy?'

'She is! You have a beautiful daughter,' I told her, smiling through my tears, and was dismayed to see the eagerness swiped from her face.

'A daughter?' she echoed dully as she fell back against the pillows. 'You told me I would have a son!'

'Next time, perhaps, but for now your daughter is as healthy as you could wish.'

'What good is a daughter to me?'

'But Cat — !'

'I don't want her,' she said, and she turned her face away. 'You can have her.'

I looked down at the baby in my arms. She was tiny and red and wrinkled still and she was making little bleating noises, but to me she was

146

exquisite. I could not understand how Cat could not want her.

'I will be your mother, little one,' I swore to Cecily in a fierce whisper. 'You are my daughter now.'

12

Cat

When I think of Haverley Court — and I do that as little as possible, as I am sure you do too — I think of peacocks. Do you remember that raucous screech that was the backdrop to any conversation? Such an ugly cry for such a beautiful bird. I used to watch them from the window, dragging their long tails across the gravel paths that were gradually being laid in the garden. I'd wait for the moment when they would pause and haul their feathers upwards in a flamboyant fan. There was a time when I loved that startling blue, those strange, shimmering patterns like otherworldly eyes watching me.

But that was before I knew what it was to be watched. Now I cannot think of peacocks without a shudder of disgust.

My wedding night was just the start of my shame. I hoped, I think, that once we were settled at Haverley Court, George would become more . . . normal. I thought we could spend more time together and get to know each other, and that we would become, in the end, like any other husband and wife.

I was such an innocent in those days.

The first night at Haverley Court, George invited Anthony to dine with us. The three of us sat around the table, and I thanked God for

148

Anthony who could coax George out of ill humour far better than I could. He was charm itself, cutting the choicest morsels from each dish to offer me, while George drank and watched us. I was afraid that he might be displeased by the attention Anthony showed me, but instead his expression was brighter than I had seen it before, and his eyes were lit with an intensity that made me shift uneasily on my stool as they flickered from Anthony to me and then back again.

Ah, Anthony was so fair in those days! I have never seen a man more comely. Merry brown eyes, white teeth, a smile that creased his cheeks just so. Good legs, broad shoulders, a kind of careless grace in everything he did. Anthony could make passing the pepper box seem like a flourishing bow.

You never trusted him, did you? But, Mary, you did not understand. Anthony could make me *laugh*. He made me feel beautiful. He made me feel desired. He made me feel as if what we did together was normal. Is it any wonder that I wished that he had been my husband instead of George with his simmering temper and strange desires?

He was a younger son of a good family that had fallen on hard times. Like yours, I suppose. I had not thought of that before. But Anthony admitted cheerfully that he was penniless and dependent on his post as George's secretary. I was never really sure what he did. He wrote letters, I think, and carried out business for George, standing in for my husband in tedious matters, like talking to his wife, amusing his wife . . . oh yes, and fucking his wife.

I did not realise at first. For the first few weeks I was just happy that Anthony was there as a buffer between me and the chilling intensity in my husband's eyes. It felt strange eating alone with just the three of us. When the meal was over, George would call for more wine, and more and more. He would drink steadily until his eyes were glassy, but his voice did not slur or his expression slacken the way mine did. I was not used to such strong wine, and my head soon swam, but when I tried to protest that I had had enough, he would fill up my glass anyway.

'Drink it,' he said.

It was not that he raised his voice. His expression did not change. But something in me quailed anyway, and I found myself lifting my glass to my lips with a hand that was not quite steady. And the more I drank, the easier it became to forget that I was his wife. You tucked in the corners of your mouth when I complained of a headache every morning. You demurred when I asked you to bring me wine to make me feel better. You told me that I should not drink so much. You thought I should be ashamed of myself.

You did not understand, Mary. I *was* ashamed, and that was why I drank. I could not bear it otherwise.

Wine, and Anthony. I craved them both. And George was happy for me to have them both. He encouraged Anthony to flirt with me, and when I saw that my husband did not mind, I flirted back. Why not?

One evening, Anthony was tickling me with a peacock feather, running it along the bare skin just above my bodice until I shivered with pleasure and giggled at his daring. We were both drunk, and laughing, and George was watching us, his face blazing.

'Your hair is the colour of summer corn.' Anthony stroked the feather under my chin and teased beneath my ear. 'Why do you not take it down? Let me see it.'

I glanced at George. 'Take it down,' he said in a strange hoarse voice.

So I lifted my hands to unpin the hair you had dressed so carefully, and I let it tumble about my face and down over my shoulders. I knew quite well how shocked you would have been if you had seen me, and I was embarrassed, I was, but Mary, I was aroused too. My blood was trembling beneath my skin and my breath had shortened, and after all, I was just obeying my husband. Even you could not have said that I was wrong to do that.

'Beautiful.' Anthony wound a lock of my hair around his hand and tugged me gently towards him. 'You are the fairest of the fair, my lady.' With his other hand, he flicked the feather over my bodice, teasing at my laces. 'Is the rest of you as fair, I wonder?'

Drunk as I was, my smile slipped at his boldness, and there was a moment when I was able to see myself as you might see me, sprawled on the cushions. 'I . . . am tired,' I said carefully,

151

trying not to slur my words. I put down my glass. 'I will retire.'

George's expression did not change. 'Fill my wife's glass,' he said to Anthony without looking at him, and Anthony rose gracefully to fetch the jug of wine. Bending over me, close enough for me to feel his breath on my cheek, he poured wine into my glass.

'I don't — ' I began, but he interrupted me.

'Drink,' he said softly so that only I could hear. 'It will be easier for you.'

'Now, undo your laces,' said George.

'No,' I said, understanding at last. 'No, I — ' I began to struggle up from the cushions, but George's expression stopped me. You will say I could have got up and walked out, Mary, but you were not there. You did not see his face. He might as well have had a dagger to my throat.

'Undo your laces,' he said again.

So, God help me, I did.

'Smile,' he said, and I did that too, though my mouth trembled.

From his chair, my husband directed Anthony to help me as I fumbled with my laces. He bade his secretary press his hot mouth to the swell of my breast as my bodice fell open.

'Don't be afraid,' Anthony breathed against my skin. 'You are so beautiful, Cat. I will be kind to you, do not fear. Pretend he is not there.'

Over his shoulder I could see my husband's avid stare. He had pulled his yard from his breeches and was rubbing himself, touching himself with another of those cursed feathers as Anthony groped beneath my skirts. He pushed them up until they bunched around my waist and he touched me beneath my shift, between my legs. It was still summer then, not yet dark, and in the distance I could hear a peacock screech.

My head was reeling from the wine and I closed my eyes. I could feel Anthony unpinning me, unwinding me, stripping off the layers you had dressed me in that morning. I jolted at the heat of his mouth, the wetness of it against my privy parts. I could hear the rustle of clothes being removed, George panting, Anthony grunting as he pushed into me. I wanted to be horrified at what was happening, but do you wish for the truth, Mary? I wasn't horrified at all. I was excited. Eyes tightly shut, I imagined looking down at myself, knees spread wide on the cushions, Anthony's bare buttocks bucking up and down between them, and my husband, his mouth ajar, breathing furiously as he watched us and fondled himself, and my blood pounded and there was booming inside me that beat harder and harder until it roared and I tipped my head back with an inarticulate cry. I was still floppy as George shoved Anthony aside and rolled me roughly onto my front so that he could enter me.

'A son!' he gasped. 'A son, a son, a son!' He collapsed on top of me with a grunt so that the three of us lay tangled stickily together.

When I opened my eyes, still with my husband's damp weight on my back, I saw Anthony lying next to me, his face pressed into a cushion. He was breathing hard as he turned his

153

head and our eyes met. 'It will get better,' he mouthed.

And it did. The next night we did it again, and the next, and before long I had been sucked into a dangerous game that I craved as much as I feared. It wasn't always the same. Sometimes George liked me to resist, and pretend that Anthony was forcing me against my will. Sometimes it was I who had to take the feather and seduce Anthony. George liked that. He would bid me get down on my knees before his secretary and take him in my mouth. But whichever way we contorted ourselves to his twisted desires, it ended with my husband's few pathetic thrusts. The only way he could bring himself to consummate our marriage was by watching me play the whore with Anthony first. Imagine how that made me feel, Mary! The more he watched and panted, the more I loathed him, and he loathed me back. I might as well have been a toad that he forced himself to pick up. If it had not been for his longing for a son, he would have never had a wife at all.

You have no idea how I suffered. There were the jewels, of course, and the gowns. I could buy what I liked, and so I did. I earned every pearl, every diamond. All that silk and velvet and gold embroidery was paid for in humiliation. I took pleasure in them, yes, but what else did I have to enjoy?

I wondered sometimes about George's other wives, if they had had to endure what I endured, and I vowed to myself that I would not be like them, vanquished in childbed or trailing down to the river in despair. I had suffered for my position as the mistress of Haverley Court, and I was determined to have it for myself — and for Anthony. My husband had created a craving in me that I could not satisfy. I was in thrall to Anthony's touch. I yearned for it, but I wanted him without George's gaze crawling stickily over us.

We had hardly any opportunities to be alone. George was jealous. He did not want us to exist if we were not performing for him alone, and he kept Anthony with him as much as possible. Once or twice I was able to lurk outside the study and if Anthony emerged on an errand I would grab him and we would pull each other behind a door or into a shadowy corner and go at it in frantic silence.

'We must be careful,' Anthony breathed in my ear. 'If he suspects that we do this without him, he will dismiss me.'

'No, he must not!' I clutched him to me in panic. George would find another secretary and pay him to service me, and how could I bear to do that with a stranger? 'I love you!'

'And I you, but we must be patient. If you could but conceive,' Anthony said, pressing his forehead against mine. 'With a son, you would be secure, Cat. If anything happened to George, your son would inherit Haverley Court and you, of course, would stay here to care for him. And perhaps you would need me to look after the estate for you . . . ' he said. 'You might even marry again. If you were a widow.'

I knew what he was suggesting, and my eyes

must have been brilliant as I looked back at him.

'How may we manage it?'

'First you must have a son. Your maid seems skilled in the still room,' Anthony said. I had not realised until then that he had even noticed you, and I felt a flash of resentment that he could look at anybody but me. But his suggestion was sound: you *were* skilled, and I knew that you would help me if I asked.

So I drank all those vile concoctions you came up with and when I conceived, I was overjoyed. I told George that I feared hurting the child and that I would not play his games any more. I hoped that he would leave me be for a few months so that Anthony could pleasure me alone, but I had reckoned without my husband's cruelty. He took Anthony and they went to London. What they did there, I never knew, but I could imagine all too well. I had to stay at Haverley Court growing bulkier and bulkier and picture George watching Anthony with another woman. Or with another man. By then I knew there were no limits to my husband's depravity.

My hatred of George deepened with every passing day. Do you remember how we would sit together in the parlour and I would watch you sewing? Sometimes you would look up from your needle and see me looking dreamily into the fire, and your face would soften.

'I am happy to see you so content,' you used to say.

And I would put my hands on my belly and smile, knowing that you thought I was picturing the babe, while my mind was busy planning how to kill my husband once my son was installed in the new cradle I had ordered.

'Do not forget me,' Anthony whispered before they departed. 'It will be worth it if you can only have a son.'

I did everything I should, did I not? I did not ride and I walked sedately up and down that long gallery until I thought I would scream with the tedium of it. I sat quietly and ate and drank what I was told. I listened as you and that fat old laundress assured me that I would have a son. I writhed and screamed at the pain of labour, and after all that, it was just a girl! Do you wonder I could not stand to look on her?

George was as disappointed as I when he came home, and he took it out on me with ever more depraved games. His eyes were aglitter with temper and lust as he ordered Anthony to bind me and take a whip to me, as if I were no better than a whore dragged through the town at the cart's arse! Anthony was as gentle as he could be, but oh, Mary, how can you judge me so when you do not know half of what I have suffered?

You stilled when you lifted my shift and saw the welts on my buttocks, the bruises under my ribs. You brought me warm water with herbs and a soft cloth and salves to sooth the welts. And you busied yourself brushing my skirts, adjusting the creases in my ruff.

'I know what this feels like,' you said, and I stiffened.

'You? What do you know?'

157

'Your brother used me like this,' you said painfully.

It would not have been the same, Mary. I dare say you enjoyed it really. Avery might have been a dolt, but he was a fine-looking man. He was not vile like George. He would not have made you take another man's yard in your mouth, would he? He would not have had to *watch* before his own would rise. He would not have taken pleasure in your pain.

I saw how Avery watched you, and it was with lust, not cruelty. You should have played your cards better, Mary. You are clever enough to have managed Avery, aye, and Jocosa too if you had put your mind to it.

'I could give you something to calm his temper,' you said quietly. 'To make him sleepy.'

Do you remember that, Mary? It was *your* idea.

'How?' I asked without turning around. 'I have to drink the wine too. We cannot put it in that even if Daniel were not to see.'

'I will put it in a dish,' you decided. 'Something savoury so that he may not smell it. A potage of sand eels, perhaps, or a mutton pie . . . ' I could see you planning dishes in your mind.

'He likes duck or capon the way you prepare it.'

You gave a brisk little nod. 'Duck then. But do you not eat any of it,' you warned. 'Leave it for the men to eat and then they will leave you in peace for the evening at least.'

I warned Anthony of course. We both declined

158

the duck that you sent in, and George gobbled it all up himself. And while he slept later, Anthony and I went at it joyfully in my bed with no one to please but ourselves, and I put back my head and gasped and groaned with delight.

A year went by, and then another, and still I did not conceive again, though no one could say that Anthony and I did not try. We were mad for each other then, and George's cruelty just made us want each other more. After that first time, I asked you to give me the potion so that I could slip it into George's wine more easily. You warned me to be careful. 'Too much and you will kill him,' you said.

'That is useful to know,' Anthony smiled when I told him. 'We must remember that for after your son is born.'

It was so tempting to use the potion more and more often so that Anthony and I could be by ourselves. We would lie naked together in my bed, the curtains pulled tight around us. I would eat sweetmeats off his belly, while he licked the sugar from my breasts, and we would plan. Oh, such glorious plans! We would wrap ourselves in velvets and furs, and wear rings on every finger. We would go to France! There would be nothing to stop us leaving the child with a nurse and travelling. I longed to leave that horrible house and see something of the world. When we were married, we might find a place at court, even. We would be rich. Why should we not do whatever we wanted?

'Oh, my dove, I cannot wait!' I sighed, but Anthony always cautioned patience.

'We can do nothing until you have a son.' He threw himself on his back. 'After that, we can put an end to George.'

'Why can we not act now?' I asked petulantly. 'I am so tired of him. I am raw from his whippings. I begin to see why his last wife took herself to the river!'

Anthony laughed. 'You are nothing like her, Cat. She was a poor thing. George might as well have been torturing a little mouse.'

'Did you service her the way you do me?' I asked jealously, and he rolled himself on top of me.

'What do you think?' He slipped his hand between my legs, making me squirm with lascivious delight. 'But there was no pleasure in it, the way there is with you, my heart. And no chance of making a profit from it. For that, a woman of spirit is necessary, and that is you, Cat.'

I was mollified. 'I wish we could rid ourselves of him now.'

'If we do that, the estate will go to George's nephew. His heir,' Anthony reminded me with an edge to his voice. I knew it was because he had explained it so many times before, but I was impatient for this time to end. 'Your daughter will have a dowry, but nothing more. As for you, you will have to go back to your brother.'

'Never!'

'But with a son . . . ' Anthony's eyes gleamed as he gestured around the bed. 'This bed, this chamber, this house, this estate . . . it would all be ours, to do with as we will. So be patient a little longer, love — and do not give George the sleeping potion too often. I fear Daniel may be growing suspicious.'

'He is just a servant,' I said dismissively.

'Not so. Have you not seen the way Daniel looks at George? Everyone else looks at him with loathing, but Daniel's eyes hold only yearning.'

I made a sound of disgust.

'It is true,' Anthony insisted. 'George uses him when he feels like it. Daniel will do things even more degrading than you can imagine. What we do, we do for duty so that he — and we — can beget a son, but Daniel would do anything for George's love, and he asks nothing in return.'

Unlike Anthony, whom George showered with gifts. I guessed that I was not the only service Anthony was called on to perform for my husband, but I closed my mind to what else he might do.

So I did try to leave days at a time before giving George some more of your potion, but it was too tempting to use it when I saw George's temper was particularly bad and I could not face whoring myself for his pleasure one more time. Your potion was powerful and I was careful not to give him too much, just as you said. It made him sleepy and listless without feeling ill.

That night, I slipped it into his wine as usual, and indeed, George soon began to yawn and slur his words. He fell asleep in his chair, his mouth open, his legs splayed and the empty goblet dangling from his fingers. Anthony and I tiptoed out to my bedchamber. I was straddling him, and we were going at it so hard that neither of us

161

heard the latch. Neither of us heard anything at all until the bed curtains were wrenched open with a roar.

'What is this?' George's face was congested with rage and great flecks of spittle gathered at the edges of his mouth, as we gaped at him in shock. 'Daniel whispered that you were cuckolding me and I boxed his ears for his insolence. You would not dare, I said. I sent him away. But tonight I woke and the fire was cold and my head was spinning and you were both gone. I came to find succour, and see what I find instead!'

'You are unwell, husband,' I tried, clutching at the idea that the potion might take hold again and that he would remember nothing in the morning.

'Unwell, am I?' George's hand closed cruelly around my arm, pulling me off Anthony and sending me tumbling to the floor. 'Not so unwell I cannot whip you until your blood runs, madam wife! And as for you, Anthony,' he went on, and his voice was low and vicious, his eyes rolling with vengeance. 'You have betrayed me . . . after all these years, you do this to me! I will kill you now.'

'No!' I scrambled to my feet, horrified as I saw his hands around Anthony's throat. 'George, please, it is not what you think!' I tried to pull at him, but he was too strong. Anthony was choking and flailing, at a disadvantage lying in bed. Frantically, I looked around for something to stop him killing Anthony, and that is when I saw the poker by the fire. It was in my hand

162

before I knew it, and heavier than I thought, but I hauled it up with both hands and brought it down on George's head. He cried out and fell sideways, sliding off the bed with a heavy thud, but he was roaring still and struggling to get up, vile words pouring from his lips. He would wake the whole house. I knew most would pretend they heard nothing, but what if Daniel came?

I had to quieten him, you must see that. I had to, but it took four blows before I felt his skull crack, and he stopped roaring and vomiting at last. I was breathing hard, and Anthony was still clutching his throat.

'You've killed him!' he wheezed, his eyes wide and staring.

I let the poker drop from my nerveless hand. 'I had to,' I said in a small voice. 'He wouldn't be quiet.' I stared at him. 'What are we going to do?'

Anthony struggled up against the pillows. 'You'll have to get help. Call that cool maid of yours.'

'You can't be here,' I said, calming down. 'This is Mary's fault. She cannot have made the potion strong enough tonight. Or she has made it wrongly, and it has driven him to madness at last. Yes, that is what must have happened.'

'He is dead!' You turned a horrified face up to me. I had run to scratch on your door, whisper to you to come and help. You dropped to your knees beside him and pressed two fingers to his throat. 'Cat, what have you done? You have killed him!'

'I didn't mean to.' I was shaking violently. 'He would have killed me otherwise. That potion you

163

made. It drove him mad.' I clutched my robe around me. My toes were sticky with blood and vomit and I rubbed them desperately against the floorboards to rid myself of the feeling. 'What are we going to do?'

I saw you work it out, click, click, click in your busy brain as you massaged your neck, as if already feeling a rope there. What would happen if I were tried for killing my husband? Would you be implicated for making the potion? I know you were not thinking of me then, Mary. You were thinking of yourself, and the child perhaps. You were besotted with her, and treated her as if she were your daughter, not mine. You were in a panic lest you and she should find yourselves with nowhere to go. You did not care what would happen to *me*.

'We must make it look like an accident,' you decided, rubbing at your scarred hand the way you do when you are thinking, and you took control. You called for Anthony, who gave a very good impression of a man roused from sleep, and made him help you push George to the bottom of the stairs. You spoke quietly to the servants, and were solicitous to Daniel, the only one who had cared anything for George. You gave him something to help his grief, and it made him dull when the coroner came. You had George's corpse carried to the church. You arranged the mourning.

You made the potion that drove George mad, Mary. I did not want him to die, not then. Not until I had a son to inherit. You covered up *your* crime. It was all your idea. You did *everything*.

13

Mary

Haverley Court, October 1578

For the first few days after Lord Delahay's death, we crept around, almost as if we feared he would rise up and berate us. The events of that night come back to me still in jolting images, like snatches of a nightmare remembered: the stomach-turning stench of vomit and of blood as I knelt on my hands and knees to scrub up the mess on Cat's chamber floor. The smell of the wine I threw over Anthony to set the scene. He was to pretend that he had been drinking heavily with George instead of swiving his wife.

Of course I knew what he and Cat had been doing. Did Cat think I was blind?

I remember the weight of Lord Delahay's body as Anthony and I hauled him to the top of the grand new staircase and then hurled him down it. It was not as easy as I thought to make it look like an accident. At first his body only slumped down a few steps. We had to try three more times until he eventually lay at the bottom and I had to twist his head so that it looked as if his neck were broken. As if the bloody dent in his temple had been caused by falling against a step and not by a poker. The cold clamminess of his skin, the grease in his hair, made me gag as I touched him, but it looked plausible enough when I had finished.

And all the while I was cleaning and arranging and thinking and planning, I was terrified for my immortal soul. Mine was the hand that had prepared the potion. The same hand that had pushed the vagrant child from the cart all those years earlier. I had told Cat to be careful, yes, but I had made it. I could not deny it. I was a murderer, twice over.

But I could not stop to pray or do penance. I had to keep Cat safe. I had to keep Cecily safe. I had to keep us all safe.

I was worried about Daniel, who would surely be suspicious, but when we had staged the scene, I told Anthony to rouse him and pretend that George had been drinking, that he had tripped, that it had all been a terrible accident.

Anthony was as good as a player, acting his part of a shocked and not quite sober friend as he roused Daniel, who staggered in shock and wept for his master. Perhaps he lacked anyone else to tie his fortunes to, just as I was tied to Cat. We led him away, and I made him a drink to calm him and help him sleep while we sent for the coroner.

The coroner twisted his hat in his hands, plainly out of his depth and uneasy at having to ask questions in a noble house. He allowed me to point out the smell of wine, and agreed with my suggestion that Lord Delahay must have stumbled and fallen down the stairs. But from somewhere he dredged up a remembrance of his duties, and said that of course he must speak to

166

witnesses too. I bent my head in acquiescence but I was dismayed. The more people he spoke to, the more suspicions might arise.

But the drink I had given Daniel kept him groggy and the coroner soon tired of questioning stolid servants who had heard nothing, seen nothing, suspected nothing. 'A terrible accident,' he decided, and we were free to bury Lord Delahay. Cat refused to make a show of sitting with the body.

'He can lie on the village midden for all I care,' she said.

So he lay alone and unmourned in the chapel that was never used, although I was able to convince her that we must have a priest and a funeral according to his position, else questions would surely be asked. I cannot lie and say that I mourned him, but I spent long hours on my knees, praying for forgiveness for my part in his death.

Daniel roused himself from his bed and came to see me. His face was white and waxy, and malevolence gleamed in his eyes. 'I do not believe my master fell down those stairs. He drank himself into a stupor every night, but not once did he fall. There is something going on between his lady wife and Sir Anthony,' he said. 'They have been cuckolding my master, I am sure of it.'

'That is untrue,' I said calmly. 'You are distraught over the loss of your master, and I am sorry for it, but you must not make accusations you cannot prove.'

Daniel's expression twisted. 'I may not be able

to prove it, but I know it in my bones. Your lady pushed my master down those stairs.'

'Indeed she did not.' I was glad for once to speak the truth. 'It was an accident. Lord Delahay had drunk so much he was unwell. Sir Anthony saw him fall, and so he told you.'

'He would say that, wouldn't he? I will go to the coroner.'

So it is not grief for Lord Delahay, I thought. He wants money. It is as simple as that.

'And say what?' I asked. 'It would be your word against Sir Anthony's, and he is a gentleman.'

'What choice do I have?'

'You will want to go away, I am sure. Haverley Court can have only bad memories for you now. A manservant of your skill will surely find another post,' I suggested. 'I am sure my mistress would want to reward you for your loyalty,' I added carefully.

'You promised him *what*?' Cat was angry when I told her that she would have to give Daniel a purse of silver. We were walking along the gravel paths in the new knot garden. I trusted the servants, but there were some conversations we needed to have where we could not be overheard. Anthony walked with us, elegant as ever. I remember the crunch of his boots on the gravel, the scent of rosemary and thyme released as our skirts brushed the plants.

'You do not want to make an enemy of Daniel,' I said. 'Be generous. Send him on his way. He suspects too much.'

Anthony agreed. 'Let us be rid of him,' he said

negligently. He smiled at Cat. 'My dove, you can afford it now.'

Cat laughed at him over her shoulder. 'So I can!'

Only until the new Lord Delahay came to claim his inheritance, I thought.

George's heir was his nephew, a young man who had been last heard of in Italy. Anything might happen to him, I could see Cat thinking to herself. Travelling was a dangerous business. He might never come, she reasoned, and she could stay forever at Haverley Court with Anthony, just as she had planned.

For a few months, indeed, it seemed as if she might be right, but the laws of inheritance do not favour daughters or widows. It was clear to me that we were on borrowed time. Sooner or later, a new Lord Delahay would come riding up to the door, and then what would become of us?

Cat told me to stop fretting. 'We are free now,' she said. 'Let us enjoy it, Mary.'

She was happy, and just as at Steeple Tew, when Cat was happy, the whole household was happy too. The other servants turned a blind eye to the fact that Anthony shared her bed. They treated him as her husband, and he was, to all intents and purposes, master.

I was the only one who gave thought to the future. 'You may be free for now,' I said, 'but for how much longer? George's nephew will inherit sooner or later, and we will have to go home to Steeple Tew — and you won't be able to take Anthony with you.'

'Go back to Steeple Tew?' Cat said in

astonishment. 'What for? Anthony and I will be married as soon as may be.'

'Your brother will not allow it.'

'It is not up to Avery! I am a widow. I can make my own choices.'

I shook my head. 'How many of us can do that? You will have to be ordered by your brother,' I told her. 'When George's nephew arrives, there will be no place for you here. It would be different if you had a son, but Cecily is only a girl child. She has no claim on the estate.'

'He is not come yet,' Cat pointed out. 'There is sickness in the country and no one is going anywhere.'

Did she really believe Avery would leave her be? She wrote eventually to tell him of George's death, but even I was surprised at the speed with which he responded, summoning her back to Steeple Tew in a letter. With no regard for her period of mourning, Avery had arranged another marriage for Cat already with one of his business associates, a prosperous London merchant called Gabriel Thorne.

Cat stared incredulously when I read the letter out to her. 'A *merchant*? How can he think it?' she exclaimed. 'I would not so debase myself.'

'Anthony has few prospects,' I pointed out.

'What does that matter?' Cat rose in a furious flurry of skirts and paced around the chamber. 'He is at least a gentleman! His family were *nobles*.'

Anthony! The pair of them thought they could live here in their dream world forever. I was out of patience with Cat. She thought only of

170

Anthony, and not once of Cecily. How was her daughter to be supported? Where was she to live? Who would feed and clothe her? Not Anthony, for all his gentlemanly connections.

'Why do you not at least hear what Mr Thorne has to say?' I tried. 'You could be comfortable with a wealthy merchant.'

'Comfortable?' Cat sneered. 'That is all you ever think about, Mary. Being comfortable, being safe. You would rather go and live in a merchant's house and let him put his great paws on you than follow your heart. You know nothing of passion.'

'And I am glad of it if it means that I would not forget those who depend on me,' I said quietly. 'I would rather live in a cottage than see my daughter and my servants starve.'

Cat sighed. 'No one is going to starve, Mary! Do not make me a tragedy. Write back to Avery and tell him that if I marry again, I will marry to please myself.'

I had no desire to go back to Steeple Tew either, but I could not imagine the new Lord Delahay would house us, and nor could I see Anthony supporting us. He had nothing but good looks and a certain sly charm to recommend him. Another marriage for Cat would be the best option for Cecily and me. So I couched the letter in more temperate terms. Cat was in mourning, I reminded Avery on her behalf. She was not ready to contemplate another marriage yet.

My attempt at diplomacy was wasted. Avery wrote back in a rage, or so I deduced reading between the lines of what his clerk had written for him. Avery, it seemed, was under a great obligation to Gabriel Thorne. He had no intention of allowing Cat to rule herself. There was sickness at Steeple Tew, but he had told Mr Thorne to present himself at Haverley Court where he could expect to be received favourably.

Cat was incandescent when I read the letter out to her. 'I won't see him!' she said furiously. 'How dare Avery do this!' Tears stood in her eyes. 'A great obligation indeed! Avery is in debt to this merchant, mark you my words. Jocosa has ruined him with her pretensions. There will be glass in every window at Steeple Tew now!' She paced up and down the chamber, her skirts swishing irritably on the rush matting. 'And now all the money has been spent, I am to be sold off to pay for it all!'

'What about your dowry? Avery must have made some arrangement with Lord Delahay.'

'It is to revert on my widowhood, but to Avery, not to me. Oh!' Cat clenched her fists to her temples. 'After all I have suffered, why can I not be allowed to be happy now? It is not fair!'

'What harm will it do to at least see this Mr Thorne?' I said soothingly. 'If Mr Thorne really is displeasing to you, you will be able to tell him no. Or you could put him off by saying you would like the chance to get to know him better, or mourn George longer.'

'Or that I am a gentlewoman and have no intention of being sold off to a merchant!'

'Cat . . . my lady . . . please, think of what may be,' I urged her. 'George's nephew may come at any time, and then what will you do? You can marry Anthony, yes, but where would we go? How would we live?'

'I have my jewels. I can sell them.'

'Jewels will not last forever,' I said. 'Do not turn away Mr Thorne without seeing him. Surely it is better to keep your options open?'

'You see him, if you think it is so important,' she snapped.

'But it is you he will have come to see.'

'Then do you take my place, Mary.' Cat clapped her hands together at the thought. 'Yes, indeed, it will be the very thing! We will change places for the day. You shall be mistress, and I your maid. Then I will take a look at this Mr Thorne, and make sure that you send him away.'

'We cannot do that!' I was scandalised. 'He would know I was not you, for a start.'

'Pah, he will see what he expects to see,' said Cat. 'You can wear my best gown, and I will wear yours. He will be shown into a room to meet Lady Delahay, and you will be sitting there with your maid standing behind you. Why should he question it?'

'You should tell him yourself, in that case,' I said. 'To deceive a man in such a way is wrong, and folly.'

I argued, but Cat was determined. There was no point in writing to Avery. Gabriel Thorne must be rejected to his face, and Avery must make good his great obligation some other way.

When only a week or so later a message was brought to her chamber that Mr Thorne begged for an audience with her, she squealed with excitement.

'Quick, Mary, let us change gowns!' To the servant, she snapped an order to tell Mr Thorne to wait. 'Offer him some ale or whatever merchants drink,' she said carelessly.

I worked as quickly as I could, but it takes time to unpin sleeves, to unlace a bodice and unfasten skirts, and then they all had to be pinned and laced and fastened anew on me. Cat ran around, amusing herself with playing the part of maid. She found me a ruff and draped some pearls from my waist, before helping me into her gown and twitching it into place with a laugh.

'Oh, Mary, you look quite the lady!'

'I do not think we should be doing this,' I said weakly, but Cat was having none of it.

'Come, help me into your gown. How dull it is!' she said, brushing it down with distaste.

'You had better wear a cap too,' I said, resigned. 'Your hair is too beautiful a gold. Mr Thorne would be sure to notice.' Cat liked that.

At last we were ready. We made our way to the great chamber, and Cat took her place behind the chair with a smothered giggle, while I sat, feeling stiff and uncomfortable. We sent the servant for Mr Thorne.

When he came in, I was too embarrassed to look at him directly at first. He took off his hat and bowed low over my hand, and I smelt clean hair and luxurious fabric. When I made myself meet his eyes, they were the colour of a winter sky, keen and cool, and they seemed to reach

174

right inside me and pluck at my nerves.

'My Lady Delahay,' he said.

'Mr Thorne,' I said nervously. 'You are welcome.'

Was it my imagination or had Cat tsked behind me?

I invited him to sit and we exchanged small talk about his journey for a few minutes. Gabriel Thorne was a steady, solid-looking man with a quiet face. He would have been unremarkable were it not for the levelness of his gaze, and a calm voice that was like a hand gentling down my spine. He made me feel safe just by sitting there.

What did he make of me? I wondered. Could he tell that I was in borrowed clothes and that the pearls I fidgeted with belonged to another woman entirely?

Behind me, Cat was getting restive. 'Bring wine and cakes,' I said over my shoulder to her.

'Certainly, *my lady*,' she said with venomous sweetness.

'You know why I am here?' Gabriel said when she had gone.

I nodded. 'My brother proposes a marriage between us.'

'That is so,' he said. 'I lost my wife last year, God rest her soul. I have three sons, good boys all of them. They need a mother, and I need a wife. God has blessed my business and I have prospered.'

And now you want a gentry wife to improve your standing, I thought, but did not say. There was no need. We both understood the reality being discussed: Cat's status for his money.

I peeped at him under my lashes. Perhaps he was not handsome like Anthony, and there were pockmarks scattered over his cheeks, but there was something pleasing about the intelligence in his face, the acuteness of his eyes. He was not repulsive, not at all.

If I were Cat, I decided, I would have been happy to marry him. He was sober, yes, but Gabriel Thorne would be a good balance for her gaiety, if only she could be brought to consider it.

'A marriage between us would be pleasing to me,' he was saying. 'Your brother has given his consent — indeed, he is eager for the match. I understand that your position is uncertain now,' Gabriel added carefully, 'and that the new Lord Delahay may come to take up his inheritance at any time. I can offer you a fine house in London and a home for your daughter. I would bring her up as my own if you would wed me.' He paused, and his eyes searched mine until I squirmed in my chair. 'What say you, my lady?'

'Will you give me time to consider?' I said after a moment. I could not bring myself to reject him outright as Cat had so foolishly commanded. 'It is not long since I buried my husband.'

He bowed his head courteously. 'I understand,' he said, but his gaze was puzzled. No doubt Avery had assured him that Cat would do as instructed. He should have known better.

'I . . . I will think about it, what you have said,' I told him.

'I hope that you will,' he said, and a sudden

smile lit the severe features. 'Write to me when you have made your decision. I will wait for your letter.'

'*Think* about it?' Cat was outraged, of course, when I told her what I had said. 'Did I not tell you to reject him?'

'It seemed sensible not to reject him straight away,' I said. 'He would go back to your brother, perhaps, and then you would have Avery haranguing you. As it is, Mr Thorne will wait for a letter from you, which will not come, and the matter will be quietly forgotten.'

Cat sniffed. She never did like to be out-argued.

'Would you not at least think about his offer?' I tried. 'You had a chance to see him for yourself. He was quite gentlemanlike, was he not?'

'Gentlemanlike is not the same as being a gentleman,' Cat snapped. 'My father raised me to marry into the nobility. Do you think he would be content with a mere merchant?'

'He would want *you* to be content,' I said.

'Well, I will not be content as a merchant's wife.' Cat tossed her head. 'Stop trying to persuade me otherwise, Mary. You become tedious. Quite apart from anything else, what do you think he would say if he came to betroth himself to you and found a quite different Lady Delahay waiting for him?'

'He would be delighted, I would think, to find himself with a wife so much fairer than he had thought,' I said levelly. 'We could tell him the truth: that we swapped places so that you could see him.'

I could tell that my reference to her fairness pleased Cat. She arched her neck and preened, but at least she had the grace to laugh when she caught my eye. 'Mary, you will not persuade me,' she said, wagging her finger at me. 'I would not make a good merchant's wife. You marry Mr Thorne if he pleases you so.'

★   ★   ★

Barely a week later, a letter arrived announcing the imminent return of George's nephew, the new Lord Delahay. Cat took the news as a personal affront, forgetting that I had been warning of this for months.

'What shall we do?' I said, equally dismayed. 'Now we have no choice but to go back to Steeple Tew.'

Cat stilled suddenly. 'No,' she said, resolute. 'I am not going back. Put together my jewels, Mary, and any coin that you can find.'

'What are you going to do?'

'Anthony and I have talked about what we would do if this came to pass. We will be married whether Avery wills it or no,' she said. 'We will leave this very afternoon. I will not wait for George's nephew to turn me out. I will not be married off to a man of my brother's choice.' She put up her chin stubbornly. 'This time, when I marry, it will be my choice, and I choose to be happy. I choose love.'

I gaped at her. 'But how will we manage? What about Cecily?'

'I cannot take her. You must see that.' Cat

178

seized my hands, blue eyes imploring. 'You care for her, Mary. I give her to you! Take her back to Steeple Tew,' she said. 'Avery will not turn away his own niece. Anthony and I are bound for France. We have often talked about it, and now we must do it.'

She bundled up the jewels and her gowns, chattering wildly about her love for Anthony. She would not listen to reason. Love, love, love was all she would talk about, as if that made it all right to abandon her daughter.

To abandon *me*.

That night, when she and Anthony had climbed into the carriage and bowled away, the house yawned emptily without her. It was the first time we had been apart since I had arrived at Steeple Tew all those years earlier. I had not believed, not really, that Cat would leave me alone.

My throat was tight as I sat in the nursery and held Cecily on my lap. She was but a babe still, and her huge eyes, so like Cat's, sparkled as she chuckled and bumped her forehead against mine. Her chubby hands clutched at my hair but I welcomed the pain as she pulled.

'I will look after you,' I promised her, but I was not sure how.

When the messenger arrived, I thought at first that the letter he brought would announce the arrival of the new Lord Delahay, and my fingers trembled as I broke the seal. The wax splintered over my skirts like drops of blood, and I brushed them from me in horror. How would I explain to him that Cat had gone? Would he be kind, and let Cecily grow up as part of his household? What if he were cruel, like George? Would he let me stay to care for and protect her? Or would he send us back to Steeple Tew with the shame of Cat's elopement to hang over Cecily forever? The questions hammered at my brain so remorselessly that it was a while before the words stopped dancing on the parchment and settled so that I could take them in.

The letter was not from Lord Delahay at all. It came from Steeple Tew. The sickness Avery had mentioned in his letter to Cat had spread and taken hold, sweeping through the village. Avery and Jocosa were both dead. If only Cat had waited a few days was my first thought, but in the end, what difference would it have made? The manor would pass, like Haverley Court, along the male line. The new owner was likely to have little use for a maid turning up with a child who she claimed was Cat's daughter.

Like a startled coney, my mind ran frantically in different directions, stopping, starting, bolting afresh in search of a way out. Oh, if only I were Cat and could have married Gabriel Thorne, all would be well, I thought.

If only I were Cat . . . The idea dropped through me like a stone into a well.

Write to me, Gabriel had said.

Avery and Jocosa were dead. They would not be at the wedding to point fingers, and who else would know or care that I was not Cat? No one.

Who would know me in London? No one.

It was wrong, I knew that, but what else was I to do? I had Cecily to think about. I could

180

consign her to the uncertain care of indifferent guardians, who would treat her with contempt, the unwanted poor relation as I had been, burdened with the scandal of a runaway mother. Or I could take her to a comfortable home.

I thought about Gabriel's cool eyes, the steady way he had looked at me. I thought about his sons, who needed a mother, and Cecily, who needed a father. *I would bring her up as my own*, he had said.

It was a monstrous deception, but I dared not wait to see what George's nephew might be like. He might be kind — but he might not.

I went to George's closet and found some parchment and some ink. I had considered his offer, I wrote to Gabriel Thorne, and I had made up my mind. I would marry him. My daughter and I would come to London as soon as would please him.

I signed the letter: Catherine, Lady Delahay.

PART III

14

Cat

London, Little Wood Street, June 1590

Oh, what a dreary June it has been! Sullen clouds weeping a perpetual warm drizzle that has turned the streets claggy and spangled the heavy woollen cloaks that made us all sweat. The dullness of the weather is as nothing to the dullness in the house, though. Three weeks since, Gabriel and his young son Tom took ship for Hamburg, and nothing feels quite the same.

You are pining for your husband, I can tell. Oh, you manage him very well, I must admit. You have him dancing on a string. When the rest of us were singing and making merry that night, you sat and rubbed your scar and looked sour, and then you took yourself off to bed, knowing that Gabriel would follow. 'A headache,' he explained, but I felt sure that you had no headache when he excused himself a few minutes later. No, you and he will have been going to it in that soft bed of yours while I was left to entertain the others. I could smell it on you both, see it in the way you looked at each other. The next day your skin glowed at morning prayers and a small satisfied smile lurked around your mouth.

It chafes at me that you should find so much

pleasure with the merchant. I confess that on closer inspection he is not as doughy as I thought at first. He has none of Anthony's style and elegance, but he has a certain quiet appeal, I will grant you that. There is something reassuringly solid about him. I am sure you know just what I mean. He has a nice mouth, and though his smile is rare, when it comes, it is a pleasant jolt, a kick to the heart.

It did not take me long to persuade you to have a feather bed laid over the flock mattress so that I can sleep more comfortably. It is still not as comfortable as *your* bed, though, is it? No curtains for me, no cushions, no embroidered coverlets or furs. Not that I need fur when it is so hot, but it is the principle of the thing. The knowledge that your bed is better than mine is a tiny piece of grit on the fine sheet, digging into me whichever way I turn.

And you share yours with Gabriel, while I sleep alone.

So, yes, I can quite see why you glow so. Your husband pleases you mightily.

It is not fair that on top of everything else you have pleasure too. But so it has always been. You have whatever you want. You have never suffered, Mary, not truly. You looked down your nose at me when you saw how bedraggled I had become, but you know nothing of what it is to be at the mercy of a man. All those years I protected you, and in return you took everything that was mine: my name, my kin, my status, my daughter.

Gabriel could have been mine too. I may have made a mistake that day I left him to you. I dare say he would have been happier with the real Lady Catherine. I'll wager I know some tricks that you have never learnt as a staid merchant's wife.

I sigh regretfully as I fasten my gown. Of course, it would have been better if Gabriel had bought himself an estate and a title. I would have been more than content with him as a husband then. He would not have wanted to watch me swived by another man, or use my beauty to attract foolish men with coins in their purse, mere pigeons for the plucking at cards or dice.

Of course you can never tell. That I have learnt.

Still, no fucking for you for a while, not until Gabriel comes back from Hamburg, and that will be some weeks away. Your husband's absence weighs heavily on you, does it not? I see you pretending to put a brave face on it, but you are pale and scratchy, and the truth is that I am feeling more cheerful knowing that your perfect life is not quite as perfect as it normally is.

And today, for once, the sun is shining. Those depressing clouds have lifted and there is a lushness to the air, a startling greenness to the trees hanging over the garden walls and the grass in the churchyards. A smell of summer that drifts into the city in spite of the stench of too many cesspits close together, and the pungent odour of streets crammed with people and horses and pigs and geese and sheep and cows and ducks and hens and dogs and cats and rats and all the other creatures that scuttle along the gutters or are driven through the city gates. But to my relief, I have not seen or heard a single peacock here.

Gabriel left you and John in charge of his business while he is overseas. Tedious work, it seems to me. Men's work, and if you had any sense you would leave it all to John, but no, you must spend long hours down at Gabriel's warehouses. What is it that you do there? Surely you are not standing on the quayside supervising the loading and unloading of ships? Perhaps you inspect everything as you do in the market, turning things over, lifting them to your nose, prodding and poking, pursing your lips and bargaining.

John is quite capable of managing the business by himself, but no, you must always know best. If John had any backbone he would tell you to take your nose out of his affairs, but he is distracted of late. My fault, I fear. The moment his father had taken ship, he declared his love for me, and what could I do but laugh at him? I may sing with him, but I have no desire to tie my fortunes to a young man who can do nothing for me.

'John is too young for you,' you whispered furiously, and I could not agree more. I have married for status, and I have married for passion, for all we did not bother with witnesses. If I marry again, it will be for wealth and comfort and security.

It will be so that I can have what you have, in fact.

Now John is languishing. His heart is broken, he thinks. His smile is not so quick, his eyes not so steady. He bought me gifts, but what do I want with gloves and trinkets? He may bring me jewels, a ring or a bracelet perhaps, and I will look more kindly on him, but until he has your husband's wealth, he will never win me.

So he is sulking like the boy he still is, and thinks to punish me by leaving us in the evenings to go to the taverns with his friends. As if I care that we do not sing any more.

You have been at the warehouses from first light and no sooner are you home to break your fast than a message comes from Goodwife Blake who lives off Milk Street. The woman is fretting as usual about her precious child. Every week it seems he has some rheum or other, but instead of rebuking her for her insolence in sending for you, you rush off at her summons. I cannot understand why you do not tell her to stop fussing, but no, you must always please everyone. What is it you are constantly making amends for, Mary? Why must you always be liked, no matter what cost to yourself? You have no idea how tiresome it is for the rest of us who care less what others think and say.

Cecily and I are entrusted with going to market while you make speed to save another soul. I will shop, but I will not sew, sing but not scour. Cecily and I smile at each other with equal insincerity when you give us our instructions. I am inclined to protest, as a matter of principle — am I really to be ranked with a snippy girl? — but the day is so bright and inviting after the gloom that I am glad to get out, Cecily or no.

Baskets over our arms, we trip down Wood Street to Cheapside. It always makes me think of the time I saw you again. I have stopped fearing that Anthony will see me. I have seen no sign of him, heard nothing about him. Besides, he will surely have moved on by now. He talked grandly of finding a position at court, or at least with one of those who hang around the edges of court. I thought it was unlikely in the extreme that his fortunes should change after so long, but I would be glad to know that he is not in the city any longer, I must say.

Still, I no longer look fretfully over my shoulder as we make our way along the stalls. You have sent us out to buy provisions, half of which I cannot remember, and Cecily is no use. 'I don't know,' she says unhelpfully when I ask if we are to buy strawberries or cherries, cabbage or cucumber. 'It is your job to remember.'

And then, when I decide on strawberries, she stares as they are tipped into my basket. 'You should have checked they were good,' she says. 'Mamma always checks.'

You have spoilt that child, Mary. You treat her like that horrid wooden baby you carried around at Steeple Tew as if it was something precious instead of a burned stump dressed in a rag. Cecily might mind her manners while you are by, but when we are alone, she is pert and impudent. You must have noticed, too, how she puts herself forward. It is most unbecoming in a maid. But you never chide her when she plays the wrong note or makes me sing off-key. 'She is just learning to play,' you say. If you ask me, Cecily knows perfectly well how to play if she chooses. She just does not like it when I sing because everybody looks at me instead of at her.

She is like a gnat buzzing at my ear, and frankly, I am glad when she spies a friend and drifts off to irritate someone else. It leaves me free to pretend that I am mistress once more, and not a mere companion. I imagine myself in a costly gown, out to shop for velvet and silk, some lace perhaps, or some pearls, not cabbages and flour. That the goodwives who stop to speak to me admire my gown, instead of inquiring respectfully after you. I amuse myself by hinting that you are not quite as virtuous as they believe. It is easily done, after all. A raise of my brows, a widening of my eyes and then a rather too obvious recovery.

'Yes, indeed,' I say. 'It is good to know that we can put our youthful mistakes behind us. Oh, did you not know? Please, forget that I spoke.'

Or when they speak admiringly of how devout you are, I look doubtful for a moment, and then smile when they ask if something is wrong. 'Oh no, no, nothing at all,' I assure them. 'She is devout now indeed.' But *now* trembles in the air. I can see them thinking there must be more to know. One or two even try to probe our relationship, but I cast down my eyes and simply say that I have known you a long time. I laugh to myself to imagine what they would say if I told them the truth, that their respectable Mistress Thorne stole my identity and lies every day of her life. Hah! Perhaps one day I will, but for now I am minded to bide my time. It is better to keep the truth in my armoury for now. I hold it like a weapon over you. It gives me power, but like an arrow, once unleashed it is beyond my control.

When I get back to the house in Little Wood Street, you are in the kitchen, looking pale and cross. 'Where is Cecily?' you demand, rubbing your throat. I see the scar from when you rescued your wooden baby from the fire still livid on the side of your hand.

'With her friend,' I say carelessly, plonking my basket on the table. 'The pudgy one.'

'Joan Parker?' You frown. Cecily has lately abandoned your gossip Anne's daughter for the daughter of Mistress Parker, she who hides her jealousy and resentment of you behind a mask of fawning smiles, and you do not like it. Joan has a flouncing way with her that you fear will encourage Cecily. 'She should be with you, though, Cat. She is only thirteen. I do not want her wandering around the city on her own.'

'Oh, she is safe enough,' I say. 'Besides, I have no authority over her. She does what she will.'

'She can be headstrong,' you acknowledge.

'I wonder where she gets that from?' I say innocently, and you shoot me a look.

'Did you get everything?'

'I think so.' But when you unpack my basket you find fault with it all. The strawberries are crushed and rotten. The oats are powdery. Did I not dig my hand deep into the sack to check? And why have I brought home a limp cucumber?

I see Amy and Sarah exchanging glances behind your back, and I burn with humiliation. How dare you speak to me like this? Anyone would think that I really was your servant!

I am not often grateful to Cecily, but when she

dances into the kitchen, her appearance at least cuts short your carping. 'Where have you been?' you demand. 'You should have stayed with Cat.'

'Oh, she had *no* idea what she was doing, Mamma,' Cecily says, the little vixen. 'Do you know, she never inspects anything before she buys it. She just takes what she is given. The countrywomen all love to serve her!'

'That's enough, Cecily,' you say, which is little enough reproof. You sound tired rather than cross, and your voice is squeezed and scratchy. Cecily doesn't notice. She is too busy unpacking her own basket, which is full of fripperies that are all she has seen fit to buy. She sets them all on the table — a ribbon, some lace, a pomander that will not be nearly as good as the ones you make yourself, a trumpery ring — and then pulls out her last treasure, and my heart gives a sickening jerk.

It is a peacock feather.

'Look what I have!' She flourishes it with an air of triumph. 'Is it not beautiful?'

'Where did you get that?' I ask, fear sharpening my voice, and she stares at me, the puppy-brown eyes full of insolence.

'It was slipped into my basket, from an admirer, I suppose — although I do not see what business it is of yours, Mistress Nosey,' Cecily retorts, and my fists clench in frustration. If the feather comes from Anthony . . .

Perhaps I am alarmed for no reason. A peacock feather is not that unusual, I suppose. But the sight of it makes my skin shrink over my scalp and sets a dull dread thumping in my stomach. It takes me back to Haverley Court and the depravity I endured there. I am sure that Anthony has sent it as a message to me: that he is watching, that he has not forgotten, that he has not forgiven me for abandoning him.

Chewing my lip, I glance at you, hoping that you will force Cecily to say where the feather came from, but you are swaying slightly, your hand to your head and the colour quite drained from your face.

'Mistress?' Sarah asks in concern. 'Are you quite well?'

'No, I . . . I feel strange,' you admit.

They all start to flap around you with contradictory instructions, to sit down, to go to bed, to drink wine. In the end, I am so irritated by the fuss that I have to do something.

'Stop crowding her!' I snap. 'Cecily, do you go and turn down the bed. Amy and Sarah, warm some wine. Now, Ma — , mistress,' I catch myself just in time, but you are feeling so unwell you do not even notice. 'You must lie down.'

'Not yet,' you say in a feeble voice. 'I promised Good-wife Blake a remedy for little Peter. He has a rheum and she wants something to make him feel better.'

'A rheum!' I click my tongue in exasperation. 'He will not die of a rheum. You are iller by far. If you must make a remedy, make one for yourself.'

'I just need to rest,' you say. 'I will be fine.'

You must always be a martyr.

'Well, then rest!'

'I will. Just as soon as I have made the remedy for Peter.'

'May as well let her do it,' Amy advises me in a low voice. 'She'll never rest otherwise.'

I huff out a sigh. 'Very well. I will come and help you, and *then* will you go to bed?'

'I promise,' you say with a shadow of your usually startling smile. 'Thank you, Cat. I own, I would be glad of some help.'

So off we go to the still room and I am set to running around, rummaging for sage and rubbing it to a powder, grating nutmeg, hunting for honey and raisins, while you sit on a stool looking positively green, but still able to order me around, it seems — not so close to the fire, skim off the filth, no, not like that, it needs more nutmeg, let me taste — until I wish I had let you do it yourself, ill as you are. If I am not careful, *I* will be the one collapsing with exhaustion.

At last you are satisfied. We have a linen bag of herbs to be heated and laid on the wretched child's neck, and a honey drink for his cough. 'Do not forget to stopper it,' you say. 'When the potion is sealed, will you send it round to Goodwife Blake with the herbs straight away?'

'I will take them myself,' I say tiredly, 'if you will just go to bed.'

'Thank you, Cat.' You let me help you up. 'You'll tell her that she has no cause to worry? That it is just a rheum and a cough as I said, and the remedies will help him?'

'Yes, yes, and you prepared them with your own hands.' I am quite short with you and am glad to hand you over to Cecily and Amy, who take you between them and bear you up the grand new staircase to your chamber.

195

I walk back into the still room. I can smell the sage and the sweetness of the honey. A blob clings to the edge of the pot and I wipe it off with my finger and suck it, thinking.

Remembering.

I do not pluck chickens or scrub vegetables or beat rugs. The dust gets up my nose and under my fingernails. Ugh. But I have not minded helping you in the still room, and I must admit you are knowledgeable. You pull out drawers and let me rub seeds and herbs between my fingers, or sniff at roots, telling me which ones I can use for what. Mr Hawkins's manservant, William, had swollen, red eyes the other day, and we went outside the city to gather hemlock, which I had often seen at Steeple Tew but had never known the name of before. You took the leaves and bruised them and laid them on William's forehead to ease the swelling.

'But look,' you said. 'See how like cow parsley the leaves are? And note how disagreeable the root smells. You must never, ever confuse these, Cat. If you were to eat either, they would strike to your heart.'

'What, and I would die?'

'Yes,' you said seriously. 'Strong wine or vinegar can be a cure, but it must be taken instantly, and if there is none to be had, or no one near to help, then yes, you would die.'

I lick my finger, taste the honey fizzing on my tongue, and I look at the cabinet where you keep the seeds and roots you warned me of, and I cannot help thinking how convenient it would be if *you* died. Would I not be in the perfect position to console your husband? But I do not know enough to succeed without casting suspicion on myself, and besides, I am not such a monster that I would plot to *kill* you. Not you, not after everything we have shared.

It is merely that if you did not recover, perhaps I would not mourn overmuch.

There is Anthony to be thought of now. I touch my little finger to the corners of my lips, delicately. What if it was he who gave Cecily the feather? What does he mean by it? Nothing good, I fear. I am safer under your protection for now at least, so perhaps I need you to survive after all.

Still, you humiliated me in the kitchen and I can't forgive that. Did you do it deliberately? I remember the look Amy and Sarah exchanged, the way they pursed their lips to stop themselves smiling too broadly at my discomfort, and my cheeks sting. It really was too much, Mary.

I pick up the honey potion and shake it around. Do not forget to stopper it, you said.

I may not be able to kill you, but I can kill your reputation. See how you like the humiliation of people looking askance at you. I reach into one of the drawers at random and take a large pinch of seed. I flick it into the potion and brush the dust from my fingers. I stop up the pot and seal it with wax and give it another good shake. There! Let us see how well your precious remedy works now, Mary.

Pleased with myself, I put the pot in a basket with the linen bag of herbs and cover it with a cloth.

'Where are you going?' Cecily asks sharply from the stairs. She and Amy are coming down together, looking worried.

I am tempted to demand what business it might be of hers, just as she did to me earlier, but I assume a virtuous expression instead. 'Your mamma asked me to take this remedy to Goodwife Blake,' I say.

Amy nods approvingly. 'That is good of you, Cat. Mistress is fretting about it, and it will put her mind at rest to know that you are doing what she would do.'

I smile, thinking of the musty smell of the seeds I dropped into the potion, the unpleasant powdery feel on my skin before I brushed it off. 'I hope so,' I say. 'I am only thinking of her.'

15

Mary

Oh, John, come kiss me now, now, now.
Oh, John, my love, come kiss me now.
The tune strums and scratches in my ears and
terror hums along with it. I toss my head
frantically from side to side to rid myself of it,
but it keeps on playing and playing and *playing*,
beating out the rhythm along my veins,
thrumming over my skin in time to Avery's
grunting as he pushes into me, and somehow
that turns into the groan and creak of huge
cartwheels rumbling closer, closer, closer . . .
They are going to roll right over me, crush me
into the dust, but nobody will help me. Certainly
not Avery who is laughing with the others now
and they are all singing: *Oh, John, come kiss me
now, now, now.*

'No, no! Stop it!' I weep in horror. 'Make
them stop!'

'Hush now.' There is a moment of blissful
coolness, a damp cloth wiping my face, and for a
moment it seems the fiddlers cease and the
cartwheels slow, but then the musicians strike up
again, and the singers raise their voices and the
cart picks up pace once more. They spin faster
and faster as the music gets more and more
manic and the voices are shrieking, or maybe
that is me, me screaming as the wheels thunder

towards me and the singers blur into grotesquely stretched mouths and the fiddlers scrape discordantly, and in the still centre of it all, a vagrant woman — no, it is Peg, my wooden baby. It is Peg who stares at me with hate-filled eyes and curses me again and again.

May you never have a child of your own.

May you never be safe, never.

You will die kicking and choking on the gibbet.

And the curse tightens vicious hands around my throat, and I choke and claw desperately at my neck until the darkness swoops mercifully and blots it all out.

★   ★   ★

It feels as if there are great weights attached to my eyelids but I drag them open. I am aching all over and there is a booming in my head. I am afraid, terribly afraid, but I cannot remember why. It hurts too much to think.

The chamber is dim and close. A figure is sitting on a stool by the bed, idly playing with Peg, flicking at her leather arm, bouncing her up and down on a knee, and the sight of the wooden baby shrieks an alarm in my head and makes my heart jerk with horror.

'Cecily?'

'You're awake! It is I, Cat.' There is a thump as she drops Peg carelessly on the floor. 'How do you feel?'

'Cat?' I stare at her, astounded and aghast. How can Cat be here? She was standing over

Lord Delahay's body, and then she was gone.

'Do you not remember? You have been very sick,' she tells me.

'Thirsty,' I manage, and she pushes a pillow behind me to prop me up and holds a cup so that I can sip at some ale. It is doctored with something, but I am too weak to ask or care.

'Not too fast.' Cat takes the cup away and I slump back, exhausted by that simple effort, my head whirling with confusion.

'Is the coroner come yet? Is Avery here?'

She puts her face down to mine. 'Mary,' she says quietly but very distinctly. 'Your mind is addled. That is all in the past. You are in London, and all is well. Do not say anything until you are clearer. Do you understand?'

'Do not say anything,' I agree, but I do not understand. My mind is full of images that jump out at me, shrieking, and I cannot tell what is real and what is not: those wheels rolling towards me with their monstrous creaking, the frantic fiddlers, and Peg cursing me . . . but Peg is just a toy, that cannot be. I close my eyes, hoping that will still the swirling in my brain, but that just lets other thoughts come crowding in. Avery, thrusting and grunting. The weight of George's body. I snap them open again as memory returns at last.

'Where is Gabriel?' I whisper fearfully.

'He is in Hamburg. He will be home soon, God willing.' Cat gets to her feet. 'I will leave you to sleep,' she says. 'It is a good sign that you are awake. We feared for your life many times.'

We? I want to ask who she means but it is too

hard to speak, too hard to think. I watch, bemused, as she goes out of the door and closes it behind her. Peg is still lying on the floor, discarded. I blink at her. I would like to pick her up but I can't seem to move. I can only stare back at her wooden face and wonder why she looks so terrified.

★　★　★

The next time I wake, a girl is sitting by my bed. 'Oh, Mamma, I am so glad you are better!' she cries as I stir.

Mamma . . . She means me. 'She said I would not have a child,' I murmur, still disentangling myself from the coils of a half-remembered nightmare.

'Who did?' she demands, bristling. 'What nonsense! I am your child, am I not?'

Cecily. Cecily, my daughter. I remember now, and my heart warms.

'Yes,' I say, and I squeeze her fingers to reassure myself that she is real and alive. And mine. 'Yes . . . I am a little confused . . . '

'I can tell.' She helps me sit up so that she can shake out my pillows and then lowers me back, before straightening the coverlet and sheet and patting them both into place. 'Until the fever broke, you were shouting and crying out . . . Who is Avery?'

Thrusting. Grunting. Hurting. I turn my face on the pillow. 'No one,' I say.

'It has been so awful while you have been ill,' Cecily chatters on. 'Cat has been ordering us all around. Sarah dislikes her as much as I do. The barber surgeon came and bled you, even though I said you did not believe in bleeding, but no one would listen to me. She — Cat — has been treating me like a child! She has John wrapped around her finger and he gives her authority to do whatever she likes while Pappa is away. I wish he would come home! But now you are better, you will make it all right.' She smiles radiantly at me.

My head is reeling but at least I am myself. I know who John and Sarah are, and I remember now why Cat is here.

I remember why I was afraid.

'How long have I been ill?'

'Days! It was Tuesday when you fell ill, and now it is Saturday.' Tears stand in her eyes and her beautiful mouth wobbles tragically. 'Mamma, I was so afraid that you would *die*!' Dropping to her knees, she buries her head on the coverlet beside me and I stroke her hair with a trembling hand.

'I am not going to die just yet,' I say with an effort. 'Did anyone else get sick?'

'No, just you.'

'That is good. I will get better now, but you must be patient with Cat. She has been nursing me, has she not?'

'And Sarah, and I helped. Sarah doesn't trust Cat at *all*.'

I promised to get better, but it took longer than I thought. It was some days before I could even get out of bed, and then could barely get to the chair, but I was better enough to insist that the curtains at the window were pulled back and the casement opened. The chamber was so hot and stuffy I could barely breathe in it.

When it was clear that I was not infectious, I had a constant stream of visitors to sit with me: Cecily, complaining about Cat; Sarah, clumsy as ever, but touchingly glad to see me better; Amy, of course; and Cat herself, who seems to have acquired a new authority while I have been ill. In spite of her concern, there is something sleek and satisfied about her now, a sheen of purpose, and I find myself wondering why I am the only one who has been ill. Is it *possible* that she gave me something? But no, it was a fever, not a poison. Of course Cat would not do that to me.

But now the suspicion has lodged in my mind like a raspberry seed in a tooth, and I cannot winkle it free.

My neighbours, too, come to see how I do and to pass on all the neighbourhood news. Joanna Felton's husband has fathered a child on their maid and will have to pay for its support. Joanna is not happy about it, Anne Hawkins says. She does not mention the maid. I wonder what has become of her. I wonder if Richard Felton forced her, the way Avery forced me. I wonder how she feels now that the child has been taken away to be brought up as a charge on the parish. How must that hurt, to give birth, to hold your own babe in your arms, and then give it up?

My gossips have already moved on from Joanna Felton's woes. William Dinsdale has spent a morning in the stocks for short-changing his customers. There is talk of another Spanish invasion. The Queen is at Greenwich and oh, have I heard about poor Agnes Blake?

That was Isabella Parker, her pale eyes snapping with a secret glee.

'No?' I confess my attention has been slipping but I sit up at the familiar name.

'So sad.' Isabella shakes her head, but there is a suppressed pleasure in her pursed lips.

'What has happened?' Something cold creeps up the back of my neck and makes me shudder.

'That poor woman . . . ' Someone else sighs.

I press a hand to my chest where all at once my heart is threatening to beat its way through my ribs. 'Tell me.'

So Isabella does. Agnes's body was pulled from the Thames yesterday. Her husband says she could not bear the grief of losing her child, she says.

'Peter is *dead*? No,' I say, shaking my head firmly. 'No, that is not possible. He only had a rheum. It was nothing.'

'It was not nothing. Agnes sent for you, but you were sick by then, and anyway, he died. They had to prise her off him so that they could bury him. She was out of her mind with grief. You know how devoted she was to that boy. She lost so many babes before him, and he was all she had.'

Now they will have to bury her outside the churchyard, away from her child.

I stare blindly over their heads at the chest, where Peg looks back at me. Is it the fever still, or does she look as aghast as I feel?

'Agnes said that he was getting better until she

gave him the posset you sent,' Isabella says pointedly.

'But it was just a mild remedy. There was nothing really wrong with him.' I twist my fingers together on the sheet, trying to remember. I was feeling ill, I do remember that. I went to the still room. I made the posset for Peter. But was I confused? I was feverish and sweating.

'I am sure you are right.' Anne lays a soothing hand on my arm. 'No one who knows you would believe that you deliberately gave Peter the wrong potion. But it is better that you know what some ignorant people are saying.'

'You were there,' I say to Cat when they have all gone. 'Do you remember what I did?'

'You were very feverish,' she says. 'I begged you to leave it until your head was clearer or to let me make it for you, but you would not.'

I rub my temples. Did I make the potion? I have a wisp of memory: Cat stirring a potion while I slumped on the stool, but it drifts away when I try to grasp it. It may not be a memory at all. I am so confused. Cat says I made the potion. Why would she lie? 'I just can't remember . . . You would have seen if I had done something wrong, would you not?'

'Of course I would, and so I shall tell everyone who asks.'

But they will all think that she is lying for me, I know. I lie feeling wretched. How many more deaths will I be responsible for? The vagrant child. Lord Delahay. Now Peter, and Agnes. I did not mean for any of them to die, but they did anyway.

I wish Gabriel would come home, but he is in Hamburg and not likely to return for at least another month yet, when he is sure that Tom has settled in. I am adrift without him. I have lost all sense of purpose, and I am tired all the time, and it is Cat who has taken charge of the household in my place. I am glad to see that she is taking more of an interest in the domestic matters, although Cecily complains long and loud that she orders her around.

To me, Cat is very solicitous, pushing cushions behind my back, encouraging me to rest, bringing me tasty dishes to my chamber to tempt my appetite. I squirm with guilt at that vile suspicion I had that she meant me harm. I must have been ill to think such a thing.

It is nearly two weeks before I feel well enough to leave my chamber. I have been dreaming of sitting outside, but I am so weak still that Cecily has to help me down the stairs and I have to sit in the chair in the hall before I can make it as far as the bench in the garden. It is high summer at last, and the sun is warming the bricks beneath my feet. I turn my face up to the light and close my eyes. Here at the back of the house, the hustle and bustle of the street feels very distant. It should be peaceful, but it seems that even when things are blissfully silent, I am straining to hear that nightmare tune: *now, now, now.* I begin to think that I can hear it in the drowsy drone of the bees in the lavender. The sparrows chirruping around my feet cannot possibly be chirping in tune, but the harder I listen, the more certain I am that I can hear it, and I lift my hand to massage my throat against the feel of an invisible noose tightening.

If only Gabriel would come home! I miss him. I have had to leave John to deal with the business. I've tried to ask him how things are, but he is worryingly evasive. He tells me all is well and that I should concentrate on getting better, but I don't like the way the muscle jumps under his eye. He is short with everyone now, too. I barely recognise the merry young man who came home from Hamburg only a few months ago. Cecily tells me it is because of Cat.

'She is toying with him, Mamma. Oh, she is well named! She plays with him just like a cat with a mouse. John brings her gifts and she just *laughs* at him. It is terrible to see the way she treats him. Can you not send her away?' she demands.

I worry at my scar. How can I tell her that Cat may stay as long as she likes? 'I am sure you are exaggerating, Cecily,' I start feebly but Cecily tosses her head.

'I am not exaggerating! You must speak to her, Mamma!'

So when Cat appears in the garden, I brace myself to talk about John, but she brushes me aside.

'Never mind that,' she says, and I notice for the first time that she is looking pale and edgy. 'We have something more important to worry about. I have bad news.'

'Gabriel?' I am struggling to my feet in panic as she flaps a hand at me to sit.

'No, not your precious husband.' She glances

over her shoulder and leans towards me. 'Anthony,' she says quietly.

I am so relieved that Gabriel is safe that I cannot think at first who she means. 'Who?'

'*Anthony!* Where have your wits gone begging?' she snaps. 'Anthony, who was my lover. Anthony who was at Haverley Court.'

'Oh . . . yes, of course.' My mind is still on my husband. 'What of him?'

'He has found me,' Cat says tensely. 'And he has found you, too. He knows where we live. He knows exactly what we did, Mary, and he is going to make us pay.'

16

Cat

London, Little Wood Street, July 1590

'Pay?' You look blankly back at me. 'What do you mean?'

Dear God, what do you think I mean? Your illness has made you dull and stupid. I suck in a frustrated breath and make myself speak clearly, as if to a dolt. 'He wants money,' I say, separating out every word.

'But . . . what for?'

'For not bringing our world down around our ears just like *that*.' I snap my fingers in front of your face, so close that you blink and jerk back. 'Do you not understand? Anthony knows who I am, which means he knows who you are *not*. And he is talking about journeying to Wiltshire to see the coroner there, to tell him that he has just remembered how George really died. If we do not pay him, we will both hang. Do you want that?'

Your hands go up to circle your neck as if you can feel the noose already, and when you speak at last, your voice is thin and scratchy. 'Blackmail,' is all you can manage.

'Yes, blackmail,' I say impatiently.

Your eyes are unfocused as you stare ahead, and under your breath I hear you humming:

now, now, now. Something about your expression sends a quick, convulsive shudder down my spine.

'Mary,' I say urgently. 'You must concentrate!'

You turn to me at last. 'How did he find you?'

'He found *you*. He saw you on your way to visit that wretched Blake child one day and guessed then where I had gone. He followed you, he said, and you brought him here. After that, he watched. I thought I was safe,' I say, not bothering to hide my bitterness.

It was Anthony who slipped the peacock feather into Cecily's basket that day you fell ill. He was playing with me. Who knows better than he what the feather means? He was telling me that he had found me.

I was on my guard after that, but we have been at sixes and sevens while you have been ill, and I have scarcely been out. It was only this morning that I ventured to market to buy eggs and cheese. The street was crowded and I was on the alert, but I still did not see Anthony until something tickled my cheek. A feather.

I spun round, and there he was, Anthony, as handsome as ever, but with a cold gleam in his eyes. He mocked me with a flourishing bow. 'Why, madam wife,' he said, 'I did not think to find you a maid again! Let us repair to the tavern to celebrate our reunion.'

What could I do? I could not outrun him, and all I could hope was that I would be able to outfox him instead. So we went back to the Dog's Head — 'for old times' sake' Anthony said — and he shouted for wine, so I supposed his

211

luck must have been good of late.

'So, you thought to leave me, Cat,' he said when we had our wine and we were facing each other across the rough wooden table. 'That was not kind of you, was it?' His eyes were hard, his lips twisted in a sneer I didn't like.

'I did not mean to,' I said quickly. 'I meant to come back and find you, Anthony. But I — '

'Saw a better chance, and did not think to include me in it?'

'Mary found me. She would not let me go back to you and I had no money,' I said tearfully, but Anthony was not impressed.

'As if anyone could ever withstand your wiles. If you had wanted to come back, you would have found a way, aye, and made her pay to help you.'

'You do not know her.'

'Oh, I remember her. I recognised that straight back of hers the moment I saw her in the street. She was ever cool and resourceful, as I recall. We would not have brushed through George's death without her.'

When he talked about how you took charge when George died, directing him to carry the corpse to the head of the stairs, to throw it down and position the body, how you dealt with the coroner, he sounded admiring. But so it is with many men, I have noticed. They like to be ordered about by women on occasion. You probably reminded him of his nurse, when he was her darling boykin.

'There is one other here in London who remembers that night,' Anthony said, and I stared at him.

212

'Who?'

'Daniel.'

'*Daniel?*'

'George's manservant. You remember him, I am sure.'

'I don't believe you,' I said.

'It is quite a coincidence, I agree. We have all found ourselves in London, but then again, they say all roads lead here in the end.'

'Where did you meet him? I suppose you saw him in the street too?'

'No, in a tavern which specialises in more . . . refined . . . tastes, where there are men who will pay well for the privilege of hurting or being hurt.'

'And what were *you* doing there,' I couldn't help asking. 'Or need I ask?'

His mouth thinned. 'Unlike you, dear Cat, I have not been living comfortably these last few months. A man does what he must to survive, when his sweetheart runs away and leaves him with no means of support. The cards have not been kind to me since you left.'

There have been times over the last few years when I have wondered if he shared George's tastes more than he claimed. I suppose I should be grateful that he never put me to work in such a place. Perhaps he would have done if I hadn't met you, Mary.

I nibbled at a thumbnail, not sure whether to believe him or not. 'Did Daniel remember you?'

'Of course he did, but not as well as he remembers *you*, my lady. Revenge has festered in his breast these twelve years. He would pay

213

dearly to know where you are now. He has a plan to take you to Wiltshire and put you on trial for George's death.'

'And why not you too?'

'Because you are the one who killed George. And I was able to persuade him that I had my own bone to pick with you. Let me but find her, I told him, and we can both have our revenge.'

I drew back, my hand to my throat. 'You cannot mean it!'

'We think the new Lord Delahay would want to know exactly how his uncle died,' Anthony said. 'We think it our duty to present the facts, that Lady Delahay took a poker to her husband's head. I am prepared to swear to it, and so is Daniel.'

'Daniel was not there!' I protested.

'Perhaps not, but he has his suspicions. And I was, as you know, Cat, and I can swear in good faith. We think Lord Delahay would press for his uncle's murderer to hang, lady or no lady.'

Hang? You cannot know how I felt then, Mary! But I was thinking quickly.

'There is one problem with that,' I told him. 'I am not Lady Delahay any more. Mary has taken my place, and she has a wealthy and powerful husband to protect her now.' I leant over the table so I could put a hand on his arm. 'Anthony, Daniel may be able to scrape together a few groats, but would you not rather have a hundred sovereigns?'

Anthony paused, his goblet halfway to his mouth. 'A hundred sovereigns?'

'Mary's husband is richer than you or I could

214

have imagined. She married the merchant I refused. And he has no idea that the woman he wed is not Lady Catherine Delahay. Do you not think she would pay handsomely to keep that secret?'

You had been living a lie, I told him. You were the one who had made the potion, after all. You had told me it was poisonous if given in too great a quantity, but you had still made it, and it had driven George mad.

'Why should she not pay for the security she has now?' I asked Anthony, and I smiled and rubbed my foot against his leg. 'And why should you and I not share the profit? Forget Daniel. Revenge is a poor thing. It might satisfy him, but you are lustier than that, my love. We have a chance for a much more profitable partnership, the two of us together again.'

I thought I had him, but Anthony grabbed my wrist and clamped it between his fingers so hard that I had to bite back a cry. 'So you think I should just forgive you for running out on me? Why should I trust you now?'

'Because you have a hold over me now. You can discover me to Daniel at any time. But this way, you will have me and the money to start afresh. What could we not do with a hundred sovereigns?' I felt his grip relax a little. 'But you will have to pretend to threaten me as well,' I told him, and he laughed unpleasantly.

'Why, that is easily done, sweetheart,' he said.

Now I assume a frightened expression and take your hand. 'Anthony says that he and Daniel will testify against us both for George's murder. It matters nothing that Daniel was not there. He will perjure himself with Anthony's help. He will say you and I killed George.'

'I did not kill him!'

'You prepared the potion, Mary,' I remind you. 'It was a poison, you said that yourself, and it drove him mad in the end. I was only defending myself. But the jury will not care for that. They will hang both of us unless we can make Anthony go away. He wants a hundred sovereigns,' I whisper, and you gape at me.

'A hundred sovereigns! I cannot find such a sum!'

'Your husband has left you in charge of his business. You cast the accounts when he is gone. You must be able to find a hundred sovereigns somewhere.'

'I cannot help myself to Gabriel's profits!'

'Then ask John. Say you need it to invest. Say it is to be a surprise for your husband.'

'I cannot,' you say, rubbing your palm over your scarred hand.

'Mary, you must,' I say firmly. 'Or do you wish us both to hang?'

Rub, rub, rub. I almost strike at your hands to make you stop.

'Of course not,' you say at last. You swallow. 'Very well, I will ask John tonight. But even he will not be able to find such a sum immediately. Will Anthony wait?'

'He will if I tell him it is coming.'

You are grey with fatigue by the time John comes home, and he looks scarcely better. Perhaps I *have* been a little hard on him, but

216

what started as a harmless flirtation to annoy you spiralled too quickly into obsession on his part, and that is hardly my fault, is it?

I slip out to find Anthony in a tavern round the corner. I am tired of the Dog's Head. The Rose and Crown is much less raucous but still has plenty of shadowy corners. I tell Anthony that you are going to find a hundred sovereigns and he shouts with jubilant laughter.

'A hundred sovereigns! By God, Cat, we have wasted years a-gambling. We should have tried our hands at blackmail a long time ago. Easy money, if she comes through with it.'

'She will,' I say confidently.

'Aye, I'll wager you know how to manage her,' he says with a smirk.

I know how to manage him too. I marvel at how long I spent looking over my shoulder, being afraid, when all I had to do was show him how to make a profit. He tells me that when he first found me, he was hot for revenge, but now that I am here — he squeezes my knee through my demure gown — he is hot for me instead.

I am giddy with excitement and the wine, and what harm can it do to let Anthony have what he wants? Besides, I am hot for him too. I have spent too many nights imagining you and Gabriel together while I lie alone. So I let him take me back to the rooms he rents in Seething Lane, near the Tower. A great improvement on the stinking hovel we shared before I met you, I have to admit.

'My luck has changed,' he says as he shovels up my skirts. 'I told you it would.'

No miserable mattress this time, but a bed. Not as good a bed as yours, mind, but still, I had almost forgotten how it feels to go at it with abandon. If nothing else, Anthony was always good at that.

And yet, when he is pounding into me and I am on the verge of breaking, it is your husband's face I picture, Mary. It is the thought of *him* that tips me over the edge with a shudder of release.

Afterwards, I lie with Anthony, both breathing hard, and it is almost like old times. I want him. I want Gabriel. I want respectability and I want the excitement of playing a chance. I want money. I want to be you, and I want to be myself, too.

I want everything.

Two days later, you call me to your chamber. 'Here.' You hand me four heavy bags of coins, piling them into my arms until I buckle beneath their weight. 'Anthony must be satisfied with this.' You blink tears of fury from your eyes.

'I cannot carry all this at once.' I wish I could run round to Anthony's rooms and toss the coins everywhere, but I have not thought about the weight of it. Foolish of me. I hesitate. 'I am afraid of what Anthony will do to me if I take only a portion. He must come here.'

'I do not want to see him,' you say instantly.

'You need not.' I put on my best soothing voice as I set the bags back on the table. I am itching to dig my hand into all that gold and let the coins run through my fingers. 'I will deal with him.'

'I have a good mind to have the constable waiting for him!'

I raise my brows. 'That is a risk,' I say. 'What if Anthony counters with his accusation against us? Can we afford any suspicion of what happened in Wiltshire?'

'Oh no, I suppose not!' You are pacing up and down, fretting at your scar. 'I wish to God there was some way out of this. How will I explain such a loss to Gabriel?'

'Your husband loves you. He will forgive you.'

'You may tell *your* husband that I will not forgive *him*,' you snap. 'Tell him there will be no more after this.'

Oho, your temper is definitely on edge. I lower my eyes so you do not see the flash of satisfaction. I should not enjoy seeing you agitated, Mary, but I am afraid that I do. You have always been so calm, so capable. Easy to let nothing ruffle you when life has been as easy as yours. It feels good to be the one that is in control for once.

Of course, I must not let you see just how powerful I am.

'I will, I promise.' I hang my head cravenly and let humility creep into my voice. 'If it were not for you, I would be facing the hangman. I am so grateful for everything you have done, Mary.'

'Sweet Jesu, how many times do I have to tell you not to call me that?'

Definitely on edge.

I hunch my shoulders and turn my head away as if from a blow, but it lets me hide a smile too. 'Your pardon. But I have been so afraid that

Anthony would go to the coroner. That I would be asked where I got the potion, that they would not listen when I told them that you were only trying to help me.' No harm in reminding you that you have as much to lose as I. 'The coroner will not see how George beat and whipped me. The bruises are long gone now. It is only the ones inside that remain.'

A strange expression sweeps across your face. 'I know.' Really, I almost shake my head. Is there anything you won't believe? 'I am sorry I snapped at you,' you say. 'I just wish things could be different.'

You wish things could be different? You with your wealthy merchant and your comfortable house? You who have everything that once was mine.

'Tell Anthony to come and collect the money,' you say, as I struggle to conceal my rage. 'I do not want any more to do with it.'

So I am to do your dirty work for you.

When I send for Anthony, he comes to the door complete with new clothes and a stolid manservant. He is all smiles and bows, while I make sure I play the part of the victim, just in case you are watching from the stairs. I would be. I tell Amy that I have business on your behalf and that she should leave us alone in Gabriel's closet.

Anthony exchanges a significant look with me as we walk through the hall. I know he is taking in the tapestries and the silver, the beautifully carved staircase.

I close the door behind me and lean back

220

against it, and only then do we allow ourselves a grin.

'I see you found yourself a comfortable hiding place!' Anthony says, running his eyes assessingly around the closet, until they come to rest on the bags of coins on the desk. 'Is this . . . ?'

I nod and go over to pull open the bags so that we can scoop up great handfuls of the coins and let them stream back into the bags, chinking and gleaming: fine sovereigns, ryals, angels, nobles . . . you have even scraped up some silver shillings.

Anthony lets out a long hiss of satisfaction, and he pushes me onto the coins so that he can kiss me and stifle our laughter.

'We are rich,' he says. 'Just as we planned to be all those years ago. And now there is no George, just bagfuls of coins!' He kisses me again, urgently this time. 'Come with me now, Cat. You do not have to play the maidservant any longer. Let us go and spend this money together!'

For a moment, I am tempted. I have a choice. I can go with Anthony now, and leave you alone. I know that is what you would like.

But how long will this money last? I know Anthony. He is like to gamble it all on the turn of a card, and then where would I be? Besides, Gabriel will be home before too long, and I have a strange yearning to see him again, to know if this obsession I have with him is real or not.

Why should I not have everything? I have suffered, not like you, and now I am due my reward.

Perhaps Gabriel will be my reward.

221

I do not suppose you would like that, but you might not be here then. Anything might happen between now and then.

And meanwhile, where there have been a hundred sovereigns, there will be more.

I ease myself out of Anthony's embrace with a last kiss to keep him sweet. 'I have a better idea,' I say.

17

Mary

Whenever I think about how I had to buy Anthony off, guilt lumbers inside me, lurching queasily from side to side, bumping into humiliation, tangling together and tripping over my guts until I am ready to vomit at the memory. I had to ask John for the money. I dreaded answering his questions, but he barely seemed to take in what I was saying.

'Yes, yes, whatever you need,' he said, but he was pre-occupied.

So now I am worried about John, too. Something has happened between him and Cat. She was all smiles and fluttered lashes with him for a while, but it seems a long time since they sang together. Cecily is cross at the moment, prone to flouncing out of the room. I should rebuke her, but I have been so tired since my illness. It is not just the after-effects of sickness, though. I miss Gabriel. Worse, the household he entrusted me to keep safe seems to be crumbling and worry is rubbing away at me, wearing at my edges, whittling down to a great weight that presses constantly on my chest.

Amy is talking about finding another position, Sarah is sulky. I still straighten Peg every morning, but her painted expression looks somehow peevish nowadays. I cannot decide if I am imagining it or not, but are my neighbours less respectful than they were? Since Peter Blake's death, I have hardly been asked for my advice. I thought it was out of kindness, that I had been too ill myself, but now I am starting to wonder.

Since Cat came, my life has unravelled, and no matter how hard I work to keep things the same, I cannot find a way to spin it back to the way it was before. The air is curdled with unspoken resentments, and instead of the welcoming sense of home that used to settle over me when I stepped through the door, the house seems to be hunching its shoulders in sullen silence and turning its back on me.

Only Cat is thriving. No one would guess that her lover, the man she lived with as a husband, has threatened to betray her secret to the coroner.

It is as if she is feeding on my misfortune. The more tired and fretful I grow, the brighter her eyes sparkle. As my happiness leaks away, she blossoms and glows. She is more beautiful than I have ever seen her. I am not surprised that John was smitten with her.

He was always such a sturdy, cheerful boy, always ready to shoulder responsibility. Now his open face wears a shuttered look and instead of his quick smile, he is more likely to offer a careless shrug. I suppose it is inevitable that he should have been bowled over by Cat. A woman of her beauty and charm must have been alluring. I see that. I just wish that she had quashed that interest straight away and turned him aside. She could have done it easily, but instead she toyed with him, just as Cecily complained, and he has turned surly as a result, his pride wounded as much as his heart, I guess. He spends every evening in the alehouse. When Gabriel was here, we would gather every evening to sing and to talk and play games, and John was glad to join in. Now he comes home dishevelled and disorderly, and I know he has been drinking and dicing. Sometimes he has a high flush and his eyes are unnaturally bright as if he has a fever, but when I ask him if he is well, he snaps at me.

At night I lie awake, worrying at my scar. Somehow I must make things right before Gabriel returns.

At least Anthony has gone. Cat has assured me of that. 'He was more than content with the money,' she tells me. 'Do not be so downcast,' she says. 'To be sure, it was unfortunate that he should find us, but he has gone now. Your secret is safe. You have everything,' she says with a tinge of bitterness.

It is true. I have everything I had before Amy's toothache sent me to Cheapside that day. I have a husband, I have a home. John, Tom and Cecily are healthy. We are prosperous. I am fortunate indeed.

But it all feels precarious now. Things are not the same. I was a fool to be so content, to let myself feel safe. I will never be safe as long as Cat is here. That much is clear.

'You are right.' I force a smile. 'If Anthony has truly gone, then it is time to make your situation more secure. We must find you a husband.'

There is a tiny pause, so tiny I wonder if I have imagined it. It is just long enough for a flash of something in Cat's face, something that scares me, but then no, she is smiling.

'Why, what an excellent idea!' she says. 'Yes, let us have some entertainment. We have been too dreary with Gabriel gone! It is time to amuse ourselves. What we need is an evening of good cheer, and you may invite all the widowers you please. In fact, let us all invite our friends.'

Our friends? 'Do you have friends here?' I cannot help asking. 'I thought you knew no one in London.'

'Oh, I have become very friendly with Anne Hawkins since you became ill, you know,' Cat says. 'She came to see how you were, and we got talking. You know how it is. She is quite my gossip now!'

Yes, I know how it is. I remember the times I have sat talking with Anne, the pleasure I have taken in her uncomplicated company. Anne has a humorous way with her and is easy with everyone, but I thought that I was a special friend.

'May I invite Anne?' Cat prods.

I want to invite Anne. She is *my* gossip, I want to say. Instead I smile stiffly. 'Of course.'

'And Cecily can invite her friends. Fat Joan Parker and Anne's Bess. Surely when she sees them side by side, she will see how superior Bess is? I know Anne is worried about the rift in their friendship,' she adds to underline how much she knows about Anne nowadays, how excluded I

226

have become. Anne has said nothing of this to me.

Cat claps her hands, all delight and merry smiles, and the thought slides into my head before I can stop it: *I hate her.* 'We should have thought of this before,' she tells me. 'Do you make sure John is there, and he may invite his friends, too. Do not scold him for spending time in taverns but make it pleasant at home for him — '

She breaks off, pretending (I am sure) consternation. 'But I should not say anything. You have been ill, Mary. It is hard for you without your husband.' Clasping my hands, she shakes them as if to shake up my spirits. 'But I promised Gabriel that I would not let you fall into a fit of the dismals.'

That is news to me. I cannot imagine Gabriel asking Cat to do anything of the kind, but what do I know? I am not sure of anything any more.

I drag up a smile. 'You are right. We should be keeping John amused, not driving him away. I will think of who to invite for my part. We will make a feast for all to enjoy.'

'Exactly! Now, you look tired, Mary. Go and rest,' Cat says. 'Leave everything else to me.'

★   ★   ★

Cat is true to her word. She organises everything. There is to be feasting and music and conversation, with a banquet of sweetmeats to round off the evening. 'Just like my mother used

227

to serve in the banqueting house at Steeple Tew,' she reminds me.

Miserably conscious of the hundred sovereigns I have given to Anthony, I wonder how much all of this will cost, but I do not have the heart to protest. The house does feel more cheerful. The idea has achieved that at least. Cecily is going to play and sing, and spends long hours practising. The summer days have turned long and hot, and all the casement windows stand open in the hope of catching some stray breeze. Cecily's lovely voice spills out, so sweet, I think, that at times I could swear that the birds are singing along with her. John's eyes have lost that red-rimmed look, and he has brightened at the prospect of a feast. He has invited his friends, he tells me, and they are all coming. I hope they will be young men we already know, sons of Gabriel's connections or our neighbours, but I am afraid he may have befriended other, less reputable types in the taverns he has been frequenting of late.

Amy and Sarah, too, have entered into the excitement of planning a feast, and Cat is amusing herself devising ever more grandiose dishes to impress: a great sirloin of beef, a haunch of venison, roasted swan, a dish of larks. Pasties of red deer, a breast of mutton, stewed. Custards and a quince tart. Gingerbread. A peacock made into a pie, its feathers on display. Cat laughs when she tells me about the peacock pie, I am not sure why.

There will be roasted porpoise and woodcocks served with a mustard and sugar sauce. There will be jellies and fricassees and fritters. There will be salted salmon, minced and served with verjuice and a little sugar, and a marrow-bone pie. Cheeses and pears and pippins.

Oh, and we are to have salads laid out on dishes in the form of flowers. The petals will be made with preserved gillyflowers, parsley stalks will act as the stem, and thin slices of cucumber will be carefully cut to make the leaves.

'Anne told me of this,' Cat boasts, and jealousy pinches at me that she should refer so easily to my friend, my gossip. When Anne visits, she sits dutifully with me, but I am poor company and quickly tired still, and I see her face brighten as she takes her leave, hear her laughing on the stairs with Cat.

Once I would have taken pride in setting such a feast in front of my guests, but now I feel only weary at the prospect. I offer to help, but Cat shoos me out of the kitchen. 'I can supervise Amy and Sarah,' she says.

My head aches too much to read, so I sit in my chamber with Peg on my lap and I smooth her skirts over her burned stump as unease curls through me, fear lingering in its wake like the smell of smoke.

I am glad when the day of the feast comes. All day the house has been in a frenzy of activity, with Amy and Sarah shrieking at each other as they meet in doorways, laden with dishes and tablecloths, and Cecily scrabbling through chests in search of a special ribbon she is *sure* she put away safely. Cat orders the silver to be polished, the candles trimmed, the pepper boxes carefully aligned. She picks up the glasses and holds them to the light, flicks them with her fingernail so that they make a satisfactory ping.

Gone are the days when she refused to take an interest in the running of the household. Since I have been ill, she has discovered the pleasures of being mistress. I hope it means that she wants to be mistress of her own house. I am afraid that she is enjoying being mistress of mine too much.

I have invited as many widowers as I can think of, hoping that one at least will offer marriage to Cat. Now that she has learnt some housewifery, with her beauty and her charm, she might make a good match. Not the kind of match her father promised her, but it was her choice to run away with Anthony, I remind myself. I do not need to feel guilty about that.

I have so much else to feel guilty about.

Cat asked meekly if she could refurbish up her old gown for the occasion. The memory of the hundred sovereigns I have squandered burns in my throat, but I want Cat to look her best. I want a man to come tonight and be dazzled by her, to desire her so much that he takes her away from here. If she were only gone, the way Anthony is now gone, I could be happy again. Besides, she has worked hard to make the evening a success.

'Cecily is having a new gown,' I said. 'Do you come with us to the tailor, and I will buy you a gown of your own too.'

She chose red. A sober colour would have been more suitable, but I had not the strength to argue. She looks beautiful as we wait for the guests to arrive. John can scarce take his eyes off her. I am hoping some other man will react the same way. Someone older and richer who can please himself.

The trickle of guests is slow at first, and then abruptly, it seems, the hall is full and the walls are ringing with the noise of conversation and laughter. The windows are open, but they let in little air and it is still very hot. The back of my neck is damp, and my smock is unpleasantly clammy against my skin. I keep my spine straight, though, and my head high as I greet my neighbours and bid them welcome. I am not imagining it. The women in particular have shrunk back. It is slight, almost imperceptible, but the change is there. Ever since Peter Blake's death, I have felt my position slipping. Like the foolish man who built his house on sand, I have built my reputation on a lie that shifts and shudders beneath my feet.

But I smile and make conversation. I agree that it is too hot for comfort, that some rain would be welcome to dampen the dust. I keep an eye on Cecily as I talk, and my heart swells with pride at how charming she looks in her embroidered bodice with the slashed sleeves and blue satin skirts.

Beautiful as she is, she is outshone by Cat in her red gown. Poised and smiling, she has made herself the centre of the room. Mine is not the only gaze following her.

'A good turnout,' Richard Martindale comments, appearing at my elbow. He has no wife, and claims he is too much of a sea dog to settle for one, and besides, he has too simple a heart for me to wish Cat on him, but I invited him anyway as he always enjoys an evening's entertainment. I am fond of him, too. I like his bluntness and his simple affection. 'No one wants to miss out on one of your feasts, mistress.'

'Is that why they come?' I ask him with a trace of bitterness. 'For the food?'

'And for the company, I dare say.' He examines me closely. Too closely for comfort. 'You are not looking yourself, Mistress Thorne.'

I smile faintly at his straightforward approach. 'I have been unwell,' I admit, 'but I am better now. I confess, I will be glad to see my husband home soon.'

'I have a cargo bound for Hamburg in a few weeks,' he tells me. 'If we get any wind. I expect to bring Gabriel home with me. Give me a month or two and I will have him safely home, mistress.'

Even a month seems a very long time to wait, but I summon a smile. 'I will be glad of it.'

Richard stands by my side in companionable silence. Cat has snagged at the edge of my vision, and he follows my gaze. 'What has happened to make that one look like the cat lapping at cream?' he asks.

'I am hoping I might find her a husband,' I confess, low-voiced.

'Get rid of her? Very wise,' says Richard briskly.

'I do not suppose that you know of anyone in want of a wife?'

'Not I!' he says, recoiling with such an

expression of abhorrence that I cannot help laughing.

'I did not think you,' I reassured him. 'Where is Jacopo tonight?'

'It is a fine night. He is happier waiting outside.' Richard leans towards me confidingly. 'He told me once that crowded rooms remind him of prison.'

'Prison!' It is the first I have heard of it, but knowing Jacopo, I am not surprised. 'Where was that?'

'He did not say. Picked up some tricks, wherever it was,' says Richard. He wipes a hand over his face. 'This cursed heat! I'll be glad to get to sea again.'

'What cargo do you take with you?'

Richard is always glad to talk business, and I am happy to listen, nodding, sparing only a casual glance at the door for late arrivals.

All at once there is a commotion at the door, and four or five lusty fellows jostle through it, laughing and shoving at each other, their voices loud and jarring. A frisson of disapproval runs around the room, and Richard breaks off in mid-sentence.

'Your guests, mistress?' he asks in surprise.

'I do not think so,' I say, frowning. 'They must have mistaken the house. Excuse me.' Embarrassed by the rowdiness, I make my way across the hall, only to see that John is heading over towards them. Relieved, I hope that he will deal with the situation quietly and persuade them to leave, but to my horror he gives a shout of laughter and they all clap each other on the back, the way men do.

'Come in, come in,' cries John jovially. 'Now we shall see some entertainment!'

'I have brought my dice.' One tosses them in his hand. 'What more do we need?'

'John . . . ' Quickly I move towards him. I am not sure how I will be able to get rid of these men, but somehow I must. John turns to me, all smiles.

'Mother! These good fellows have come to join us. I bid you make them welcome!'

A voice cuts through the babble. 'Perhaps we are not welcome, my lady?'

I do not see who is speaking at first. My gaze passes over them, little more than a herd of young men, indistinguishable as bullocks, until it jerks back as I register that one is older, and shock stops the breath in my throat.

Anthony.

It is as if a bucket of icy water has been dumped over my head, and as the chill ebbs, darkness roars at the edges of my mind. For a moment, I fear that I am going to faint. Beside me, John is talking, apparently eager to present the men to me. They are his particular friends, he tells me. How glad he is that I bade him invite them all.

It is twelve years since I have seen Anthony, but I could not mistake him. He looks coarser now. Mottled veins have turned his skin ruddy and his nose more bulbous, but there is that negligent charm still.

Look at him, standing there in his handsome suit of velvet, his buttons gleaming, cross-garters at his knees, a fine lawn collar at his neck! His sleeves are puffed, his shoes decorated with slashes and loops, and a cloak hangs with careful casualness from one shoulder.

All paid for with my hundred sovereigns, I have no doubt.

He even has the gall to use his own name. 'Sir Anthony Cavendish,' John presents him proudly, and Anthony steps forward. For one terrible moment I think he is expecting a kiss of welcome, but in the end he only bows, and when he glances up at me, his brown eyes are mocking and sickeningly familiar.

Cecily's eyes.

I stand numbly as John presents the others and sweeps them off. 'Bring wine!' he calls to Sarah, and they are soon straddling benches, roaring with laughter and tossing dice on the table in front of the scandalised gazes of my neighbours, although all have done their best to resume their own conversations.

What is Anthony doing here?

Oh, but I know the answer to that at least, don't I? I was a fool to think he would have gone so easily.

Instinctively, I turn to look for Cat. She is laughing with Anne Hawkins and Edward Parker. Across the hall, Isabella Parker is watching them too, her expression venomous.

Did Cat *know*? Did she plan this? Surely she has as much to lose from Anthony as I do, though? I need to talk to her, but I cannot confront her now, not with all these people around.

How will I endure this evening now? The bullocks, as I think of them, are persuaded to clear their dice from the table, and we all sit for the feast. I see my neighbours talking and laughing, their mouths opening and closing, growing ruddy-faced with the heat and the wine, but I am separated from them all by an invisible wall, cut off by a dread that churns queasily in my stomach. I am here, but I am not part of things. I see my guests enjoying the feast, sharing dishes with their neighbours, but I cannot force any food down my throat.

After the feast, we move up to the great chamber. I see Cecily playing at the virginals, I see friends singing their parts, but all I can hear are the words of 'John, Come Kiss Me Now' beating in my brain. I hear the gasps of delight at the display of sweetmeats that Cat has ordered specially, little sugar goblets and plates, sugar birds, sugar beasts . . . so much sweetness for a bitter evening. What use is sugar when danger is sitting at my board, in a velvet suit and a neatly trimmed beard: *now, now, now?*

The evening wears on and on. It grows louder and louder. It is as if Anthony's presence has unleashed something coarse and reckless into the air. My neighbours, usually so carefully mannered, are squabbling. There is a lewdness lurking at the heart of every conversation, every song. People stop looking askance at the dice-playing. They barely blink when the cards come out. I am mortified.

John is in high good humour, slapping cards onto the table and gathering his winnings towards him with a great shout of triumph. His expression is avid as he studies his cards. He barely knows the rest of us are here, I think, and when Cecily tries to persuade him to sing with her, he shrugs her aside so carelessly that tears stand in her eyes.

I see Cat go over to help persuade him, which Cecily does not like at all, but even Cat cannot tear John from his cards. Cecily stalks off, her shoulders rigid, and Cat lifts her hands gracefully with a charming smile of surrender. She says something I cannot hear and everybody laughs.

I am watching Anthony now, who has strolled away from the card players and is making himself pleasant, as he well knows how to do. My neighbours are mightily impressed with him. If they only knew. At last I manage to get Cat alone. She has seen Anthony of course, and professes horror. It seems genuine, but with Cat you can never tell.

My head is aching so, I fear it will explode. I want nothing so much as to go to my chamber and pull the curtains on my bed so that I can lie quietly in the dark. But I cannot leave while Anthony is here, prowling around my home.

He is playing with my family like a cat with a wounded bird, patting them this way and that for his amusement. He has John enthralled. I have no doubt that they have diced together and that he has flattered John with his attention. He is older and more assured, and doubtless a better card player too. Perhaps he has been advising him how to deal with women, and curing him of his heartsick love for Cat. But John will not see how gradually Anthony will fleece him, luring him into gambling deeper and deeper until there is no way out. He can ruin John as easily as look at him. John has ever been open and trusting; he is no match for the likes of Anthony.

And then there is Cecily. Anthony makes sure he flatters her with his attention, and I watch grimly as she unfurls and blossoms. Her lashes dip, her eyes peep, her smile trembles invitingly. Where did she learn to flirt like that? Never have I seen her look more like Cat and my heart cracks.

He is standing with her by the virginals, their heads close together as they sort through the music, choosing what to sing next, poor Joan Parker ignored beside them. I want to stalk over and slap him away. I want to scream at him to leave my house, to leave my family alone. But I cannot do that. He knows too much about me.

Will my guests never go? Can no one else feel the menace trembling in the chamber? Can they not see the tension spitting and crackling in the hot air?

'You look tired,' Anne Hawkins tells me bluntly as she sits down beside me in the window seat.

'I have been ill.'

'I know, but you cannot hide away in here any longer. We need to see you out in the street once more, else these rumours will not go away.'

'What rumours?'

'That you sent Peter Blake the wrong remedy.'

'It was not so, I am sure of it!'

'Now they are saying that it was deliberate. That it has happened before. Who can tell where rumours start? Cat does her best to quash them, but it seems that you do not want to face the world at the moment. People think you are ashamed, that you must feel guilty. I'm sorry,' she says. 'I thought you would want to know.'

I rub my temples. 'They do not think me so guilty that they refuse to come here.'

'No, but the dicing and the card-playing will not have done your reputation any good,' she says frankly. 'How came you to allow John to invite those men?'

'I did not know.' I am overcome with weariness. 'I have lost control of everything, Anne,' I confess.

'Come,' she smiles. 'It is not that bad. They will forget this evening soon enough.'

The words are barely out of her mouth before a screaming and a shrieking erupts on the other side of the chamber. I jump to my feet and hurry across to find Joan Parker sobbing in her mother's arms and Cecily, her eyes blazing, slapping at Cat's attempts to restrain her.

'What has happened?' I demand.

'Your daughter has no decorum,' Isabella Parker snaps. 'She slapped Joan's face and pulled her hair. I knew this would happen. Cecily is no suitable companion for Joan. She is a hurly-burly girl with no manners!'

I bristle. Nobody talks of my daughter like that, least of all Mistress Parker. 'I fear that she has learnt lack of manners from *your* daughter!'

'How dare you! Fine talk from someone whose

239

house is little better than a tavern,' she blusters.

'At least I offer some hospitality, which is more than can be said for you, madam.'

And with that we are off. I know I should stop, but I cannot help myself. The pent-up tension of the evening explodes as I tell Isabella Parker everything that I have ever thought of her meanness and her pretension, while neighbours stand agog, half horrified, half enthralled. We have exchanged every insult we can think of before Isabella sweeps off with her husband and Joan, two spots of high colour in her cheeks, vowing to take me to court for vile slander.

There is an awkward silence as she leaves, broken at last by an embarrassed murmur as the rest of the guests decide that they should go too and all trail back down to the hall. I am glad of it. I stand stiffly by the door to bid them all farewell, burningly aware of how badly I have behaved. Almost last of all comes Anthony, smirking as he bends over my hand.

'I fear we have all outstayed our welcome,' he says, and the touch of his lips on the back of my hand makes me shudder. 'Thank you for a delightful evening. I have rarely enjoyed myself more.'

I look into his eyes. I see the cold calculation there, and I understand that money is not enough for him. He is determined to make mischief too. I know without being told that he is prepared to lead John along the road to damnation, that the dicing and the drinking will only be the beginning. Before long there will be an invitation to a house where there will be all kinds of debauchery, the likes of which John has never even dreamt of. Then perhaps Anthony will ask John for a temporary loan, or ask him to settle his debts, and John will be lost.

Anthony will do whatever he can to ruin Cecily too. He smiles at me, and his smile tells me that he can lead Cecily astray just as easily. That if he chooses, he can fascinate her and tease her until she forgets every duty that I have taught her. He can lead her into temptation and ruin her, and care nothing for it.

Unless I stop him.

18

Cat

Anthony is almost the last to go. I watch him bow insolently over your hand, see you flinch from him.

Oh, this evening has been better than a play! I cannot remember the last time I was so amused. Laughter has been bubbling in my throat all night. Where to begin? I made sure to greet Anne Hawkins most affectionately when you were watching.

You don't like the fact that Anne likes me, do you? She used to be your gossip, but now she is really mine. You never were good at giving up what you had, Mary, that is your trouble. You never had much, like that unchancy wooden baby of yours, but you held onto it for dear life. You would never share. I had to share my family and my home and my life with you, but what did you ever give me in return?

Anne dared me to flirt with that dullard Edward Parker, which was easy to do, and I enjoyed making that hag, his wife, glare. I thought it would stir trouble between you and her, but I could have spared myself the inconvenience, could I not? It turned out you were quite capable of making trouble by yourself.

Oh, and then there was John, ignoring Cecily

as she tried to drag him away from his cards. That pretty little nose of hers is mightily out of joint. She must have everyone at her beck and call the whole time. She treats John as a lover, not a brother, she wants him to jump up and down and turn her music for her and tell her the sun rises in her eyes or some such nonsense. Faugh! I have tried to hint that what she feels for him is unnatural, but you cannot see it. 'She loves her brother,' is all you will say, puzzled. 'What is wrong with that?'

Cecily can forget John now. He is lost to the cards. *I* might lure him back if I choose to, but I do not.

I thought my sides would burst with the effort of holding in my laughter when Anthony arrived and I saw your face! True, you kept your cool then, but those rowdy youths he brought with him, tossing their dice and dealing out their cards . . . Will your reputation ever recover? Your neighbours were shocked. I heard the disapproving murmurs all evening, but even that was not the best. That was when Cecily and Joan fell to squabbling and pulling each other's hair and *then*, oh then, there was your quarrel with Isabella Parker! In front of everyone! The names you called each other! You were like two fishwives scrapping over a herring down on the staith! I could have died laughing, but I had to appear shocked like everyone else. You will never be Mistress Perfect again. What *will* Gabriel say when he returns?

Of course, it was I who told Anthony the taverns where he might find John, and how easily

243

he might be lured into gambling. I who suggested that the feast would be the perfect time for him to threaten you without saying a word. I was conscious of a tug of pride when I saw him come in. He looked very fine, even distinguished, in his new suit. I think about this afternoon when we were going at it in his rooms, and a small, satisfied smile tugs at the edges of my mouth. I am the one glowing now.

I cannot imagine why I was so afraid of Anthony finding me. I have the best of both worlds. When Gabriel comes home, why then perhaps I will make a decision, but for now, I may as well make a profit while I can.

Anthony offered to buy me a new gown, but I could not risk you wondering where the money had come from. So I asked you if I could refurbish up my old gown for the occasion, and of course you let me order a new gown altogether. I knew you would. This one is cherry red, and I know I look my best in it. I felt the way people looked at me tonight, the envious glances of the women, the heat in the eyes of the men, both warmed me.

Of course, I made sure to appear properly horrified when I sought you out, pretending that I had just noticed Anthony. 'Have you seen who is here?' I asked you, letting my voice tremble.

'I have.' Your eyes were hard as you looked at me. 'What is he doing here, Cat?'

'I do not know! I thought my heart would stop when I saw him!' I pressed my hand to my throat. 'He told me he would be gone,' I whispered as if terrified. 'Does he want more money? Has he said anything to you?'

'Anthony wants more than money,' you said. 'He means mischief.'

Your gaze rested on him as he bent courteously over Cecily at the virginals, and I almost flinched. I hope you never look at me like that. Perhaps you are not as easily frightened as I thought.

I twisted my hands together. 'What shall we do? Anthony knows too much.'

I have not forgotten that Anthony is as great a threat to me as he is to you. It is just that you have more to lose now. And the pull of passion is strong still. For now, he has remembered his desire for me, and the situation amuses him, no doubt. Anthony has never cared for the humdrum. There is part of him that craves darkness and depravity. He was a good apprentice to George, after all.

'We will bring out the sweetmeats,' you answered coldly. 'We will pretend nothing is wrong. We must serve him and watch him. And then,' you said, 'we must be rid of him.'

The implacable expression in your eyes took me aback, I confess. I wonder if I should warn Anthony? But what can you do? Anthony needs only tell one or two of your neighbours who you really are, and your pleasant life would be torn asunder.

Of course, he could also tell the coroner in Wiltshire what happened twelve years ago. I have no desire to find myself on trial for murder. But for now, Anthony is captivated once more, and I can control him.

I find myself torn. It is unusual for me. I usually know what I want, but now . . . I cannot decide. I want Anthony again, yes. The secrecy has added spice to our fucking, or perhaps it is the knowledge that you would not approve. More, you would be horrified if you knew what I was about. Why does that make it so much better for me? You are so good, so dutiful, so dull, that you allow me to be the opposite.

I am enjoying this game Anthony and I are playing with you, too.

Anthony is giving me pleasure, for sure. But I am not the impractical fool who ran away with him before. There will be money as long as you pay up, but Anthony will never keep it. Coins run through his fingers like water, and I am grown used to comfort again.

Anthony is for now. Gabriel is for the future.

My obsession with your husband has taken me by surprise, I confess. It is not just his wealth, whatever you would surely think. And it is not just because he is yours, although that does add piquancy to my desire. It is *him*. I keep thinking about the set of his mouth, the deft way he peels an apple to please Cecily. I think about his sudden smile, and how the air steadies and settles around him. When Anthony is thrusting into me, shoving between my spread knees, I think about Gabriel doing it to you, and how it will feel when he is doing it to me, and there is a pounding in my blood and a need that gathers and gallops until it explodes out of me in a great shout of release.

I must have him. I *must*.

But first, I can have some fun with Anthony and with you. I think I deserve that, don't you, Mary? You have had all the luck so far. It is my turn now.

★   ★   ★

Oh dear, Mary, you don't look well, really you don't. Your face is drawn and you have lost that prosperous glow I used to envy so much. It is as if someone has rubbed away at you and left you looking blurry around the edges.

Your life is not so perfect now, is it? I told Anthony where to find John, who was easily lured into the pleasures of gambling. Gabriel will be so disappointed in you when he finds out, will he not? Cecily is sulky, your neighbours shun you, your servants are beginning to accept me. All except Sarah, who is surly with me still.

As for your husband, he is still overseas, and who knows what trulls he will be consorting with while he is away.

And you dare to find a husband for *me*? When you suggested dangling me in front of a parade of fat widowers, it was all I could do to keep my tongue between my teeth, though in the end it has suited my purposes perfectly. I was happy to let you invite some widowers to inspect me. You can waste your time and your reputation if you wish. I will take none of them. I have quite a different husband in mind.

Yours.

Now the last guests have trailed out of the

door, and the energy ekes out of the house. We are left with the debris of the feast. Sarah and Amy have already cleared away most of the dishes, but there are goblets abandoned on chests and windowsills. Wine has spilt stickily onto the tiles and the tablecloths are stained and scattered with crumbs.

John clatters down the stairs, shrugging on a jerkin. 'Where are you going?' you ask.

'Out,' he says. 'I promised Sir Anthony I would join him for a drink. The night is young yet.'

'But there is so much to do here,' you protest.

John looks around him as he bounds down the last steps. 'Women's work,' he says. 'What else are maidservants for?' His eyes meet mine briefly, and I acknowledge the hit with a quirk of my lips.

'Oh, John, don't go!' Cecily rushes over to him and clings to his arm. She pouts up at him adorably. 'It is so dull when you are not here. Can we not go to the parlour and be comfortable?'

John barely glances at her. 'I am sorry, chicken,' he says carelessly as he removes her hand from his arm. 'I have promised.'

The door clunks behind him as he goes out, leaving us standing in the empty hall. There is a defeated slump to your shoulders, you who have always been so straight-backed, and you look weary, though in truth you have done nothing tonight. I organised everything. If anyone has a right to be tired, it is I.

Cecily's face is thunderous. 'I am exhausted,'

she says when you direct her to fold up the tablecloths.

'We are all tired,' you snap.

Mary, you must be worried. Cecily never receives the sharp edge of your tongue. You treat her always like a little princess.

'What did you say to Joan Parker? Did you slap her?' you ask her, and Cecily's face crumples.

'She is hateful!'

'I thought you liked her?'

'Well, I don't. She is rude and jealous and spiteful!'

'In other words, she made the mistake of telling Cecily the truth,' I murmur at your shoulder. 'Joan told her that it was obvious she was only flirting with Sir Anthony to get John's attention, and that it wasn't working. I have noticed Cecily does not care for uncomfortable truths, but then, few of us do, do we?'

Cecily stares at me. For a moment I think she is going to burst into tears and flounce off, but no. She laughs instead. 'What nonsense is this?' she cries. 'Joan said no such thing.' She dances over to you and winds her arms around your neck. 'Do not listen to her. Forgive me, Mamma. I am sorry I am so cross, truly I am. Joan was jealous and I was scratchy. It is just that I miss Pappa so! I wish he would come home and make everything right.'

'So do I,' you murmur tiredly, your arms closing around her to hold her tight. 'So do I.'

Over your shoulder, Cecily's eyes meet mine in triumph. She knows how to manage you to a nicety. Nothing I can do or say will ever make you see what a little madam she is. All she has to do is smile or press her cheek to yours, and you let yourself be blinded to her selfishness. You are a fool where Cecily is concerned, Mary, I tell you that.

'Come,' you say after a moment. You let her go and rub the back of your neck, and I can almost see you pulling together the tattered rags of your strength. 'We will all help. Amy and Sarah can clean up properly tomorrow, but for now we will leave everything tidy. It looks . . . ' You look around as if the mess pains you. 'It looks debauched,' you say eventually.

I almost laugh. A few crumbs, a few spills? You have no idea about debauchery, Mary dear.

I am longing for my bed too, but no, we have to toil backwards and forwards, carrying dishes, sweeping up crumbs of sugar, collecting goblets.

'What about Anthony?' I ask you, low-voiced, when we are alone in the hall. I want to know what is in your mind. 'What can we do?'

You are mindlessly gathering up discarded goblets. 'Get word to him tomorrow,' you say. 'Tell him that I want to meet him, after dark.'

'Here?'

'No.' You hesitate. 'At a tavern. Near the docks.'

'Near the docks?' I echo, astounded. 'It is too rough an area for you.'

'It is near Gabriel's warehouse. I go there often.'

'Not at night,' I say bluntly. 'You cannot go there by yourself.'

'I must.' You look at me. 'He knows enough to hang the both of us,' you say, and you put your hand to your throat as if you can feel the rope there already, and for a moment, I can almost feel the hemp tightening against my own skin.

'I know,' I say with a shudder. 'But what can we do?'

'I will talk to him,' you say.

Talk to him? Is that it?

I wrinkle my brow. 'What good will talking do?'

But it seems you are not going to confide in me any more. Mary, Mary, could you be growing suspicious?

'Just get him to meet me,' you say.

19

Mary

I half expect Anthony to refuse to meet me, but no. Cat comes back from who knows where and tells me that he will be at the Cock and Pie at nine of the clock. I do not ask how she knew where to find him. I do not want to know.

'Are you sure about this?' she asks. 'Anthony is not a man to cross.'

Nor am I a woman to cross, I think. Anthony has crossed a line, from greed to cruelty, and he has threatened what is mine. There will be no easy end to this. It is not just about my safety, and hers. He knows enough to hang us both, but he knows too how to destroy my family. He will ask for more and more and more. There will never be enough money to satisfy him.

'I am sure,' I say.

At nine it will be almost dark, I think. That will suit my purposes well, but I will need a good excuse to be out at that time of night. I send Cat out again, ignoring the tightening of her lips. She does not like it when I treat her as a servant, but there is no one else I can trust with this and her sour expression is the least of my problems.

'Find a boy who will bring me a message tonight to say that I am wanted,' I tell her.

'Wanted for what?'

'You can think of a reason,' I say impatiently. 'I

am needed at a childbirth, or a sickbed, or some such reason.' Cat knows that I am rarely consulted since Peter Blake's death, and I stare her out, daring her to say so. 'The boy does not need to know. He needs only knock at the door and speak to you. Then you will come to me and say that I am needed urgently. All I need is some reason to give in case anyone should question why I put on my cloak and hurry out. Surely that is not too hard to arrange?'

I am too tired, too sick with anxiety, to be tactful.

I pretend it is a normal day. I shop and cook and direct the servants. I go to the warehouse, as I often do. There is nothing remarkable about that, except for the fact that it is so hot. Few folk are out unless they have to be. We are all sluggish and scratchy, and it is an effort to draw in the thick air. The streets lie slumped beneath the suffocating torpor that lies over the city like a discarded cloak.

I am glad of the linen smock that soaks up my sweat as I walk down to Gabriel's warehouse at Three Cranes Wharf. It is a long walk with my basket over my arm, and were it not for Anthony, I would turn back for the shelter of my garden which at least is calm and well ordered.

But there *is* Anthony, so I set my mouth straight and stick to the shade, much good that it does. Flies lift and fall in clouds over piles of stinking filth as I walk down Wood Street to Cheapside. Their buzz accompanies me all the way along Bread Street, past the Vintners' Hall and then at last into Three Cranes Lane, where the stench of rotting fish mingles with the briny smell of the river.

I usually like being by the river. I like the noise: the bellowing between ship and dock, the raucous squabbling of gulls, the shoving and shouting, the creak and groan of ropes and the slap of palms as bargains are struck. The quays reek of the scent of fish and salt air, and the refuse stranded on the beaches at low tide. Beggars pick over the debris in the mud, or snatch at scraps around the stalls. Tall ships and sturdy cogs jostle at the quays, sailed in from who knows where, destined for somewhere far from here. They set sail across the wide seas, the seas I have never seen, ploughing through the waves, bucking and rearing like horses in the wind, or so Gabriel tells it. They anchor in distant ports and fill their holds with exotic spices, with peppercorns and cinnamon bark and nutmeg. They bring wine and salt, oil and dyes. So much of what brings savour and colour to our lives must come on a ship. And when it comes to London, the mariners roll barrels down their gangplanks before hoisting great sacks of English wool onto their shoulders to run nimbly back up and load the ship once more. The crane hauls heavy weights on and off the ships, the loads dangling precariously. I always give it a wide berth, remembering what happened to Jacopo and how easily it might have been Gabriel lying on the dockside.

But I mustn't think of Gabriel, not with what I have to do tonight.

Today, though, the Thames lies oily and still at

the end of the lane, its mud banks slimy. There is none of the usual activity. Even the gulls cannot summon the energy to screech and swoop as they usually do and perch surly-faced on stewps and posts. The great ships are pinned down by heat, their sails slack, and sailors lounge on the docks, waiting like the rest of us for a stir of breeze.

John is slouched on a barrel outside the warehouse, tossing dice twitchily from hand to hand. He stops and rises when he sees me noticing him so idle, and a dull flush rises in his face.

'Mother, I did not expect you today. You said nothing this morning.' There is a sheen of sweat over him. 'It is too hot to be out.'

'Too hot to stay inside, too,' I say. It is true. The shade offers little coolness now. The heat has spread into every crack and crevice, even the deepest, darkest cellar, and there is no relief from it anywhere. 'Is there news of that shipment of cinnamon?' I ask John, but he shakes his head.

'No wind, no ships. Pray God this heat ends soon. There is a bad feeling in the city at the moment. Everyone is on edge.'

I know what he means. Folk are too hot to be courteous. They snap and snarl at each other like dogs and will pull a knife as soon as move out of the way.

'They say we will have a storm later.' We both glance up at the sky which has the same glazed glare it has held for what feels like weeks. There is no sign of any clouds, but the air is twanging like a lute string. It may come. Please God, let it come soon. Let it come tonight, I think.

'I may as well take a look at the account book while I am here,' I say.

John ought to ask me why, he ought to care, but he doesn't. 'If you wish,' he says indifferently and settles back on his barrel.

The warehouse is dim but the heat is suffocating and pungent with the spices that once filled the empty barrels lined up against one wall. The smell of hessian tickles the back of my throat, and all at once I find myself remembering the sacks stacked on the cart behind me on the way to Steeple Tew.

May you never be safe, never.

I push the memory of the curse away. As with Gabriel, I cannot think of that now.

At the back of the warehouse is a little counting house with a locked chest where Gabriel keeps his accounting books. The key is hidden in a jug. Time after time, I have chided Gabriel for his lack of security, but the last time I mentioned it, he only lifted his shoulders. 'If a thief is determined to steal, the lock will not deter them. I keep what is most valuable safe at home. And that includes you, wife,' he said, smiling, and the memory rises up my throat and lodges there, crowding out my breath with the pain of it.

I must not think about Gabriel. It will undo me.

Wiping the sweat from my face, I draw out the book from the top just in case John follows me in after all and asks what I am doing. I learnt to cast accounts at Steeple Tew, and for the look of it, I open the book and run my eyes down the figures. I frown. It looks as if we made great profit on the sale of wine from Gascony, but where has it gone?

Was this where John found the hundred sovereigns I gave to Cat to give Anthony? Or has it gone on gambling?

Oh, Gabriel, I think bleakly. I have done badly by you.

I have a bag of coins and some oats in the bottom of my basket. The air in the counting house is so thick and taut that it presses against me like a body as I twist my head jumpily from side to side and hide the bag in the chest. It is a relief to have it done. I put the book back on top, drop the key into the jug with a chink and go outside again.

John looks up from the barrel. 'Done already?' he asks without interest.

I nod. 'We should sell that salt,' I tell him. 'The accounts do not look good. We have had too many losses lately,' I say. 'Your father will be home soon and we have not given a good account of ourselves lately.'

John's eyes slide from mine. 'I will make it good,' he mutters.

'Have you seen Richard Martindale today?'

John shakes his head. 'I've seen no one.'

'I will go to his lodgings. I promised him this remedy for his gout.' I gesture to my basket, not that John cares. I am talking too much, I know. It is almost as if I want John to get suspicious, to question me, to stop me. But he says nothing, just nods, uninterested.

Richard has lodgings hard by the Cutlers' Hall. I walk back up Three Cranes Lane, my basket lighter without the coin. As I hoped, Richard is out, but Jacopo is there, squatting by the door, smoking his pipe. He straightens as I approach, and I think about what Richard told me, about the tricks Jacopo learnt in prison, about the innkeeper who quarrelled with his master and was found the next day, about the ferocious, unquestioning loyalty to those to whom he feels he owes a service. He is a small man, but wiry, quick. A dangerous man to have as an enemy, a good one to have as your friend.

I look him straight in the eyes. 'I am come to call in your debt,' I say.

★　★　★

The air is tense and wavering when I say goodbye to Jacopo on the doorstep, and at last, dark clouds are boiling up behind the rooftops. Jacopo glances up at the sky, eyes narrowed in his monkey-like face. 'Best stay here, mistress,' he advises. 'The storm will break at any moment. You should wait until it passes.'

'I will hurry,' I say, anxious to get home.

I bid him farewell and set off up St Thomas's Lane, but the air thickens with every step that I take, and the tension winds tighter and tighter as the light gets blacker and blacker until it is almost dark. I see candles hurriedly being lit as shutters are sparred, and the countrywomen keep a wary eye on the clouds as they gather up their vegetables and herbs. Thunder rumbles

258

ominously. All this time we have been longing for rain, but now that the storm is here, its power frightens us. I keep looking over my shoulder as if it is stalking me, prowling along the streets in search of sacrifices to its rage. If I can just get home . . .

But I am only at St Mary-le-Bow when the darkness splits with a deafening crack and a jagged dazzle of lightning, then another and another, and at last the rain comes, emptied out of the sky as if from a bucket. It cascades onto my head, bounces off the dust, swirls furiously along the gutters. I turn my face up to it, welcoming the sudden cool, and I am drenched to my smock in no time at all. Is this what it is like to fall into the sea? I wonder.

By the time I get back to Little Wood Street, my sodden skirts are dragging in the mud. Sarah clucks when she sees me. 'Oh, mistress, look at the state of you! You'll catch your death, and no time since you were so sick.' She hurries away to bring me a cloth to rub my face and hair as I stand dripping in the hall. She helps me off with the sodden gown and promises to send Cat to me as soon as may be. I climb the staircase to my chamber, abruptly cold and very weary. I am so wet, I will have to strip to my smock.

My fingers fumble with the knots of my bodice and I am glad of Cat's help to untie them.

'What have you been doing out in the rain?' she asks in a low voice.

'Business,' I say shortly. Over her shoulder, I can see Peg. She is leaning in her usual place on the chest, but her expression is worried, and in

259

spite of myself, I shiver.

'Get into bed,' says Cat, dragging back the covers almost crossly. 'It was foolish of you to go out in this weather,' she scolds me. 'You have been ill, Mary. You must get warm.'

I almost protest, but then I realise that I will not be able to deal with Anthony if I am unwell, so I climb meekly into the bed and close my eyes while Cat fusses around, ordering Sarah to take away all my wet clothes and bring a warm wine. I would like to tell her that she has turned into a good servant, but I don't think she would like it.

'Have you made arrangements for the message?' I ask instead when Sarah has gone, and Cat clicks her tongue with annoyance.

'It is done, but you will be in no state to go anywhere if you do not stop being foolish.'

I lie in bed all afternoon, listening to the rain crashing onto the roof and remembering how it rained when Amy had the toothache, and I insisted on going out into it. Remembering how Gabriel had told me not to go, to send Sarah instead, but I hadn't listened. And so I met Cat. If I hadn't gone out that day, there would be no Cat fussing around my chamber now. No Anthony, rubbing his hands with greed.

But I did go, and now I must go out into the rain again, and Gabriel is not here to tell me to stay at home.

★ ★ ★

The rain has dwindled to a light patter by the time I get up and dress in an old, dry gown and

260

pull a cap over my still-damp hair. It is cool inside and out now, and a breeze moves busily around the streets, knocking at shutters as if announcing — too late — that the weather has turned. Hard to believe that only hours ago we were waving our hands in front of our faces, plucking at our collars and barely able to move for the heat.

I have no appetite, and my drenching earlier gives me a reason to stay in my bedchamber while Cecily plays the virginals next door in the great chamber, banging peevishly at the keys, and John, who came home nearly as wet as I for dinner, has gone out again, no doubt to some tavern where he will dice away Gabriel's business if he is not careful. I must take him in hand, I fret. But first, I must deal with Anthony.

When the message is brought to the door, Sarah is at first inclined to turn the boy away, but Cat intervenes just in time, and says she will take me the message and allow me to decide. So I override Sarah's concern for my health, and Cecily's fretful complaint about being left alone, and announce that a fellow wife is in sore need of my help.

'I will take a basket with some herbs and remedies,' I tell them, acting the part. The basket I have prepared earlier, and it lies covered with a cloth so that no one sees what it holds.

'Cat, do you keep Cecily company,' I order her as I leave.

I am not often out on my own at this time of night. It is alarming but exciting at the same time. The rain has stopped and the shapes of the houses are bulky against the dark sky, where a moon flitters fitfully between scudding clouds, giving me just enough light to see by. The trees and gutters rustle and dark shapes of creatures slink and scuttle. I think longingly of my quiet house, but I cannot turn back now. The night is blessedly cool after the rain, the air smells different, fresher and more pungent somehow, and the sounds are more intense: a dog barking, a babe's thin wail, quickly shushed as it is put to a breast. It is as if all my senses are alert tonight. I cannot believe what I am about to do.

A hand falls on my arm and I gasp and shrink back in fright.

'It is I, Cat.'

'What are you doing here?' I whisper, still shaken from my fright. 'I told you to stay behind!'

'I do not think you should go alone,' she says. 'You do not know Anthony or what he is capable of. It is better if there are two of us.'

Perhaps it would be better, I think. I know Jacopo will be there, but still, I am nervous, and Cat's presence steadies me. I do not entirely trust her, but I have known her for so long, it is as if she is part of me, and it feels right for us to be walking together through the night. I am more glad of her company than I expected to be.

The quays are furtive in the dark. I sense people standing in shadows, and I wonder how many of them think that Cat and I are trulls on the lookout for clients. My cheeks burn at the thought. The breeze is rattling the lines against the masts, and the water is slapping against the great hulls of the ships as they groan and tug at their ropes.

In spite of the torrential rain earlier, the alehouses by the docks are busy and music spills out onto the slimy cobbles as we walk past. Somewhere, I can hear a drunken crowd singing: *Oh, John, come kiss me now, now, now*, and I am not surprised, not tonight. If they had not been singing it, the tune would have been playing in my head in any case.

The singing grows louder and more raucous as we pick our way through the puddles to where a tattily painted sign creaks in the breeze, and I look up, knowing without being told what I will see. This is the Cock and Pie.

Of course it is.

A curse be on you.

Cat pushes open the door and the tune shoves itself through the fug like a bully in the street, wrapping itself around my throat, strangling me as surely as a hangman's noose, and I baulk in panic, my hands scrabbling at my throat.

Cat holds the door, looks back impatiently. 'Well? Do you come or not?'

Inside waits Anthony. I think of John, red-eyed. I think of Cecily, my daughter, and the way Anthony bent over her, the tiny smile that curved her mouth as she peeped at him through her lashes.

I swallow the painful clog in my throat. 'I am coming,' I say.

20

Cat

The Cock and Pie is a squalid place, even by Anthony's standards. The stench of ale and piss and sweat stewed together in the heat of the past weeks wraps itself around our faces in a foetid embrace and I see you recoil and cover your nose and mouth with your hand. The tavern is crowded with leering, drunken sailors, singing and shouting. Between the noise and the smell, I feel battered. This was my life before I found you again, Mary. Can you blame me for not wanting to go back to it? For doing whatever it takes to stay where I am?

Anthony is lounging in a corner, looking slovenly and unkempt. I can tell by the slackness of his mouth that he has been drinking, the fool. My lips tighten. If anything had been needed to persuade me to choose your husband over Anthony, this visit has done it. I could have stayed warm in bed and let you come here by yourself, but I could not trust what Anthony might say in his cups.

And in spite of everything, I do not like to think of you out at night by yourself. This is not your world. You are rigid with shock and disgust. Oh, you think you have seen how hard life can be, Mary, but what do you know of it, cossetted in your fine house? I am torn between

264

impatience and a strange desire to protect you as I take you by the arm and drag you through the press of bodies, your hand still pressed over your nose and mouth.

Anthony does not even bother to get up when we approach. 'Well, good ladies, here is a change of scene for you,' he sneers. 'Sit you down.' He gestures mockingly to the stools across the table.

You glance at me and I nod. We sit side by side facing him. It feels right like that.

Anthony shouts for wine. A serving wench brings it over and slops the jug down in front of us, clattering the goblets onto the table beside it. Anthony pours unsteadily and we both shove our stools back as wine trickles over the edge of the table.

'Anthony, have a care!' I snap at him without thinking. 'Why have you chosen this vile place to meet?'

'Down by the docks, you said,' he counters. 'Is this not by the docks as my lady requested?'

'It will do well enough,' you say tersely.

'There, she says it will do.' Anthony picks up his goblet and tips it towards us and the spark of malice in his face is unmistakable. 'Come, let us drink to friendships rediscovered. What, you don't drink?' he says to you, pretending offence. 'There is nothing untoward in this wine, I assure you. I would not be so free to drink if *you* were pouring the wine. I know what a hand you have with poisons, mistress.'

'I did not poison anyone,' you say. 'We all know what happened. It was an accident.'

'Well now, Daniel says different.'

265

'Daniel?' You flinch as if remembering George's servant with his goat-like eyes and his smirk. 'What has he to do with us?'

'He will say that he knows how his master died, and that you are both responsible.'

'Daniel was not there,' you say after the tiniest of hesitations. 'He knows nothing.'

'Perhaps,' Anthony allows, 'but he suspects much. About how you two put poison in his wine, how you pushed him down the stairs. He will say he saw it all.'

I make a dismissive noise, determined not to seem daunted. 'If Daniel exists at all now, he will say whatever you have told him to say.'

'He will not be any less convincing,' Anthony points out. 'A devoted manservant and a devoted friend against a scheming wife and her maid. I would not care to take my chance at trial, would you?'

I look at Anthony, my eyes narrowed, wondering. What game is he playing? I told him to treat me as his victim, just as you are, and so he is, but I do not trust him.

'Why are you doing this, Anthony?' you ask quite coolly after all. 'What did we ever do to you?'

He nods his head at me across the table. 'Well, this one ran off without telling me. Does that seem very polite to you?'

'She barely knew what she was doing.' Mary, you are defending me. I had not expected that. 'She was cold and hungry. You had not cared for her.'

'Is that what she told you? I cared for her for

266

all those years until her jewels ran out, and then the first chance she gets, she takes off. Next time I see her, she is a fat little pigeon, well fed and well gowned, while I, I am left in squalor. I think I deserve some compensation, don't you?'

'Compensation? Is that what you call it? I name it blackmail!'

He shrugs. 'Call it what you will. The fact remains that I know the truth of what happened to George, and neither of you want anyone else to know. But I am very willing to share my knowledge, if you wish. It would be a relief to unburden myself and ease my conscience after all these years.'

'No one would believe you,' I say, and he smiles unpleasantly at me.

'Would they not? Do you wish to put that to the test?'

'Enough,' you interrupt with an impatient gesture. 'Lord Delahay's death is old news. I am not here for that.'

Anthony's brows rise. 'Indeed? You are very brave.'

'Let us not pretend, Sir Anthony,' you say briskly. 'You have taken a hundred sovereigns from me, but you are greedy. You want more. Well, you can have more,' you say. 'One more payment, that is all I can do. My husband will be home soon, and I will not be able to find such a great sum again. After that, you will have to do your worst. Go to the coroner, produce Daniel if you can. Cat and I will take our chance at a trial.'

That is all very well for *you* to say, Mary, I

think. I try to look as if I know what you are about.

Anthony looks taken aback. 'If you are so ready for a trial, why ask to see me at all?'

'Because I care about the present, not the past. And because you mean mischief,' you say. 'You have found a way to hurt me through my family. Oh, do not try to deny it. I know quite well what you are doing with John. He was a good and worthy man until you weakened him with gambling.'

'The poor boy was so unhappy,' says Anthony with a glance at me, inviting you to blame me for putting an end to John's infatuation. 'We all know why. I offered him friendship when he found none at home.'

'Friendship?' You spit out the word. 'No friend would lure another to the tavern and teach him to squander his money on dice.'

Anthony is unmoved. 'I fear you do not understand the fever that grips you when you know how much depends on the fall of the dice, the turn of a card.'

'Do I not?' you say, grim-faced.

'You cannot teach someone to feel that,' Anthony says. 'The fever was always in him. If it has taken hold while I bore him company, am I to blame?'

'You are the carrier of that particular sickness,' you say. 'If you leave him alone, I believe he may recover.'

'So you care more for John than for the threat of the gallows?' Anthony turns a mocking face to me, widening his eyes. 'What say you, Cat? You, I

268

am sure, care more for your pretty neck than an idle gambler.'

'It is not up to Cat,' you snap before I have a chance to reply. 'She has nothing to give you in any case. You have already gambled away her jewels. Everything she has now she owes to me.'

For now, perhaps, I think, glancing down at the gown that, yes, you gave me. But there is no need for you to speak so contemptuously of me, Mary, none at all. Especially when the truth is that everything *you* have, you owe to *me*, or have you forgotten that? You came to Steeple Tew with nothing but a grubby apron and tattered wooden baby. If it were not for me, you would have no name, no husband, no family.

'I will give you three hundred sovereigns,' you say, your voice cool, and you do not even look at me when I gasp.

Three hundred sovereigns! Where have you got such a sum, Mary?

Anthony stills. 'Three hundred?' he repeats cautiously, as if he cannot believe his ears.

'They are yours if you will take them tonight and go,' you say. 'I care not where, but somewhere far from John, far from me. From my house and my daughter.'

'*Your* daughter?'

You lean forward. 'Come, there is no need for play-acting. We know the truth, we three. Cat gave birth to Cecily, but I am her mother. You have neither of you given her a moment's thought, and now I will protect her the way you should have done. If that means paying you to go away, then that is what I will do.'

269

'But she is so very charming,' Anthony says provocatively. 'I would wish to know my daughter better. For she is mine, is she not? And if she is mine, she is not entitled to the dowry she has as Lord Delahay's daughter. That would be a sad blow for her marriage prospects, would it not?'

But you are not impressed. 'Do not waste my time, Sir Anthony. The choice is yours. Three hundred sovereigns in your hand, or nothing at all.' You smile, but not nicely. 'I understand you are a gambler, sir. Here, I offer you a wager, all or nothing. Which will you take?'

I stare at you. What are you thinking, Mary? Surely, *surely*, you do not believe that Anthony will keep his word, whichever he chooses. He will always come back for more. You will never satisfy him.

I have almost forgot that the idea was mine. It was a small thing, tossed into a broth, but it has boiled and bubbled up and now I can see no end to it, save tipping up the pot and pouring it all away.

Anthony glances at me over the rim of his cup. I can see him thinking as he drinks: *three hundred sovereigns*. He is not thinking of me, I can tell. He is thinking of keeping all three hundred for himself. He is thinking of spending them on cards, on dice, on wine and women. He is thinking that he does not need me now.

We will see about that, my heart.

He puts down his cup abruptly. 'You have the money with you?'

'In a warehouse, hard by.'

'Very well. I will take your three hundred sovereigns.'

'And in return, you will go away? You will make no attempt to contact John or Cecily or any of us again?'

'It is a fair deal,' he says, and he spits on his palm and offers it to you. 'We are agreed.'

You do not take your eyes from his as you spit on your own palm and shake his hand. Look at you, Mary, cool as a winter sky, sealing your bargain with a black-mailer! If Gabriel could see you now, he would not recognise his drab and dutiful wife. I scarce recognise you myself.

I fear you are making a terrible mistake, though. Three hundred sovereigns! Where will you find any more when Anthony comes back? As come back he will. I will have to throw in my lot with Anthony after all, but then, what about Gabriel? Oh, I am out of patience with you!

But it is too late to persuade you to another course. Anthony drops some coin on the table and pushes back his stool. 'Let us go now.'

It is a relief to leave the tavern to the darkness and relative quiet of the quay. My head is aching from the racket and the piss-poor wine. I do not like not knowing what is happening, or why you are behaving so foolishly. You seem so sure of yourself, Mary. You know something I do not and it makes me uneasy.

You and Anthony walk together, both apparently content with the bargain that has been driven. I am left to follow behind, picking my way over the cobbles that are still slippery from the rain, my shoes skidding on who knows

271

what filth that has been discarded underfoot.

I do not like following behind.

The warehouse door opens with a creak when you unlock it, releasing a reek of stuffiness and spices. You gesture Anthony inside.

'If it is all the same to you, I will let you go first into the dark,' he says. 'We may have agreed, but that does not mean I trust you, mistress.'

You shrug. 'Wait then while I make some light. There is a tinderbox here . . . '

A spark jumps in the darkness and you light a candle set in a lantern. 'There,' you say, holding it aloft so that the shadows leap and swirl on the walls. 'You can see that there is no one here.'

Satisfied, Anthony steps inside. The candle-light judders over us as we walk through the warehouse. The barrels lined against the wall are bulky in the darkness, and my shoulder blades twitch as if they are soldiers, gathering themselves for a leap.

You open the door to a counting house at the back of the warehouse. 'Cat, do you hold the lamp while I find the key,' you say, beckoning to me, and like an obedient servant I step forward and do as you say, burningly aware of Anthony's amused eyes on me.

You rummage around in a jug and draw out a key. For all your briskness, I notice that when you draw it out, your hand is not quite steady and that makes me feel better. You step over to a long chest and bend down to unlock it, lifting the lid up and pulling out an account book, or so I assume.

'Come,' you say to Anthony. 'I have the money

here. Cat, bring the light so that he may see.'

You are grown far too firm in your orders, Mary. I do not like it, but I step reluctantly closer as you step back from the chest to let Anthony bend down and dig his hands into a bag of coins with a chuckle. Thinking that you cannot see his expression, he looks up at me with a grin and puckers his lips in a secret kiss.

So, perhaps he has been thinking of me after all. Well, that is something. I am careful not to smile back, but a warmth spreads from my belly.

'It is a pleasure doing business with you, mistress,' Anthony says, letting the coins run through his fingers. They glint in the light as they fall, chink, chink, chink, back into the bag. Anthony and I watch them, mesmerised. Images jostle in my mind: costly gowns, furs, jewels, a carriage of my own. Feather beds piled high, the bedstead hung with silk, sheets made of the finest linen.

But who will lie with me there, Anthony, or Gabriel?

I cannot decide, I really cannot. Is it wrong to want both?

You give me no warning.

I am looking at the coins, dreaming of what they will buy, and Anthony is stooped, chuckling, over the chest, when you step closer. Out of the corner of my eye, I see your arm lift, the flash of metal in the candlelight. I turn, my mouth opening in surprise, or perhaps it is to warn Anthony, I am not sure, but anyway it is too late for that, and I can only watch as you coolly drive a knife deep into his back.

273

21

Mary

It is not as easy as it looks to stab a man. I aim just above his kidneys. If I hesitate, he will knock me aside before I can kill him, but I think of how he smirked across the table at me, of how he toyed with John and threatened Cecily's security, and when I remember that, it is not so hard to kill him after all.

It is fortunate that it has been so hot. Anthony is wearing only a fine linen shirt open at the neck and a thin jerkin made of damask, which offers little resistance to the point of the knife. It might have been harder had he been wearing a padded doublet, I find myself thinking inconsequentially.

In any case, I have sharpened the knife well and Anthony has no time to react before I shove it into him and it slides easily, soundlessly, into his skin. I do not let myself think any more. I close my eyes and imagine that I am in my kitchen, dealing with a chunk of meat. This is not human flesh swallowing up my knife. These are not a man's veins, a man's sinews. I am not glancing off his bones or ripping through his membranes. He is just a carcass to be butchered.

But a joint of beef lies inert on my slab. It does not flinch and groan or resist the blade. It does not jerk or choke as Anthony is jerking and choking and retching in shock.

The horror of what I am doing makes me wrench out the knife and stab him again, and again, and again, frantic to make him stop that awful noise. He slumps over the chest, gasping, groaning in pain, and Cat gapes at me, the lantern shaking in her hand and sending the light jumping frenziedly around the counting house.

'Mary! Dear God, Mary . . . what are you doing?'

I don't answer her. It must be obvious what I am doing, what I have been driven to do.

Anthony won't die. There is a terrible gurgling sound coming from his throat, and his fingers scrabble weakly at the coins, and I have the terrifying conviction that he will never die, that I will have to stand here forever, stabbing the knife into him, smelling the blood and the loosening of his bowels, while the shadows swing wildly in time with the candlelight. My gorge rises, but I cannot stop now.

Again and again I push in the knife. It is like a nightmare: the soft squelch of knife in flesh, the sound of my harsh breathing, the grotesquely lurching shadows. And the smell, sweet Jesu, the smell! My hands are slippery, with blood or sweat I cannot tell.

'Mary, stop!' Hampered by the lantern, Cat tries to pull me away one-handed, but it is easy to brush her aside. She almost loses her grip on the lantern and the light jolts before she manages to steady it.

'Take care!' I say sharply. 'We do not want to set the whole warehouse on fire!'

As I speak, Anthony topples from the chest

and crumples onto the floor. I have to jump back to stop him rolling onto my skirts. God save me, *still* he is not dead. There are ghastly choking sounds coming from his throat, and I crouch down beside him, my face set. I cannot stop now. He looks up at me in horror, lifting one hand feebly to ward me off. His lips part. He is trying to say 'no', but it is too late. He has threatened my family. My eyes meet his, and he knows that he is doomed. I thrust the knife deep into his heart. Blood spurts from his mouth and he gives a great twitch and eventually lies still.

It is done.

My throat closes convulsively and I gag, but there is no way to keep the revulsion inside. Retching, I turn my head and vomit onto the floor, careless of Cat's exclamation of disgust.

Trembling, exhausted, I sit back on my heels after a minute and wipe my mouth with the back of my hand while silence clangs around the little room and the candlelight shudders in the lantern. Cat is still holding it, her other hand pressed to her throat, staring at me as if I am a monster.

'What . . . what . . . what . . . ?' she stammers.

I wipe the blade of the knife on Anthony's jerkin. 'He would never have stopped,' I say, surprised at how calm I sound, how reasonable, although my hand holding the knife trembles a little. 'He would have come back, whatever he said. We would never have been safe,' I say as I stand and straighten slowly, like an old woman, stiff and bent. 'Always he would have been lurking around the corner, waiting to threaten you with the coroner, waiting to lure John to the alehouse, waiting to start a rumour for the pleasure of ruining all Cecily's prospects. This way it is over,' I tell her. 'It is Anthony's choice. He could have taken the hundred sovereigns and left us alone as he promised, but he was greedy, and now he has died for it.'

'You planned this.' Cat sounds more shaken than I have ever heard her.

'Of course I planned it. Did you really think I would be foolish enough to give him three hundred sovereigns and let him walk away?'

Clearly she did. Her eyes drop from mine to Anthony's body on the floor. I can't read her expression properly in the dimness but I wonder if she is remembering how passionately she loved him. She gave up everything for Anthony, and now he is just a carcass on the floor.

'I am sorry,' I say. 'I know you cared for him once, but it had to be done, you do see that?'

'I did not think that you would be the one to do it,' she says.

'I know how to protect what is mine.'

'Aye, you have always done that.'

A silence falls, shrieking, in the counting house. My ears are ringing with it. With one part of my mind, I note dispassionately that reaction is setting in: I am very cold, my heart is racing and nausea wavers under my skin. I don't know what to do with the knife still in my hands. My body is leaden. I should move, I should think, but I can't. I can just stand here in the unsteady light, listening to the silence, refusing to acknowledge the horror that is roaring behind it.

'What are we going to do?' Cat says at last. 'We cannot leave him here.'

I draw a breath, and then another. The worst is over. Now we just need to get home.

'Jacopo is nearby. Stay here.'

But she comes with me as I open the warehouse door and Jacopo materialises from the shadows. He looks at the knife in my hand. 'I'll take that, mistress,' he says almost gently.

Dumbly, I hand it over. I have started to shiver.

'Where is he?' Jacopo asks.

'In the counting house.'

He nods. 'You get on then.'

'What are you going to do?'

'The *Margaret* leaves with the tide,' he says gruffly. 'He will go with her.'

'How — ' Cat begins, but Jacopo holds up a hand to silence her.

'Best not to ask questions.' He nods in my direction. 'Your mistress is cold,' he tells her severely. 'Look to her.'

'Cold?' Cat laughs a little wildly. 'You have no idea!'

I gather myself together. 'Come, Cat, there is no more to do here.' I go to take her arm but she shakes herself free of my grasp.

'What about the coins?' she says.

'They are safe in the chest.' I glance at Jacopo. 'Take what you need,' I tell him. I have not asked him how he will manage it, but doubtless silver will be required to change hands. I do not care how much it costs, as long as I do not have to see Anthony again. The thought of lifting his slack body, of touching his cold skin, fills me with horror.

Jacopo knows all this without me saying anything. He nods his understanding.

I swallow. 'Thank you,' I manage, and he nods again. Our eyes meet and I know then that he will never bring me another gift. His debt is repaid, and though his presents made me uncomfortable at times, now I feel a wave of sadness that there will be no more.

I take Cat more firmly by the arm and steer her back towards Three Cranes Lane. 'Is that it?' she whispers furiously. '*Take what you need!* You have just tossed three hundred sovereigns to that Barbary ape!'

'I trust Jacopo. He will take only what he needs,' I say. 'Besides, there is not near that amount at stake. You saw some coins on the top, but I filled the bag with oats first.'

'Oats?' Cat starts to laugh again, a shrill, frenzied laugh. 'Oats!'

'Stop that,' I say, low and angry. My reserves are too low to deal with hysterics. 'Do you want everyone to look at us and wonder what we are about?'

But she is beyond reason now, and keeps on laughing until I draw back my arm and crack a palm to her cheek. 'Quiet!'

Shocked, Cat stops on a gulp and stares at me with a dazed expression.

'Be quiet, Cat,' I say again more gently. I take a breath and it shudders out of me. 'We must be calm,' I remind her after a moment. 'We have been out to attend a difficult childbirth, that will

279

explain any blood. Say nothing else of what we did here tonight.'

What *I* did. She does not need to correct me. Tonight's work is mine alone.

'We had no choice,' I say. I am speaking slowly and clearly, as if to a child. 'We are safe now.'

'Only until Jacopo talks,' Cat points out, sounding more herself. 'What is to stop him turning to blackmail too?'

'Jacopo is no Anthony. He will say nothing. Would I have turned to him unless I trusted him completely? The only people who know what happened tonight are the two of us, and we will say nothing, will we? We are bound together, after all. We know too much of each other, Cat. We always have done.'

Are secrets all that bind us to each other now? I wonder sadly. Once there was love between us, but now I have had to remind my mistress, my friend, that if she tells my secret, I will tell hers.

Though I have more to lose now, as I am sure Cat is well aware.

Cat hesitates then nods. 'I will say nothing,' she agrees.

Bone-weary, sick and shaken, we trudge in silence back to Little Wood Street. I keep my expression composed, but any minute I expect to hear a shout, to feel a constable's hand fall heavily on my shoulder, but nothing happens. It is as if when we left the warehouse, we stepped into a different world, one where we are just two respectable women walking back from helping a neighbour. Anyone passing on the other side of the street would not know that my hands are sticky with blood, that tonight I stuck a knife into a man's heart.

It is late when we get back and the household is dark and quiet. I gesture Cat inside and close the door very quietly behind us, my knees weak with relief. Lighting a candle, I hand it to her. 'Go to bed,' I tell her. 'Remember, it was a childbirth, no more.'

She says nothing, just turns and heads up the stairs. I wonder what she is thinking? Is she sad? Is she shocked? Or is she calculating how to work the situation to her best advantage? With Cat you can never tell. It might be all three, it might be none.

I watch her out of sight and then take a candle of my own and light it. In the kitchen, I ladle water into a basin, and carry it up to my chamber. There I strip off every piece of clothing, yes, even my smock. *Every time you change your smock.* I set the basin on a stool and wash my hands in water, again and again, and then I take the cloth and rub and rub and rub at my skin until it is red and raw, and still I do not feel properly clean.

As I rub myself, the back of my neck is prickling. Someone is watching me. Someone who knows who I am and what I did. But no one knows except Cat, I tell myself. Even so, I keep glancing over my shoulder, although I know there is no one there. The feeling is so strong that in the end I step round the stool until I am facing the door so that I can be sure no one else is in the room, and that is when I see Peg. She is propped up on the chest as she always is, her

281

single arm dangling by her side, her expression so aghast that I gasp and knock over the water. The basin clangs onto the floorboards, and the bloody water splashes over me and runs into the cracks.

Trembling, I turn Peg to face the wall. Then I take the cloth and mop up the water as best I can, wringing it into the basin, and only then do I climb into bed.

I have never been as tired as I am tonight. The weariness is a lead weight pressing into my eyeballs and pinning me into the mattress, but I can't sleep. Every time I close my eyes, I see my arm lifting, driving the knife into Anthony's bent back. I feel the springy resistance of his muscles, the loosening of his flesh, and my head rings with the sound of him coughing up blood, and wound through it all like dancers around the maypole is the curse, the vagrant woman's cry: *until you die kicking and choking on the gibbet.*

I can barely swallow. I can feel the rope rough around my neck already, and I circle my throat with my hands as I lie in bed staring up at the canopy.

Did I really think I could escape the curse? I am a killer, many times over. Ellen the vagrant girl, Lord Delahay, Peter and Agnes Blake . . . Mine was the hand that caused their deaths, but I meant harm to none of them. I could be forgiven them all.

Anthony, though . . . this time it was different. I took a knife and sharpened it. I planned to kill him and I did. There was no mistake, no accident. I do not expect to be forgiven such a sin, but what else was I to do?

No sleep comes this night, or the next, or the next. For two days I lie in bed, sick with guilt, sick with horror. Sarah is worried and brings me dainty dishes to tempt my appetite, but I send them away. My stomach revolts against food. I try to nibble a cake, but vomit it back into a basin. Wine has the same effect. It is as if my body is trying to rid itself of the poison of guilt.

Cat offers to make me a caudle to comfort the stomach. 'You showed me how,' she reminds me. 'Stale ale and a pint of muscadine and the yolk of new-laid eggs, have I not remembered that right? And sugar and . . . what else?'

'Some whole mace,' I say weakly.

'Of course!' She claps her hands. 'And I will soak some bread in it and you will feel much better.'

She looks sincere, she sounds sincere, but I do not quite trust her. I wish I had not introduced Cat to the skills of the still room. What is to stop her adding a pinch of something poisonous to the caudle?

Is this what guilt does to you? Is it guilt that twists me inside out and upside down, so that I cannot tell what is right and good and true any more? That coats my vision with darkness and dredges suspicion in my ears? I listen for every inflection in a voice, every flicker of expression. Is that sympathy in Cat's eyes, or sly satisfaction?

'Let me bring you the caudle now,' she says, but I stop her.

'I thank you, but I cannot face anything now,' I say. 'Tomorrow, perhaps, if I am stronger.'

283

I force myself to get out of bed the next day. I must take back the reins of the household, else all will have been for nought. I am very weak, but it is easier to eat when I can oversee the kitchen. Cat has no interest in cooking, and is content to retire to the parlour and play the lute instead.

She *seems* unchanged.

I am the one who has changed. Even when I recover from my sickness and can eat and drink again, I am edgy and irritable. I snap at Sarah and Amy, at Cecily and Cat. I am short with the countrywomen in the market and shunned by my neighbours. They turn away from me now and pretend that they have not seen me. They cross the street to avoid my greeting. Between Peter Blake's death and my disgraceful quarrel with Isabella Parker, my reputation lies in tatters. Amy tells me there are even whispers that I may be a witch, that more than one remedy I have made has caused a patient to sicken further, or that I ill-wished all of those currently suffering from misfortune. Sensible people scoff at such rumours, Amy says, but she looks uneasy.

I cannot find it in me to care. My terrible crime has divided me from the rest of the world. I think I see Anthony everywhere, even though I have seen Jacopo who came to the house with Richard soon after. 'It is done,' was all he murmured to me. He too seems to have receded. I believe him, but at the same time I cannot shake this conviction that Anthony is lurking around every corner, that he will spring out of the shadows and laugh in my face, my knife still quivering in his heart.

There is a constant queasiness in my belly, and a fine tremor under my skin. I long for Gabriel to come back, but I dread it too. He knows me so well, surely he will see that I have changed. That I have been changed. Richard tells me that he will be sailing for Hamburg next week, and that Gabriel will return with him. All I want is for my husband to come home and for everything to be as it was, but I am afraid, afraid I have crossed a line and that nothing will ever be the same again.

22

Cat

Well, well, well. I did not expect *that*. I eye you under my lashes as you walk home in silence, straight-backed, stern. Nobody looking at you would guess that you had just taken a knife and stabbed a man in the back, and then knelt beside him to finish him off, like a pig you were planning to hang for bacon.

It felt as if I were watching everything in slow motion. The way you drew your arm back, the expression on your face as you thrust: intent, implacable. Anthony arching in agony, the slow tumble onto the floor, disbelief clouding his eyes. He underestimated you, Mary. Perhaps I did too. I must say, I did not think you had it in you.

And now what? Anthony is dead. I cannot quite believe it.

When we get in, you send me to bed like a child, but I am glad enough to climb the steep stairs to my own room. I am weary, and shocked, and I let myself feel a little maudlin, remembering how madly Anthony and I loved each other once. I sit on the edge of the bed and rub my hands on my thighs, pressing down through the fabric, thinking about how Anthony once touched me. I won't feel his hands on me again. I tired of him, but lately he has made me feel desired again. Perhaps it was because we had to go at it in secret. Is there something in me that craves the forbidden? It is a mournful thought.

But perhaps after all it is for the best. I amused myself with Anthony, but he could not give me what I really wanted, and besides, he could always hold the threat of blackmail over me. You were so intent on protecting your family, you barely gave me a thought, but I was far more at risk than you. I could have hanged for what I did to George, and yes, it was I who killed him. I had to, or else he would have killed me and Anthony, too, most likely. Perhaps I should have waited longer in the hope of a son, but I was not sorry that he died then. I wanted him dead. He repulsed me. I did not want him breathing in the same room as me. I wanted Anthony, and you gave me the means to have him. It was a pleasure to see George writhing and gagging on the floor, his face congested, his eyes bulging in terror. I just watched, the way he liked to watch. I remember how heavy the poker felt in my hand, the thrilling rush of rage as I brought it down on his head. And then I put on a fine show of fear and ran to get you to clear up the mess. I knew you would not be able to resist the temptation to show me how clever and capable you are.

You have taken me by surprise tonight, I will admit. First with the murder — and let us not be shy, that is the word — and then with your lack of remorse. A little vomit, and you were quite yourself again, taking charge and dragging me along. And then, when I realised that Anthony had died for a bag of oats, putting an end to my merriment with a slap.

I touch my cheek where it still smarts from your blow. You had no need to hit me quite so hard. I was shocked — and no wonder — but you have to admit that it was funny too. Oats!

So, it turns out that you are not such a milky miss after all. I would have expected hand-wringing and protestations of guilt at the very least, but no. Although perhaps I should have known. You can be steely when someone tries to take something away from you. That look in your eyes tonight reminded me of when I tried to look at that horrible wooden baby when you first arrived at Steeple Tew. You would not let anyone near it. It is not as if I even wanted to hold the thing. I was just being kind, but you snatched it to your chest and wouldn't let me see. It is only now that I understand how very selfish you are, Mary. You give the impression of being good and devout, but really, underneath you only care about yourself. You don't care about me at all.

So I must care for myself. Things could be worse. I unlace my kirtle and petticoat thoughtfully. You have disposed of Anthony for me, but you do not know that I know where Anthony has been living. I know where he has kept the remainder of the money you gave him. Some has been spent, of course, I remember regretfully. I could not expect Anthony to keep a coin in his pocket for long and he will have gambled much of it already, not to mention his new velvet suit. But there should be a sum left that I can find and hide. A little nest egg for me, if you will. Just in case my other plans do not work out.

You didn't tell me what you planned to do, Mary. That rankles. You do not trust me. Well, perhaps you are wise. You have become a worthy foe. I despise you when you are too good. Now we are even. No longer can you flaunt your goodness over me. I know what you are.

It is stuffy in the chamber still in spite of the rain earlier and I shift restlessly in bed. I didn't like the feeling tonight that you were in control, not I. It is as if the competition between us has become real at last after all these years. Only one of us can win. I am back to where I first found you again that day in Cheapside, apart from a few coins that I may be able to retrieve from Anthony's lodging. I have no prospects, not really. Marriage is still my best option, but I do not want to marry the first stout merchant who will offer for me.

I want what you have, Mary, and what you have killed to protect. Perhaps I had better wait and see what happens when Gabriel comes home? The thought of him is a warm tingle in my bones. Is that the idea of him, or the reality of his cool mouth and steady eyes? What I feel for him is a yearning, although I am not sure what I am yearning for. Gabriel offers a tantalizing mixture of my father's security and the passion I felt for Anthony. I am not surprised you burn for him, Mary. I burn for him myself. But I am puzzled by what he sees in you. I have seen the way he looks at you, and I do not understand it.

Still, a few months away must surely temper his ardour. When he comes home and sees me, he will see me properly. He *must* do so. When I came here first I was bruised and battered. Of course he did not see my beauty then, and since then I have become familiar. This time, though, I will be at pains to be sweet and modest, and I will look my best. He will not be able to resist me.

But he cannot have us both. One of us must lose, and it must be you, Mary. It is my turn now. I must find a way to be rid of you. It would be helpful if you would die of guilt, but I don't think you are going to do that, are you? You survived the sickness too. But who knows when there might be an accident. It would be all too easy to trip on that fancy staircase of yours, for instance. All it would take would be one little push. But I couldn't be sure. And it is not as if I want to kill you, Mary: it is just that I can see no other way.

★ ★ ★

You stay abed, claiming to be sick the day after the murder. *Murder, murder, murder.* The word jangles in the air, so loud I can scarce believe nobody else hears it. But you hear it, don't you, Mary? That is why you lie abed, sick with guilt, no doubt.

I am willing to play along. Why not? And you *do* look unwell, grey and haggard, your clear eyes dull. Well, what can you expect when you go around murdering people? I shake my head

290

sympathetically and even offer to make you a caudle, but you will have none of it. You refuse quite petulantly.

When you stay in bed another day, I let myself hope that you are ailing in truth. Perhaps you will be sick again, and this time you will not recover. But no, you must always thwart me. You force yourself up and take control of the household, but there is a sourness in the atmosphere now. The others may not know what you did, but they sense the wrongness in you. Cecily is pettish, John disconsolate. He must think himself abandoned by his new friend. But Anthony has taught him well. The dice are his best friends now, and they lure him to the taverns every night whether Anthony be there or no. You watch him with worried eyes. Did you think getting rid of Anthony would make everything better? It is not so, is it?

Amy is hoity-toity, and Sarah is grown much too pert. I had to be quite sharp with her this morning, and she just gave me a surly look. When I am mistress again, I will keep my servants in better order.

Now we sit in the great chamber, and the unease festers. Cecily is showing off at the virginals, but she keeps striking a wrong note that jars in the air until I want to scream at her to stop. I am not sure you even hear her. You are straight-backed as ever, but still you seem slumped in your thoughts, and your hands are idle, resting on your lap, the cloth you are sewing forgotten.

I am weary of this waiting. Weary of playing a

servant. Weary of sitting on a stool while you sit in a chair. Weary of my narrow bed and practical gowns. Weary of listening to Cecily's playing and watching you, wondering when you will break. Because break you must, sooner or later. I cannot see you living with Anthony's death on your conscience, not you. It might be best for me if you took your own life, I think often. I would be here, ready to console your husband and step into your shoes, which are rightfully mine, after all.

Sighing fretfully, I finger the lute. If Cecily would only cease, I could play and that would soothe me. As it is, I must wait — more waiting! — until she is tired.

The door opens, and she breaks off, thanks be to God. You look up dully. It is John, looking dishevelled and anxious. 'I have news,' he says.

Your hand goes to your throat and you half rise from your chair. 'Gabriel?' You fear it is bad news, but John manages a smile. He brings a message from the sea captain, Mr Martindale, master of that monkey-like servant you trust so much. He is sailing to Hamburg on the tide and he will bring your husband back with him.

Gabriel is coming home.

*   *   *

For the past two weeks you have been in a frenzy of preparation for the return of your husband. The silver has been polished, the carpets beaten. Amy and Sarah have laid new rush matting in the chambers, and you have ordered new linen for your bed. You are planning a warm welcome, I see.

Meanwhile, I am left with nothing to do. You send me out to do the marketing, but I sense that it is just an excuse to get me out of the way. I spend more than I should and make certain to exchange friendly tidings with Anne and those few friends you have left. They were concerned about you at first. I told them that you were preoccupied, consumed with guilt about Peter Blake's death. I hinted that something similar happened before. No harm in preparing the ground just in case you oblige me by taking poison or following Agnes Blake to the river. I think I did it rather cleverly. Nothing too obvious, just hints and worried looks, and insistence that I must leave to see how you are.

You should be consumed with guilt, if not for that child, at least for Anthony. Would those goodwives feel so torn if they knew how easily you knelt to skewer a man's heart? How you looked in his eyes and killed him as if you were doing no more than snapping a chicken's neck?

You have ordered a new gown for yourself, and one for Cecily, so that you both look your best for his return. There is no new gown for me. You have deliberately arranged it that I look shabby beside you as we stand and wait for the traveller. I will not forgive you for that, Mary.

Anyway, you can order all the vibrant silks and velvets you like, you will never be as beautiful as I am. You look drawn still, and your nails are nibbled down almost to their quicks. Cecily, on the other hand, looks very well indeed. Of course, she is young, but she is untried yet. She has no allure.

It will take more than a new gown to beat me, Mary. I have planned how I will be: demure and obedient, but so quietly beautiful that he will not be able to resist.

John waits, looking edgy. The servants are beaming, their hands wrapped in their aprons. Cecily is dancing up and down. How restless the child is! Was I as bad as that? You stand very still and outwardly composed, but I see the tremor in your throat. I can almost feel the booming of your heart. Yes, you are glad to be welcoming your husband home, but how will you feel when he turns to you tonight? When you know the great wickedness that lies between you?

There is a stomping of boots and a jingle of harness outside in the courtyard and we all suck in our breaths and look at each other. And then the door is open and the hall is suddenly full of men, and it rings with greetings and laughter and excited dogs. I only have eyes for one man: Gabriel. It is strange, I have thought about him so much since he has been gone. I have wondered if I have made him up somehow, or was pretending my yearning for him, but just seeing him there in the flesh sends the breath whooshing from my body. I am frozen into place, paralyzed by the force of my desire. My eyes crawl over him, the way his eyes crease, the way his hair grows at his temples, the curve of his mouth, the four-square way he stands. He is *not* as handsome as Anthony, not near. He is not really handsome at all. But every part of me is clamouring for him.

And he, he has eyes only for you, Mary. Whey-faced as you are, he takes your hands and he kisses you fiercely on your mouth. He says something to you, something only you can hear, that sends the colour rushing into your face and a smile blooms and all at once, just like that, you are beautiful. My fingers twist in my skirts. It is you that he wants. Why, why, *why*? I do not understand it.

He has clapped John's shoulder and swept Cecily into an embrace that makes her squeal with happiness. The way I used to squeal when my pappa embraced me.

Now Gabriel is greeting us all in turn. He is a kind man, a decent man. He has a word for all of us, Amy, Sarah, and now me, it is my turn and my mouth dries. I have no clever words, no plan of seduction. I can just stare at him with dumb longing.

'Cat,' he says. It is impossible to tell if he is pleased or disappointed to see me. 'So you are still here?'

Where is my witty response to make him laugh?

'Yes,' I say.

This is what you do not understand, Mary. I am not staying to spite you, not really. I am staying because I cannot leave him.

It is madness. I lie in bed and torture myself with thoughts of you and him together in bed. I think I may be sickening for something. I am hot and cold, and then hot again, and my belly churns and twists with jealousy and longing. I have never felt this before. It was not like this with Anthony. I always knew that I could have him, and he looked on me with desire. But there is nothing in Gabriel's eyes when he looks at me, just a keen, cool stare that seems to lay me bare. You asked me to sing tonight, and I did, a song of love and of yearning that brought tears to Amy's and Sarah's eyes, but Gabriel only pushed a stray strand of hair under your cap and let his fingers linger on your cheek. I could have been any wait scraping away on a fiddle in the street. The two of you are absorbed in each other; it is as if the rest of us barely exist. And Gabriel, breathing heavily like a beast in heat, practically pawed at the ground in his haste to get you to your chamber and mount you.

I love him and I fear him. He makes me feel exposed, as if I must lay my heart out and wait for him to stamp on it.

But this must not be. I must have him, I must. He must come to love me, and he will only do that if you are gone, Mary. I will let him grieve, I am not so crass that I would make my move too soon, but he will need me then. Who else will he turn to? I am sorry, but sooner or later, somehow, *somehow*, you must die.

23

Mary

London, Little Wood Street, September 1590

When Gabriel steps through the door at last, a desperate relief swells my heart, pushing it into my throat and hard against my ribs so that it is almost painful and I can neither speak nor swallow. Until this moment, I have not let myself trust that he would come. Even when a boy ran up from the docks with the message that the ship was tied up at the quay, I could not truly believe it.

Hastily, I took off my apron, brushed down my skirts, straightened my cap. I peered into the looking glass in my chamber and saw myself, pale and sunken-eyed, a poor wife for Gabriel to come home to. There was no time to do more than pinch my cheeks to bring them some colour.

Now we are assembled in the hall, the servants whispering and shuffling their feet. Cecily is dancing with impatience, John twitching his gown into place on his shoulders. I see Cat adjusting her collar and surreptitiously tugging at her laces, and I frown.

We have kept our distance since the night in the warehouse. The night I murdered Anthony. I have to be honest with myself, even though I have done my best to keep the events of that night shut away behind a closed door in my mind. It has not been easy. Every time I kneel, I remember kneeling beside him to plunge a knife into his heart. Every time I light a candle, I remember the darkness in the warehouse. Every time I dress a joint, the memory of that night engulfs me and nausea rises up in me, choking me, making me gag and I have to put a hand to my mouth to hold it back.

Every time you change your smock.

The memories are slippery worms inside my head, constantly wriggling free from the box in which I keep them. I may lunge and grab one, but others escape the moment I lift the lid to put it back. It is exhausting, and I have barely slept since that night. Closing my eyes just takes me back to the counting house and the feel of my knife sliding into Anthony's flesh as easily as I carve a leg of bacon.

I have held onto the thought of Gabriel. As soon as he comes home, I have told myself, all will be well. The world will stop lurching like a cart with a broken wheel. I will be able to put the past behind me as I have done before.

Now he is coming. Any minute now and he will be here at last. I am gripped by a terrible fear that I have forgotten what my husband looks like. My eyes skitter frantically around the hall as I try to conjure up his image, but my mind is blank. All I can see are signs of poor housekeeping: the cobweb in the corner, a thread unravelling at the edge of a hanging, a pewter pot in need of a polish, in spite of the fact that everything has been cleaned and cleaned again over the past two weeks.

It is a golden September day and the glass panes divide the sunlight into beams that stripe the hall, trapping lazily twirling motes of dust. I am mesmerised by them. I feel cut off from everyone else, trapped like the dust in a bubble from which the noise of the street and the murmurs of the servants have receded, leaving a muffled silence behind. I am strangely weightless, and I press my shoes into the floor lest I simply float up into the air.

Into the silence, the sound of boots and men's voices outside sends a ripple around the hall, and the firm rap on the door makes me jump. Gabriel is here, but I am not ready!

I look around in panic, but then there he is, warm, solid, *real*. His skin is weather-beaten and there are lines at the edges of his eyes, but he sees me. He *sees* me. My husband, my love. How could I have forgotten him?

There is a moment when we just stare at each other across the hall, drink each other up. I cannot speak. My heart is too full. I can only wait as Gabriel moves at last. He comes straight to me, as if there is no one else in the hall. He takes my hands and he kisses me, his mouth warm and firm on mine, and the world settles into place once more.

'My heart,' he says to me, low. 'I have yearned for you these past few months.'

Light-headed with relief, I feel my face warm with pleasure. 'And I you,' I say. He will never know how much.

Now, when we lie together in bed, I press against his sleeping body. I want to burrow into him, lose myself in him. I tell myself that it is all over now.

But it is not over. I know because sometimes when I look at Peg, her expression is bleak and a trail of blood runs from the corner of her mouth. The first time I saw it, my heart jumped sickeningly and I snatched her up, thinking that someone — Cat was my first thought — had disfigured her, but when I looked closely, the blood was gone and her mouth looked just the same as always. It is only sometimes, in a certain light, when the candle flame flickers or the light slants through the window, that I seem to see the blood trickling down her chin, just the way it trickled down Anthony's chin.

I hoped that Gabriel's return would set things to rights. We pretend that life is as it always was, but the household is fractured in ways I can't explain. On the surface it seems the same, but there is something rotten hidden below, like a sack of flour when you need to dig your hand down, down, to test for mould. There is something tense in the air, an oppression that I cannot shake. Smiles seem forced, laughter too brittle, and we watch each other guardedly, even though we know not what we are watching or waiting for. I feel the weight of secrets pressing behind every door. My own secrets, Cat's. The secrets we share that are the most dangerous of all.

Ah, Cat. We are bound together more tightly

than ever, and neither can shake the other free. Cat watches me more warily now. I know she is remembering the moment I knelt by Anthony and dealt him the death blow. She likes to pretend that she was horrified, but she did the same to George. She made sure that he was good and dead before she ran to find me. We both have blood on our hands, and we both know it.

We cannot go on like this. Somehow, Cat must be persuaded to leave. I must work harder to find her a husband, but no matter how many marriageable men I invite to the house, she turns up her nose at all of them. I do not understand what she wants. She cannot want to spend her life here with me, trapped together with our secrets.

I think of the time when we were a happy household. Was I fooling myself in thinking that we were as one? Now we are fractured, but perhaps we always were. I had forgotten that we all have our own secrets and experiences, and that we do not share everything, no matter how much we love each other.

Look at how much I have not shared with Gabriel.

London, Little Wood Street, October 1590

So we go through the motions, or that is how it feels. I run a sober house, I set a fine table. I supervise the servants. I support my husband. The household still gathers for prayer every morning, but no one prays as fervently as I do, for forgiveness, for release, to forget.

Gabriel's business prospers. He never asks about the hundred sovereigns that are missing from the accounts. I know that he has spoken to John about the state of the accounts, but I don't know what was said. All I know is that John is more sober now, and attends his father dutifully. I am glad of it. That at least has come good again.

'We must find John a wife,' Gabriel says one night as he watches me comb out my hair. It falls thick and straight to my waist and is my one vanity, in spite of — or perhaps because of — the fact that he is the only person who ever sees it. Every morning I bind it up beneath a cap, but at night I let it tumble free, and when I straddle my husband and lean down to kiss him, it falls like a curtain on either side of his face. We are shut off by the bed curtains, but my hair makes our world even smaller, even more intimate. A world where nothing exists but our mouths, our kisses. Our skins, pressed together. Our desire, burning bright.

I tilt my head as I comb, thinking. 'That would be good for him. Do you have a family in mind?'

'Henry Sim has a daughter, Margaret. I dined with him last week and she was at the table,' Gabriel says. 'They call her Meg. She is a modest girl, quiet, but Henry says she is sweet-natured.'

All to the good. John needs a sweet-tempered girl. 'Does she bring any money?'

Gabriel nods, smiles. 'She is his only child, and dear to his heart. As dear as Cecily is to mine.'

302

I nod approvingly. I want John to be happy, but one must be practical, after all. 'Let us invite Henry and his wife to dine here and to bring their daughter. A family dinner, some music and good cheer. Nothing formal.'

Although, needless to say, I will plan the meal as carefully as if we were entertaining our Lady Queen herself.

There will be much discussion to be had, but first let us see if John has a fancy for Meg Sim. Gabriel is a fond father. He will not force John to wed where he has no inclination, but what, after all, is there for him to object to in a well-mannered, sweet-natured girl? A wife would be a steadying influence.

It is time, I know, but still I feel a pang. It seems not so long since I first came to this house and John was but a boy. Where have the years gone? When he weds, his wife will come to live here, just as Jocosa came to Steeple Tew when she wed Avery. I know only too well how a new wife can change a household — but perhaps change is what we need?

For a while I fear that my diminished reputation among my neighbours will make the Sims cautious about a connection, but they live in Cornhill, a different ward altogether, and Agnes Blake means nothing to them. Besides, if my reputation has suffered, Gabriel's has not. He is wealthy and respected, anyone would be eager to ally with his son, I remind myself when the Sims accept the invitation without apparent hesitation.

The young people are stiff together at first, but

I like Meg at once. She is a good, kind girl, with round blue eyes and a shy smile. I like her mother, too. We take each other's measure when we meet, but that is only natural. I see her look approvingly around the hall and picture her daughter as mistress here one day. Well, so she may be with my goodwill.

I know she is curious about Cat's position in the family, but I am unable to think of a reason to exclude Cat from the gathering. I dare not, is the truth. She has never looked more beautiful. Her skin glows, her hair shimmers gold in the candlelight. She keeps her blue eyes lowered in a parody of a demure girl, so the effect is all the more dazzling when she lifts them and smiles. She does nothing to put herself forward, I have to give her that, but she draws the eye just by sitting there. I am afraid that she will over-shadow Meg and remind John of his ill-judged passion for her, but that at least seems to be cured.

Cat sits quietly, saying little. She is playing a part, of that I am sure. I wish I knew what game she is playing but I cannot accuse her of behaving badly.

Which I am sorry to admit is more than I can say for my daughter. Cecily, until now so open and loving, has turned secretive. She has become brattish, flouncing out of the room, and spending hours in her chamber pinching her cheeks and adjusting her ruff. She tosses her head when her will is crossed and a mutinous look has settled around her perfect mouth.

I have been too ill or too preoccupied to be a

good mother and must give her more attention. I am not pleased with the pettish face she shows to Meg, or the way she does nothing to make her feel welcome. Yes, she sings beautifully and the Sims applaud, but there are more important things than singing. There is kindness and courtesy. I thought I had taught her that.

'She is jealous,' Cat says the next day.

We are in the still room making scented waters for the table to replace those we used last night. Sarah has laboured in with well water for the tub, and we are picking over dried herbs to add to it. The air is heady with the scent of marjoram and camomile. There is something about the still room that invites confidences. In the great chamber, in the hall, in the kitchen, I am wary of Cat, but here in the still room, I seem to forget.

'Jealous?' Puzzled, I drop a sprig of marjoram into the water. 'How so?'

'Cecily is used to being first in all your affections. Look at how she demands attention. That is why she must sing and play every night,' Cat says authoritatively. 'Everyone must look at her! As long as she is the centre of the world, she is happy, but let someone else be of interest and she pouts and scowls.'

I know somebody else like that, I think but do not say, reluctant to spoil the peace of the still room.

'She doesn't like the idea of John marrying at all,' Cat goes on. 'That is plain to see. She loves John.' She pauses delicately. 'And he is not, after all, her brother, is he?'

'She thinks of him as a brother,' I say.

305

'Does she?'

'Of course she does.' But I have left too long a pause before replying.

Cat notices, but doesn't remark on it. She tosses camomile into the tub. 'If I were you, I would marry her off,' she advises.

'She is not yet fourteen,' I object.

'That is old enough to marry. Do you have no one in mind for her? She is the daughter of a nobleman, after all.'

There is a short silence while we both remember whose daughter Cecily really is. She thinks she is Lord Delahay's daughter; we know better. I killed one father, Cat the other.

★ ★ ★

Summer recedes to a torrid memory. As the negotiations for a marriage between John and Meg continue, I begin to think that I will be able to put those wretched months behind me after all. John gives Meg some gloves, she gives him a handkerchief. He blows hot and she blows cold, but then warms again, in the old dance of courtship.

Anthony lies deep under the ocean, nibbled by fishes. I have survived. I avert my eyes from Peg when I pass. I cannot bring myself to put her away, but I don't straighten her skirts any more. I don't want to look at her empty eyes and see my own horror reflected there. The past is past. I want to think about the present, about being a good wife, a good mother.

I welcome the cool autumn days because they

mean that the summer is over. I like the crisp mornings, the way the wind chivvies the dead leaves along the street and swirls them into drifts that rustle beneath my clogs. The mist shrouds the Thames and drapes over the tops of the masts so that the ships tied up by the quays look stunted.

I like the longer evenings, especially when Gabriel is at home and we sit on either side of the fire in the great chamber. John is happier, and often visits the Sims. I miss him, but am glad that he seems so happy with Meg. They seem certain to wed in the spring. I have been stricter with Cecily, and she has been charmingly contrite. 'It is just a show,' Cat says, but I refuse to believe her. We are a family again. All we lack is Tom, but Tom is in tearing spirits in Hamburg from all accounts, and will come home in good time.

Cecily is singing: *Go from my window, my love, my dove* . . . Her voice is as sweet as ever, and listening to it calms my heart. I glance up from my sewing to meet Gabriel's eyes and we exchange a contented smile, before I look to my stitching once more. John is at the Sims' house on Cornhill. Amy is walking out with a young man, but Sarah is sitting on the floor, hugging her knees and listening raptly. She loves to listen to Cecily sing and can sometimes be persuaded to join in. Cat is on a cushion, inspecting her nails.

The wind and the rain have brought you back again, Cecily sings, *but you can have no harbour here.*

If only I had said that to Cat.

Gabriel is nodding his head gently in time with the music, a smile lingering around his mouth still. I know without him telling me that he is thinking about tonight, when we will be alone in our bed, and anticipation clenches within me. We have never lost our desire for each other.

I lower my head to my sewing once more, but there is a prickle at the back of my neck, something I have missed that my mind wants me to notice. Under my lashes, I look around the chamber once more. Everyone is doing what they were doing before. Cecily is singing, Gabriel nodding, Sarah smiling with pleasure. Cat is still staring at her hands . . . but as I watch, her eyes lift and she looks at my husband, and the expression on her face is one of such fierce yearning that my hand slips in shock and the needle stabs my thumb.

'Ouch!'

My exclamation makes Cecily jar a note on the lute.

'Oh, Mamma! You have distracted me!' she complains.

I suck a bead of blood from my thumb as she starts again. My mind is racing. What a fool I am to have thought myself safe from danger! Anthony may be lying on the ocean bed, but danger is still right here. There is no mistaking Cat's expression. She hungers for Gabriel, for my husband, and if I know Cat, she will be planning ways to have him, because Cat has always believed that she can have whatever she wants.

308

But she is not going to have my husband, I vow to myself. I will not let that happen.

Somehow I will have to find a way to be rid of her once and for all.

How? My mind flickers to Anthony's fate, but no, I cannot kill again. That was different. He threatened my family, not me. And in spite of everything, Cat was my friend. Once we were as close as sisters. I cannot kill her. I just want her to go away.

I must be careful, though. If she guesses that I know what she really wants, she will fight like a cornered cat. My only hope is to let her believe that I am ignorant of her desires.

Let her feel contempt for me, I care not. She does not know Gabriel the way I do. She does not love him. She wants him, but that is not the same thing at all. You can love and want, yes, but Cat does not know how to love. She only knows how to want. She can take, but she cannot give.

The autumn wears on and I am not closer to finding a way to dislodge Cat from my home. We gather apples from the orchard. Sarah and I lay them out carefully, not touching, lest any rot spread. Cat is the rot in my household. I must cast her out before she infects us all.

Somehow, *somehow*, I must be rid of her.

24

Cat

Gabriel is home. He is *here*. Any moment he may walk into the room, which means that I am constantly atremble with anticipation. I look up every time I hear a latch lift in case it is him. Men's voices sound in the street and I strain to hear if it is him. My blood thrums in my veins. I was not imagining things: I do desire your husband. And the more I see him, the more I want him. Hunger for him bangs in my belly like a drum, heavy, insistent.

At night, I think of him with you in the chamber below, and I touch myself where he is touching you, imagining that it is his hand, his mouth on me, and my breath shudders out of me. I have felt desire before, but not like this. I am made fearful by it, struck dumb by it.

I do not understand it at all. Gabriel is not a gentleman. He is not handsome, he is not charming. He writes no poetry about my beauty. He does not flatter me. Half the time I am not even sure if he notices me at all. He is just himself: steady, sure, at ease in his own skin. He moves deliberately, a man who knows exactly what he is doing and why he is doing it.

And, of course, he is yours.

Is that why I want him? I don't *think* so, but it may be partly true.

Much good my desire does me. My charm has quite deserted me. At first, I pretended to be modest and demure, hoping that Gabriel would approve of me, but it seems that the role has taken me over, at least as far as your husband is concerned. I can barely speak when he is near. My tongue feels thick and unwieldy in my mouth and my mind goes blank. How does he do that to me? Why cannot I do the same to him? Even if I could summon them at will, smiles and flirtatious looks mean nothing to Gabriel. I have no way to reach him. My beauty is not enough. When I sing or play, he watches me, but indifferently. Just so does he look at Cecily, or Sarah or Amy.

At everyone except you.

I am consumed by envy of you. You rarely touch him, I have noticed that. Gabriel is more affectionate. He drops a hand on your shoulder, or runs a finger down your cheek, and every casual gesture is fraught with his desire for you. What do you do to him behind the bed curtains, Mary, to keep him so enthralled? I wouldn't put it past you to concoct some potion in your still room, some spell to bind him to you. You could be a witch if you chose, Mary, you really could, for all the time you spend on your knees. You are always in church, or praying at household prayers, your lips moving fervently, your head bowed. It is too late for praying now, the deed is done. We never talk about what happened in the warehouse, even when we are alone, do we? But that does not mean that it can be undone, or that I do not remember.

Still, we carry on. From first light, you keep the household busy with tedious chores. There is water to be carried, linen to be washed, food to be bought and prepared, floors to be swept, clothes to be brushed. You brew ale and dry herbs and preserve fruit. You make sure the silver is polished and the rush matting replaced regularly. You entertain Gabriel's guests and cast the household accounts.

Things are better for you since your husband came home. You can hide your tattered reputation behind his, and you invite guests almost every night. There are companions for John, wholesome young men and women to remind him of the comfort of decent living, good families to eye up Cecily to see if she might be a good match for a son one day. And then there are the old men and widowers you think would do for me.

I know you want me to leave, but how can I go and not see Gabriel every day? Every night, guests or not, I sing my heart out for him. I treasure every little smile, every casual word of praise. I rack my brains trying to think of something to say to him, but the only subject we have in common is you.

I take to loitering outside his closet, hoping that he will come out and we can talk. He is usually with someone else, or you send me away, but once he comes out and catches me pretending to polish the silver.

'Good morrow to you, Cat,' he says. He has his hat in his hand and is clearly on his way out.

My heart races so fast that I fear I might faint.

'Sir,' I manage, and even now there is a part of me that marvels that I should call a mere merchant 'sir', that I should want such a man with such a fierce longing.

That appears to be it, but at the last moment — oh joy! — he turns back to me. 'Have you seen your mistress?'

'She is gone to the market.' There, I have managed a whole sentence!

There is a faint frown in Gabriel's eyes as he studies me. 'Does she seem quite well to you?'

Now is my chance. I do not miss it, but I resent you for being all that I can talk about with Gabriel. 'She is not as well as she was,' I agree. 'She was very sick while you were away. We feared for her life, and although she has recovered, ever since she has been . . . ' I trail off, wondering how far I should push it.

'Preoccupied?' Gabriel suggests, and I nod.

'Yes, that. As if something troubles her greatly, but when I ask if there is anything I can do, she will not tell me. I worry for her,' I tell him. 'We have known each other for many years, and I have never seen her like this before.'

'I am glad you have been here to care for her,' Gabriel says. 'She has no kin so it means a lot to her that you are here now. We all need someone who remembers us and tethers us to our past.'

He has no idea how tethered we are, or how desperately we wish to unshackle ourselves from it.

'She is very dear to me,' I say, and the odd thing is, Mary, you *are*. You are part of my past too. But this envy I feel for you has grown out of control. I love you, but not as much as I hate you now. 'But I fear that she has changed lately.'

Gabriel stands, his eyes unfocused, rubbing a finger thoughtfully under his bottom lip. It gives me a chance to stare at his mouth. I want to cover it with kisses, to grab that finger and put it in my own mouth, to let him know that he can do whatever he wants with me, as long as he does it now. My whole body is pulsating, as if I am about to burst into flame.

But he is thinking of you. It is always you, you, you. It is infuriating.

Gabriel shakes himself out of his study and bestows a smile on me that will keep me burning for the rest of the day at least. 'I would be glad if you would keep an eye on her,' he says. 'If you are concerned at all, I beg you will tell me.'

'Of course,' I say, lowering my eyes so that he does not see the naked need there.

I go to Gabriel a couple of times to tell him of my concerns. I cannot do it too often or he would be suspicious of me, but I hoard the chance to speak to him alone. Now I may scratch on his door and go into his closet. I know I must make a touching sight, my beautiful face creased with worry for you. How I love those minutes with him and I spin out the conversations as long as I can.

It is a strange time. Do you feel that too, Mary? As if part of you is waiting for something to happen, and the other part going about your daily business as if nothing has or ever will? Next door, the Bowmans are having a new staircase built. It seems that ever since Mistress Bowman saw the staircase here, she has been consumed with envy, and has not rested until Mr Bowman has agreed that they should have one too, although knowing Elizabeth Bowman, it will be even bigger and grander than yours. She is nearly as jealous of you as Isabella Parker. The carpenters are certainly making enough noise. Wisely, the Bowmans have gone to live with her sister for a few weeks, which is all very well for them, but we are left with the constant banging and hammering and sawing and shouting, and the smell of sawdust clogs the nostrils.

Truly, I sometimes hate the unceasing noise of the city. Even at night you can hear neighbours arguing, dogs barking and babes crying, and the dark is filled with the sound of snoring and sniffing and snorting, grunting and gasping that dances from house to house through the thin walls. And when all of that quietens down, the scavengers come to collect the night soil, waking me with the creaking of their carts, the jingle of harness. Cursing, I pull the sheet over my head and wish myself back at Steeple Tew, peaceful, comfortable Steeple Tew, the only place I have ever felt truly safe.

You go with Gabriel to a great feast at the Grocers' Hall. I am not invited, of course. Gabriel buys you a new gown for the occasion, trimmed with sable. I gasp with pleasure when I see it and stroke the soft fur longingly. It is so unfair that you should have this gown and not me. Cecily sulks because she wants a new gown, too, and for once you have refused. You are still feeling guilty about the hundred sovereigns you stole from your husband to give Anthony, are you not? I have noticed how frugal you have become of late, as if to make amends, but it is too late for that now, Mary. By all means say no to Cecily, who is abominably spoilt as it is, but I do think you could have thought of *me*. It is getting colder, and I would be glad of some fur for warmth, too. But you have never cared for me, not really.

I could use some of the coin I found hidden in Anthony's lodgings, but why should I buy my own gown when you have enough money to buy one for me? Besides, how would I explain my sudden wealth? It is frustrating to have the money but not be able to use it. I have had to hide it under my feather bed. I tried to even out the coins, but sometimes when I turn over in bed at night, I can feel the lumps of gold digging into my flesh. It is not a bad feeling, though, to know that it is there. I have enough to go and live by myself with a servant, but then I would never see Gabriel, and the thought is not to be borne.

I cannot bear it. I will not.

★　★　★

Outside, it is a bright, snappy day with a jagged light that makes me screw up my eyes. The wind is in an irritable mood, blustering between the jettied houses, leaping to grab at the shutters and shake them like a dog with a rat, only to drop eerily away without warning. The last few leaves clinging to the trees shudder under its onslaught, while the sign of the three swans above the front door creaks wildly. A draught sneaks in at every window, it seems. I really do need some fur to comfort the back of my neck.

You have taken Cecily to the market and Amy is busy in the brewhouse. Sarah is out somewhere, I care not where. Gabriel has been at his accounts in his closet all morning. I see Gabriel's manservant, Roger, leave the house on some errand, the latch rattling as he pulls the door of the study to behind him and his boots clomping on the hall floor.

This is my chance. I scratch quietly at the door. 'May I speak with you?' I ask him when he bids me enter.

'Of course.' Is it my imagination or does he hesitate? 'What concerns you, Cat?'

'It is my mistress.' I have to force the word out. You, my mistress? I am *your* mistress, though you seem to have forgotten that long ago! How I hate the fact that I have to so demean myself in order to speak to your husband at all.

Gabriel gets up and stands in front of the fire, warming himself. 'What about her?'

'There is something I think you should know.' The carpenters are making such a racket next door that I have to raise my voice over the noise. 'She is . . . not herself at the moment, as you may have noticed.'

He studies me with those cool eyes that seem to reach right inside me and squeeze my heart. 'Why do you think that is, Cat?'

I have a pretty tale ready, hinting that you have not always been as calm as you normally appear. All I need to do is tell him my story and pretend

317

that it is yours. Oh, I don't tell him all of George's charming perversions, but that he was cruel to his wife is no lie. If you really had been married to him, you would have been driven mad, of that I am sure, Mary. So I nudge the truth this way and that, always pretending to make excuses for you while at the same time trying to convince Gabriel that you cannot really be trusted.

Which is only the truth. He has no idea that you are capable of killing a man in cold blood.

But I know.

I think I do it quite cleverly. Gabriel is looking very grave, and I am on the point of confiding that you were suspected of helping George to die — while claiming not to believe a word of it myself, naturally — when you knock and walk in without even waiting for Gabriel to bid you enter. You can do that because you are his wife. I cannot do that.

You spoil everything.

You are supposed to be still at market, not here. I did not hear you come in over the sound of those carpenters, and I feel at a disadvantage. Humiliation scrapes at me and pinches my lips together.

You look at me sitting on the stool, at Gabriel standing by the fire. Your face is taut. He looks rueful, but not guilty. 'Do I interrupt?' you say coldly, and I get to my feet with an insulting lack of haste. I cannot help myself.

'Not at all, my heart.' Gabriel goes over and takes your hand, the way he never, ever takes mine. He barely looks at me as he says, 'Cat, you

318

may go. We will talk of this matter another time.'

And that is that. I am dismissed. Rage chokes me and I stalk up the stairs to the great chamber. I want to break something, but I vent my feelings instead on the virginals, crashing my fingers down on the keys in one jarring sound. The carpenters are busy next door, banging away, so no one will hear but it makes me feel a bit better. I strain to hear the sound of an argument from Gabriel's closet but there is nothing. If you are fighting, you are doing it very quietly.

At length a blessed pause in the banging lets the sound of the front door drift up to the chamber. Has Gabriel left? Have you?

Restless, I pick up the lute that Cecily has left lying about, the way she does, but I cannot sit still. What if you have told Gabriel to send me away? I will tell him the truth if you do, Mary. Do you really want that? I tiptoe out and hang over the staircase, but there is only silence that throbs with a kind of defiance. Turning, I push open the door into your bedchamber, the one you share with Gabriel, where you brought me when I first came here. I am rarely invited in here and I wander around it, the lute dangling from one hand. I don't care if you find me. We have come to the end of the pretence. It is time for me to reclaim my life once and for all.

All of this should be mine. These velvet bed hangings, these cushions, these tapestries . . . all of it. You may take away that horrible wooden baby on the chest with my pleasure. Has it always had that malevolent expression? Uneasily, I turn it to face the wall. Wooden or not, I do not care for the way it looks at me.

I sit in the window seat and imagine that the chamber is indeed mine. I will hang different bed curtains and change the tapestries. I do not want Gabriel reminded of you at all. The thought makes me smile, and I pluck at the lute strings. I find myself playing the song that always makes you flinch: *Oh, John, come kiss me now, now, now, I sing. Oh, John, my love, come kiss me now. Oh, John, come kiss me by and by, for well ye ken the way to woo.*

I wish Gabriel would kiss me now, now, now. He does not need to woo me. He just needs to stand there.

And you need to be gone.

I start again. *Oh, John*, I begin, but the door bangs open and you are there, your eyes ablaze.

'Stop it!' you say furiously, slamming the door shut behind you. 'Stop that singing!'

Deliberately I sing on to the end of the line, but before I have reached the third 'now', you have snatched the lute from me and thrown it — thrown it! — onto the settle.

'I said, stop that,' you say as the lute strings squawk in protest.

I have never seen you so angry. I stare up at you defiantly, not wanting to admit that I am afraid. I wonder if you are going to strike me, but you suddenly turn away.

'What has happened to us, Cat?' you say abruptly. 'We loved each other once.'

'Life has happened,' I say. I am not one for sentimentality. 'We are not little girls any longer.'

'No, and I am not your maid any longer. I am

your mistress. I am married.'

'As if I could forget that,' I say bitterly.

You let out a long sigh and turn back to me. 'Gabriel is not for you, Cat. He is my husband. Leave him alone.'

'I do not know what you mean.'

'Come, Cat, I am not blind! Do you think I do not notice you making sheep's eyes at him?'

Fury at the contempt in your voice sends a wave of colour sloshing into my cheeks. Sheep's eyes! How dare you? But you do not even give me time to respond before you rail on.

'You are wasting your time,' you tell me. 'Gabriel will never return your feelings, and even if he did, he would not act on them. He is an honourable man, a devout man. Do you really believe that he would sully himself with you?'

Where I was red, now I am sure that I must be white with rage. 'You forget who you are talking to!'

'Oh, I do not forget,' you say coldly. 'I remember exactly who you are, Cat. You are not Lady Catherine Delahay any longer. You threw away your name like a wilful child when you chose to play the whore with Anthony.' I gasp as if you have slapped me. 'You did not want your name or your child, so I picked them up,' you say, oh so sanctimonious. 'They are mine now. You cannot go back and play the lady after everything that has happened. You made your choice and I made mine.'

'A choice? You saw an opportunity to better yourself and you seized it.' My voice is shaking, my hands clenching and unclenching. 'That was typical of you, Mary. You always have looked out for yourself first. Don't think I don't know that. You were the one who persuaded me to marry George in the first place, because it suited you. You didn't want to stay with Avery and Jocosa, so you pushed me into marriage.'

'Oho, so it is my fault!' You give a short laugh. 'How very like you to see it that way, Cat. It is always somebody else's fault, never yours. When will you ever, ever take responsibility for yourself?'

'When will *you* ever stop being holier-than-thou?' I retort. 'I am sick of you, Mary. Your whole life you have looked down on everyone. Nobody can match you for perfection, can they? And yet it is you who has spent your whole life living off other people! You give nothing of yourself. You care only for yourself and that dull merchant of yours. I, desire your husband?' I spit at you. 'You delude yourself. I have never wanted anything of yours, but you, you have everything of mine.'

All the petty frictions come roiling to the surface like a great pot of broth coming to the boil, releasing all the rage and resentment I have repressed over the past few months. The years are blown away and we are small girls again, shouting that we hate each other, slapping at each other with tears in our eyes, as sisters do. I push at you in frustration, and you push back, savagely, and I stumble, my arms flailing as I try to regain my balance.

Everything seems to stop, as if time itself has paused, and for a long moment I am poised, trapped on the cusp of falling or regaining my balance. I have time to stare at you and see your mouth open in shock, your eyes widen in horror. Your hands come up and you step towards me and I cannot tell if you are going to push me down or pull me up. Either way, you are too slow. I am falling backwards, backwards, after all, and my heart is lurching in fear as my head slams into something hard and blackness bursts through me.

★ ★ ★

The chamber is tilting and spinning. I blink dazedly, unable to make sense of it. Where are you? A face swims into view above me, and I stare, confused. How can there be someone on the ceiling? And then I realise. I am not standing up, I am on the floor. I have fallen down. At the same time, I become aware of a terrible pain in my head and I groan.

The face smiles and then is blocked out by a blur of green. How strange. I just have time to realise that it is a cushion before it is upon me, pressing down on my mouth and nose.

Horror and disbelief blank my mind. I am too weak and groggy to lift my arms and pull it away. Instead, I try desperately to gain purchase with my heels and buck off the weight, but the cushion is held firmly. I cannot breathe. This cannot really be happening. Is that what Anthony thought before you stabbed him in the heart? 'No,' I want to say. 'No, no, no! Not yet, I am not ready.'

But I cannot speak. There is a screaming in my head, the scream I would make if I could draw in any air. It swells louder and louder until there is a great flash of bright light, a stare into the abyss, a collapse into the dark. And then nothing.

25

Mary

When Cat's head hits the edge of the fireplace, the sound is not loud, but it is unmistakable. The sound of having gone too far. The sound of losing control. It cuts through the wind outside and the carpenters knocking and banging next door.

The sound stops me dead. The world that has been spinning out of control for what seems like weeks, months, now jars to a sickening stop. What am I doing? This is *Cat*, my past, and I have hurt her. I pushed her, just as I pushed the vagrant child all those years ago, as I pushed Avery. When will I learn?

I drop to my knees beside her. Her face is a ghastly grey, her eyes rolled back in her head. 'Dear God, dear God, I am sorry, so sorry,' I mutter feverishly as I press my fingers beneath her ear. Her skin is warm and I can just feel the thread of a pulse. My own throat feels horribly constricted.

But this is no time to be thinking about myself. I must help Cat. I scramble to my feet and rush to the door. Outside I nearly collide with Cecily who is coming up the stairs with an armful of linen.

'Leave that!' I say, bundling her into the chamber and ignoring her astonished protests.

'There has been an accident. Stay with Cat, keep her still. I must go and get bandages and a salve. Don't let her move!'

Without waiting for an answer, I clatter down the stairs to my still room, but when I am there I have to hold my head to stop it spinning. I can't remember what I am doing. I stare helplessly at the spice cabinet. What can I take to help Cat? I must pull myself together. I must think!

At last I grab some bandages and a cloth and some water from the pot. Where are Amy and Sarah? Too late, I remember that Amy is in the brewhouse and I sent Sarah to the butcher. Spilling the water from the bowl in my haste, I run back to the chamber and shoulder my way through the door.

Cecily is sitting calmly on the settle, holding a cushion. I know instantly that Cat is dead. There is an emptiness to the air, a clamouring absence. Swallowing, I set the bowl down with ridiculous care and bend down to Cat once more. There is no light in her eyes and her face is congested.

A thread of green silk trails from the corner of her mouth.

My head lifts in slow jerky stages to look at Cecily. She gazes limpidly back at me.

'She spoilt everything,' she says, as if that was explanation enough.

'Cecily . . . ' I croak, the enormity of what she has done pounding in my mind. 'Cecily, what have you done?'

'When I saw her lying there, it seemed as if God had put her in my way,' my daughter says seriously. 'Cat has made you wretched, Mamma.

326

Do not think that I have not noticed! She was trouble right from the start, always insisting on being the centre of attention. Singing and showing off, and she cared for nobody but herself! She hurt John, she flirted with Pappa, she was horrible to me. I hate her!'

'But . . . ' It feels as if the world has cracked asunder, and there is a great chasm between now and a few minutes ago. When I killed Anthony it was not like this, not this great welling of horror. 'That is not a reason to kill her, Cecily.'

'I do not see why not. It is not as if anyone will miss her.'

I will, I think.

Is this all my fault? Have I not realised what effect Cat has had on the others in the household? I have been so preoccupied with my own problems that I have become as self-centred as Cat.

As Cecily.

It is only now that I realise how much she resembles her mother. I have been misled by her sweetness and light-heartedness, but she is only really charming as long as she gets her own way. Cecily is the centre of her own world and nobody else really matters. She did not like Cat coming in and drawing attention away from her. Would I ever have understood this about her if Amy had not had the toothache that day? If I had not met Cat and invited her into my home?

I close Cat's eyes with a heart turned to stone. If there is a chasm between now and the past, there is another between now and the future, and I feel giddy when I think of how deep and dangerous that gap is. How can I get Cecily across it safely? Because it is clear to me that I must care for her now more than ever. She is not responsible. She does not know what is wrong, and that must be my fault, as I have been her mother for so long. I cannot tell anyone what she has done. I must protect her.

And Gabriel? What can I tell him?

'We will say it was an accident,' I say, but my voice comes out thready and weak as if I am an old woman. 'It *was* an accident. I argued with Cat. I pushed her and she fell. You were not here,' I tell Cecily. 'You know nothing about it.'

Downstairs I hear the sound of the door opening and male voices. John and Gabriel are back.

My husband meant to be reassuring about what Cat had said to him earlier. 'She cares for you more than she knows, I think,' he said before he went out to meet his son. But I was not reassured. I was jealous, and see where that has brought me.

'Do you go down and see to their wants,' I say to Cecily. 'Pretend you have not seen me if your father asks. I will try to think of some way to make this right.'

She goes off without even a backward glance. That is what really frightens me. I pick up the cushion. When I turn it over, I can see the marks of Cat's teeth and I shudder. How can I deal with this? I stand, turning the cushion over and over in my hands, and then I hear the footsteps on the stairs. Gabriel is coming to find me, and I still do not know what to tell him.

* * *

The door opens, and Gabriel is there. As if at a signal, I drop the cushion, abruptly repelled by it. 'There you are, my heart,' he says, only to stop when he sees my face. My expression must be ghastly because he takes a quick step forward. 'What is it? Are you ill?' But then he breaks off as he catches sight of Cat sprawled on the floor.

'I pushed her.' My voice quavers, wobbling up and down so erratically that I must be hard to understand.

Gabriel stoops swiftly to feel for Cat's pulse, just as I did. He looks up at me.

'She is dead,' he says, expressionless.

'It was over in an instant. She pushed me and I pushed her back. We were squabbling like little girls.' My chest hurts so badly I can scarcely breathe. 'I don't know what happened. She tripped, I think, and then she fell and then there was this sound, her head hitting the hearth.' My hands are at my throat, massaging it desperately. Now that I have started talking, it is as if I cannot stop. I keep telling Gabriel that I didn't mean it, until he comes over and clasps my arms firmly.

'Hush now,' he says. 'Just tell me what happened.'

So I start again, rambling on. 'We were arguing.'

'What about?'

About you, I want to say, but I cannot. Even in death I will not let Cat share in him. He will never know how she felt for him. I do not want him wondering what would have happened if I had been the one to trip and fall.

'I wanted to know what she had been saying to you. You said it was nothing, but I was afraid she had been lying.' My eyes are jittery, darting around the room, unable to fix on any one thing. 'I was angry with her, but I didn't mean her to die, you must believe that, Gabriel.'

'Of course I believe you,' he says soothingly. 'It was an accident.' But something in the way he says it makes it sound like a question.

'It *was* an accident,' I insist.

'How long has she been dead?'

'I hardly know ... some minutes, maybe more. I couldn't move. I knew that if I moved, that would make it real, and I do not want it to be real.' My eyes fill with tears. 'She was my friend once.'

'Come, my heart, sit down.' Gabriel leads me over to the settle and pushes me gently down onto it. My hands are still scrabbling at my throat, and I am convinced that I cannot breathe properly.

'We must send for Edward Parker,' he says.

I can only stare at him.

'He is the coroner,' Gabriel reminds me gently. 'In a case of sudden death, he must be called. He will find it an accident of course. No one who knows you could suppose otherwise.'

'Keep Cecily away,' I manage. 'I do not want her to see this.'

'I will send John for the coroner and ask Amy to sit with you. Why do you not lie down for a while? You are shocked.'

'No, I will stay with Cat.' This last thing I can do for her, to sit vigil over her body.

It seems ages before Gabriel comes back into the room with Edward Parker. I spend the time praying, or trying to pray. I press my palms to my forehead and beg God to forgive me for all the wrongs I have done. And I remember Cat as she was, so bright and warm, the laughter and lift of spirits when she was near. Is it her fault she was caught up in my curse?

But what makes me feel worse is that there is a bit of me that is relieved too. We had come to such a pass that we could not continue living together and Cat had no intention of going. One or other of us would have had to die.

I am worried about Cecily. She seems so unaffected by what she has done. Does she even realise that Cat is dead by her hands? I cannot bear to look at the cushion. I have picked away the green thread from her mouth.

Edward Parker. A man who has ever been jealous of Gabriel's success. Whose wife I brawled with openly in the great chamber and who will not have forgiven me. Between them, they are a resentful couple. I had forgotten that he was coroner.

When he and his assistant arrive at last, he bustles in, very conscious of his responsibilities and of his importance. 'A bad business,' he says at first. 'A very bad business. But I must inspect the body and make my inquiries, and then you will be able to bury her.'

'Inquiries?' Gabriel asks.

'It is my duty to investigate any sudden death,'

331

he says officiously. 'You would not want me to be derelict in my duty, would you?'

'No, of course not,' Gabriel murmurs, but the glance he shoots at me is worried.

Mr Parker sends us out of the room. The household gathers in the hall but the silence is leaden with anxiety. It is a lifetime since I looked around and thanked God for my healthy, happy family. A lifetime receding into the distance beyond that aching chasm. I want to comfort Cecily, but I cannot. I keep thinking of Cat, hoping that she was not conscious when my daughter pressed that cushion over her face.

If only I could unspin time: but where would I go back to? To the moment I told Cecily to sit with Cat? To when I set out to buy poppy seed for Amy? When I lied to Gabriel about who I really was? Or when I encouraged Cat to marry George? Or perhaps I should go all the way back to the cart? If I had just handed Peg to the child, how different would this moment be?

It is past time to eat, but none of us are hungry. We can hear Mr Parker and his assistant clomping around in my bedchamber. I should be thinking about calling the minister. We should lay Cat out.

But it seems that I need no longer concern myself with domestic details. Mr Parker comes importantly into the hall and calls Gabriel out for a discussion. When Gabriel comes back, he is looking grey, and I know that this is the end. He will not look at me.

'This was not an accident,' Mr Parker says, looking hard around the room. 'The woman died of suffocation. We found some threads in her mouth and there is no doubt in my mind that this was murder.'

I look at Cecily, and see her flinch. Perhaps only now does she realise what she has done. Is she opening her mouth? I cannot let that happen.

I stand up. 'I did it,' I say, keeping my eyes on Mr Parker. 'I killed her.'

Mr Parker looks disgruntled as if he had hoped to have the chance to unmask Cat's killer. 'Then I must take you to prison, Mistress Thorne. You will be tried in the courts of assize, and sentenced there. If you did indeed do this terrible thing, I have no doubt you will hang.'

You will die kicking and choking on the gibbet.

Mr Parker lets me go up to my chamber and find a warm cloak to wear over my gown. He will have to go with me, he says sternly.

Cat still lies on the floor where she fell. I avert my eyes from her and walk stiffly over to the chest. Kneeling, I open the lid to my linen press to find a cloak and the sweet smell of summer herbs rises to meet me. A drumming sense of desperation swells in me as I realise that I will never gather herbs again. Never stand in my garden and feel the sunshine warm on my shoulders. Never open the door to the house and feel myself at home.

'Mistress Thorne.' Impatience feathers Edward Parker's voice and I straighten, but as I turn to go, my eyes meet Peg's where she sits atop the chest and my heart stutters to see that she is crying painted tears for me. I lift a hand to touch her gently, but Mr Parker snaps at me from the doorway.

'Leave that. You may take the cloak but nothing else.'

Next door the carpenters are still banging and hammering, oblivious.

Carrying the cloak over one arm, I follow him down my fine staircase. For the last time I run my hand over the wood to impress the feel of it on my mind. I cannot look at Sarah or Amy, at John who watched aghast as I stood up and confessed, or at my daughter, who said nothing.

I cannot look at Gabriel, my husband, heart of my heart.

I do not say goodbye. There is a muffled sob from behind me as I walk to the door. I hope that it is Cecily, but I think it might be Sarah. Numb, I step out under the sign of the three swans for the last time. I do not look back.

★ ★ ★

Push, push. Push, push. It is so easy to do. Such a small action. So deadly. My head was boiling with rage when Cat pushed me, and I did not think. My hands came up and I pushed her. She staggered back and even as she was falling, I came to my senses. I meant to catch her, but I was too late. I meant to save her, I *did*.

I am in prison. It is not too uncomfortable because Gabriel has paid my gaolers well, and Sarah has brought me food. But I am still in prison. I cannot open the door and leave, and the thought wraps itself around my face and makes it hard to breathe. I have not slept. I lie on the rough bed and I stare at the wall. I do not cry. In a strange way it is almost a relief. I have spent my whole life fighting the curse, and now it has come to pass. I have been betrayed. I will hang. I will die.

I have tried to be a good woman, a good wife, but I have not been. I stood in the court of assize, and I listened to my neighbours tell of my misdeeds. The rumours that have been whispered around the streets have congealed into something heavier and more certain. I had killed Peter Blake with a poisoned potion, they said, aye, and Agnes too if the truth be told, and who knew how many more? Was it not known that I had murdered my first husband? He was said to have fallen down the stairs and broken his neck, but someone had heard someone else say that *they* had heard he died of poison too, and all too conveniently for me. As for Gabriel, he was an upstanding citizen, and I bound him to me with a spell.

So much that is untrue, but there is truth there, too. I have killed a man, and caused the death of others. It is right that I should hang.

I told Sarah not to come again. I am too ashamed to look her in the face. The street must be afire with news of my fall from grace. Will any of my friends stay loyal to my memory, I wonder? Does Anne Hawkins deny the rumours, or does she weep for Cat instead?

Most of the time, though, I think only of the house at the sign of the three swans, of Gabriel and Cecily and John. What they must be thinking and feeling. How will they tell Tom? It is worse for them than it is for me. I just have to die. They have to live with the bitterness of knowing that I have lied.

I worry most about Cecily. She killed so calmly, so certainly. But I cannot tell the truth. It will be the last thing I do for her, to keep her safe.

Gabriel comes to see me. I have longed to see him and dreaded it at the same time, so when he appears, I do not know whether I am grateful or desperate. He has to duck his head to enter my cell. His face is drawn with grief and something in me crumples. My heart is caving in with guilt and sadness and shame.

I hang my head and wait for him to berate me, but instead he comes over and takes my hands. 'How are you, dear heart?' he asks, and his gentleness oversets me. Tears spill down my cheeks.

'I am sorry, I am so sorry,' I weep, clinging to his hands. 'Please forgive me. I have brought disgrace to your name. I have been such a bad wife to you.'

'No.' Gabriel draws me down to sit next to him on the bed. 'I do not know what has happened, but you have been a good wife. You have brought up my sons, and kept my house and loved me well. I cannot forget those things. Whatever happened, it does not change the past. It does not change the fact that I love you.'

'Oh, Gabriel . . . ' I draw a shuddering breath. 'You would not say that if you knew the truth about what I have done.'

'Tell me the truth, then,' he says.

So I tell him. I tell him everything, from my journey to Steeple Tew and the child that I pushed and the curse that has blighted my life. I tell him about Cat and how we loved each other. About Avery and how he forced me again and again. About the babe that I voided into the privy. I tell him how Avery's marriage changed everything, especially when Sir Hugh died. All I wanted was a home and to feel safe, I tell him, and Jocosa would never have rested until she was rid of me. I tell him how I encouraged Cat to marry Lord Delahay.

'But I did not know what he was,' I try to excuse myself. 'How could I have known that he would twist Cat's sweetness and debauch her?'

I falter only when I come to talk about how Cat gave birth to a daughter and turned away from her. About Cat's passion for Anthony. I am coming to the part where my lies grow great. In spite of myself, my voice softens as I remember Cecily as a baby, how small she was, how perfect.

Gabriel listens, interrupting rarely. He nods occasionally or makes a sound to encourage me to go on, but he does not exclaim in disgust as I half expect. I flick glances at him from under my lashes every now and then, but it is easier to tell him sitting side by side instead of facing him.

And now I have reached the point where I must tell him about George. The decoction I gave to Cat to mute his temper and give her some respite from his cruelty. How she had feared for her life when he woke unexpectedly

337

one night and attacked her in a rage. 'I made it look like an accident,' I confess. 'I concealed the truth, but what could I do but help her?'

But I sound as if I am excusing myself, and it is too late for that now. I tell him about how Cat reacted when Avery suggested his courtship, and my cheeks burn at confessing the deception.

'And then, when you visited Steeple Tew, I didn't know what to do. I thought Cat was mad to reject you, when you were everything I had always wanted. So . . . ' I swallow. 'I did not correct you. I married you knowing that you thought I was someone else. I lied about my name. I am not Lady Catherine.'

'I know,' he says, and I stare at him.

'You know?'

'Avery went to great lengths to tell me how beautiful his sister was, with her golden hair and blue eyes. I knew as soon as I saw your eyes. The cap could cover your hair, but never your clear eyes. I wondered that she would not want to talk to me, but I saw you and I was captivated. I let you believe that you had fooled me because it seemed important to you, and I wanted you. You are all I have ever wanted.'

'You knew,' I say wonderingly.

'And some of the story Cat told me. Oh, not deliberately, but now I understand. She wanted me to think that her story was yours, but that it can never be, because you are not her. There is only one thing I want to know.'

'What is that?'

'What is your name, wife?'

I look at him then. 'My name is Mary.'

338

Tomorrow I will die. I have stopped regretting now, but it is strange. I keep saying it to myself but I don't believe it, not really. I will *die*. Will God have mercy on me? Or will I be consigned to hell, to burn for all eternity, never to see God or Gabriel or my child again. For Cecily is still my daughter. I have told Gabriel not to bring her to see me. I do not want her to be distressed or to blurt out the truth. But I have tried to warn him, too, to be careful of her. I have asked him to watch her, to recognise that when she is crossed she is capable of acting thoughtlessly. He looked at me hard when I said that. Is it my fault that Cecily is that way? Have I spoilt her by loving her too much? I think I was firm with her as a child, as all children need firmness. I treated her and Tom the same. But I could not help loving her more. She grew up knowing that she could do whatever she wanted and I would still love her: perhaps that was my mistake, but should not a child like that be considered fortunate, to take so much for granted?

So, yes, perhaps it is my fault. Unless she was born that way, just as Cat was. I have been thinking about Cat so much, replaying that moment when my hands shot out and pushed *(pushed)* her. And if Cecily was born like that, is there anything I could have done? She might have killed Cat anyway. That was the worst moment, when I understood that I would never be rid of the personality they shared, a ruthless focus on themselves. Now I think that that is the

339

other half of me, a necessary balance. When I did not have Cat, I had Cecily. The problem was when they were both there, tipping me off balance, so that I lost control.

I hope Cecily's husband will be doting and not cross her. But she may not have a husband now. Who would want to marry the daughter of a murderess? What will happen to my household? Gabriel tells me that Sarah and Amy wish to stay, and that while some acquaintances have turned their back on the family, some friends have stayed true. 'My wealth will always buy me some friends,' he says ruefully.

So it may be that Cecily can stay with Gabriel, and not marry at all — but what if she does not care for that? Is it possible she would take her frustrations out on Gabriel? Have I created a monster? And what of John? I hope that Cat was not right when she hinted that Cecily's feelings for him went beyond that of a sister. I cannot believe that is true, but then I did not believe Cecily was capable of murder either.

I did not think I was.

The best thing for John would be to marry Meg, but will the Sims agree to the marriage now? I hope so, but I will never know.

I will never know about dear Tom, either. I hope he will not think too badly of me. He is young still and adventurous. He will be happy as long as he has a ship and a horizon to sail towards, I think. I hope he will remember me fondly, that is all, but why should he, when I have ruined his father? But he might remember instead the times I picked him up when he fell and brushed him down. When I sat up with him all night and spooned an infusion into him, little by little. The times when I cooked his favourite apple pie, or mended his torn hose, or did not tell Gabriel that he had lost his hornbook but quietly bought him a new one.

What will it be like tomorrow? They have told me what will happen. I am not a queen to merit a swift execution. Instead, they will lead me out to the gibbet. *You will die kicking and choking on the gibbet.* I have told Gabriel not to come. I cannot bear to see his pain, but saying goodbye to him this afternoon was the most painful moment of my life. My heart was torn asunder. Knowing that I will never see him again, never again wake with his warmth beside me, never be able to roll over and press my face into his bare shoulder and breathe in the scent of his skin. The scent of safety.

I can picture the chamber so clearly. If I close my eyes, I can imagine myself there, convince myself that I lie on soft beds and sheets scented with lavender. That if I open my eyes again, I will see the rich bed curtains, the tapestries on the wall, the ornately carved chair with its embroidered cushions. And on the chest, the shell that Jacopo gave me, and Peg. Peg who has been with me all my life but who now sits alone. Who cried painted tears when I turned to go. I have asked Gabriel to give her to Cecily, to watch over her.

And now it is morning, and I am ready to die. I have taken off all my jewellery, all my finery, and am simply dressed in a petticoat and kirtle.

It's cold. I am shivering, so much that I almost wish that it was over, but after the rush and blur of the last few months, everything has slowed down and seems to be happening with exaggerated slowness: the gaoler unlocking the cell, the walk outside as if he and I are lifting every foot through deep mud. I blink at the air. In the distance, I can see a tree over the wall, and a bird darting in the sky. It is all extraordinarily detailed, as if I have never seen anything before. As if I have never appreciated how beautiful life is. The gaoler is whistling through his gappy teeth. I know the tune. It is the tune that has followed me my whole life, since Jack the carter whistled it on my journey to Steeple Tew: *Oh, John, come kiss me now, now, now.*

My whole life has been leading up to this moment, to now, now, now. There is no future for me, only this endless now. I climb up onto the platform. A crowd has gathered, jostling and jeering, laughing and gossiping. Someone is selling hot pies. I can smell them. There are some people for whom death is an entertainment, as good as the players. My eyes drift over the crowd. I see a few familiar faces, neighbours come out of curiosity, and they avert their eyes from mine, until I see one who does not avert his eyes but looks steadily back at me. Gabriel has come after all, to be with me so that I am not alone.

They tie my hands behind my back and drop the noose over my neck. It feels familiar, as if it has always been there. But then they drop a hood over me, and just like that, life is blacked

342

out, gone. Only now *(now, now)* does terror rise in me. There is so much that I need to say. I want to change my mind, to shout that I am innocent, to make them take off the hood and the noose, and let me go home with Gabriel.

But I can hear boots on the boards, the murmur of a priest. A rope creaks, and then the world drops away beneath me. I hurtle down and the noose grabs my neck, throttling me. I gurgle and twitch. I have forgotten everything except the pain and the terror which has blotted out the world.

I thought that I was ready but I am not. I am not.

Epilogue

Cecily

Pappa comes home from the hanging and says not a word of comfort to me. Not one word! He shuts himself in his chamber and does not come out for a day. John taps on the door to try and get him to eat, but Pappa sends him away. He does not want to talk to anyone.

Everything is awful. How could Mamma have done this to me? It is all her fault for inviting that Cat into the house. Nothing has been the same since. You would have thought she would have been glad when Cat died. I know that she hated her as much as I did. But no, she must invite in the coroner and accept responsibility. Now our neighbours look at me askance, and our reputation is in ruins. Who will marry me now, the daughter of a murderess? When we go to church, as Pappa insists we must, everyone falls silent when we walk in. I hate it.

Everything has changed. Pappa is silent, and although he has said nothing, I have caught him looking at me sometimes with a strange expression, and when I went to embrace him the other day, because I needed comfort, I am sure that he flinched. And John, too, is sad. I thought he loved me. I thought that once Cat was gone, we could go back to how we were, but he has no time for me now. 'We must look after our father,'

344

he says. What about me? Who will look after me?

Pappa gave me Mamma's jewellery. He said that she wanted Sarah and Amy to have something, but I do not see why I should give servants jewels. I am sure she must have meant money, and Pappa will do that. He says we may move away to where nobody knows us, and I cannot decide if that will be a good thing or bad. Sarah and Amy might not come with us, so why should they have a ring or a necklace?

I am pleased with the jewels, but not with that horrible wooden baby that Mamma used to love so much. Pappa said she wanted me to have it too. Peg, she called it. It has always made me shudder. When he brought Peg to me, her expression was sly: every time I looked at her, she seemed to be accusing me. But it was not my fault that Mamma said that she killed Cat. She should have said nothing. Mr Parker would never have been able to prove anything.

In the end, I throw Peg away on the midden, and the feeling of relief with her out of the house is intense. For a day, I relax and let myself think that everything will be all right, but when I go to bed, and set the candle on the chest, there is Peg, smiling at me.

'I found her,' Sarah says, as if waiting for me to be grateful. 'I know how much she meant to the mistress. I don't know how she came to be outside.'

Stupid girl.

So I take Peg and throw her in the river. There!

That night, Peg is back, and everyone denies

even knowing that she was gone. I almost scream as her painted eyes meet mine with triumph and hatred in the candlelight. My hands shake as I turn her to face the wall, but in the morning when I wake up, she has turned round again and is facing me, smiling her sinister smile, and for a moment I think I see a thread of green silk trailing from her mouth. I understand then that I will never be free of her. No matter what I do, she will always be there, an unwelcome conscience, to remind me of my mother, to remind me of what I did and who I am.

MK